POCKET

THE QUARTET

The four novels of *The Alexandria Quartet*
interlap and interweave, sharing the same characters and events, yet presenting them from
different perspectives of time or narrator—
each imparting new color and texture to the
tapestry of love affairs that makes up the life
of the writer Darley.

THE AUTHOR

Born in India of Irish parents in 1912, and
educated in England, Lawrence Durrell has
spent much of his life in the Eastern Mediterranean which forms the background of many
of his stories.

THE ACCLAIM

Of Lawrence Durrell, *New Statesman* has
written: "Among living writers, few equal and
none surpass Lawrence Durrell." Of *Justine*,
Time observed: "It is an extraordinary novel,
sensuous and beautifully written."

Books by Lawrence Durrell

The Alexandria Quartet:
   Justine
   Balthazar
   Mountolive
   Clea
Tunc

Published by POCKET BOOKS

POCKET

Lawrence Durrell
Justine

PUBLISHED BY POCKET BOOKS

POCKET BOOKS, a Simon & Schuster division of
GULF & WESTERN CORPORATION
1230 Avenue of the Americas, New York, N.Y. 10020

ISBN: 0-671-82793-6

First Pocket Books printing April, 1961

20   19   18   17   16   15   14   13

Trademarks registered in the United States and other countries.

Printed in the U.S.A.

To Eve
these memorials of her native city

NOTE

The characters in this novel, the first of a series, are all inventions together with the personality of the narrator, and bear no resemblance to living persons. Only the city is real.

marked by the rest of his guests.

I am accustoming myself to the idea of regarding every sexual act as a process in which four persons are involved. We shall have a lot to discuss about that.

S. Freud: Letters

There are two positions available to us—either crime, which renders us happy, or the noose, which prevents us from being unhappy. I ask whether there can be any hesitation, lovely Thérèse, and where will your little mind find an argument able to combat that one?

D. A. F. de Sade: Justine

PART

one

THE SEA is high again today, with a thrilling flush of wind. In the midst of winter you can feel the inventions of Spring. A sky of hot nude pearl until midday, crickets in sheltered places, and now the wind unpacking the great planes, ransacking the great planes. . . .

I have escaped to this island with a few books and the child—Melissa's child. I do not know why I used the word "escape." The villagers say jokingly that only a sick man would choose such a remote place to rebuild. Well, then, I have come here to heal myself, if you like to put it that way. . . .

At night when the wind roars and the child sleeps quietly in its wooden cot by the echoing chimney-piece I light a lamp and walk about, thinking of my friends—of Justine and Nessim, of Melissa and Balthazar. I return link by link along the iron chains of memory to the city which we inhabited so briefly together: the city which used us as its flora—precipitated in us conflicts which were hers and which we mistook for our own: beloved Alexandria!

I have had to come so far away from it in order to understand it all! Living on this bare promontory, snatched every night from darkness by Arcturus, far from the lime-laden dust of those summer afternoons, I see at last that none of us is properly to be judged for what happened in the past. It is the city which should be judged though we, its children, must pay the price.

❊   ❊   ❊   ❊   ❊

Capitally, what is this city of ours? What is resumed in

the word of Alexandria? In a flash my mind's eyes shows
me a thousand dust-tormented streets. Flies and beggars
own it today—and those who enjoy an intermediate existence between either.

Five races, five languages, a dozen creeds: five fleets
turning through their greasy reflections behind the harbour bar. But there are more than five sexes and only
demotic Greek seems to distinguish among them. The sexual provender which lies to hand is staggering in its
variety and profusion. You would never mistake it for a
happy place. The symbolic lovers of the free Hellenic
world are replaced here by something different, something subtly androgynous, inverted upon itself. The
Orient cannot rejoice in the sweet anarchy of the
body—for it has outstripped the body. I remember
Nessim once saying—I think he was quoting—that Alexandria was the great wine-press of love; those who
emerged from it were the sick men, the solitaries, the
prophets—I mean all who have been deeply wounded in
their sex. —

*   *   *   *   *

Notes for landscape-tones. . . . Long sequences of tem-
pera. Light filtered through the essence of lemons. An air
full of brick-dust—sweet-smelling brick-dust and the
odour of hot pavements slaked with water. Light damp
clouds, earth-bound, yet seldom bringing rain. Upon this
squirt dust-red, dust-green, chalk-mauve and watered
crimson-lake. In summer the sea-damp lightly varnished
the air. Everything lay under a coat of gum.

And then in autumn the dry, palpitant air, harsh with
static electricity, inflaming the body through its light
clothing. The flesh coming alive, trying the bars of its
prison. A drunken whore walks in a dark street at night,
shedding snatches of song like petals. Was it in this that
Anthony heard the heart-numbing strains of the great
music which persuaded him to surrender forever to the
city he loved?

The sulking bodies of the young begin to hunt for a
fellow nakedness, and in those little cafés where Balthazar went so often with the old poet of the city,* the

boys stir uneasily at their backgammon under the pet-
rol-lamps: disturbed by this dry desert wind—so unro-
mantic, so unconfiding—stir, and turn to watch every
stranger. They struggle for breath and in every summer
kiss they can detect the taste of quicklime. . . .

*   *   *   *   *

I had to come here in order completely to rebuild this
city in my brain—melancholy provinces which the old
man* saw as full of the "black ruins" of his life. Clang
of the trams shuddering in their metal veins as they
pierce the iodine-coloured *meidan of* Mazarita. Gold,
phosphorus, magnesium paper. Here we so often met.
There was a little coloured stall in summer with slices of
watermelon and the vivid water-ices she liked to eat. She
would come a few minutes late of course—fresh perhaps
from some assignation in a darkened room, from which I
avert my mind; but so fresh, so young, the open petal of
the mouth that fell upon mine like an unslaked summer.
The man she had left might still be going over and over
the memory of her; she might be as if still dusted by the
pollen of his kisses. Melissa! It mattered so little somehow,
feeling the lithe weight of the creature as she leaned on
one's arm smiling with the selfless candour of those who
had given over with secrets. It was good to stand there,
awkward and a little shy, breathing quickly because we
knew what we wanted of each other. The messages passing beyond conscience, directly through flesh-lips, eyes,
water-ices, the coloured stall. To stand lightly there, our
little fingers linked, drinking in the deep camphor-scented
afternoon, a part of city. . . .

*   *   *   *   *

I have been looking through my papers tonight. Some
have been converted to kitchen uses, some the child has
destroyed. This form of censorship pleases me for it has
the indifference of the natural world to the constructions
of art—an indifference I am beginning to share. After all
what is the good of a fine metaphor for Melissa when she

lies buried deep as any mummy in the shallow tepid sand
of the black estuary?

But those papers I guard with care are the three
volumes in which Justine kept her diary, as well as the
folio which records Nessim's madness. Nessim gave them
all to me on parting saying:

"Take these and read them. There is much about us all
in them. They should help you to support the idea of
Justine without flinching, as I have had to do." This was at
the Summer Palace after Melissa's death, when he still
believed Justine would return to him. I think often, and
never without a certain fear, of Nessim's love for Justine.
What could be more comprehensive, more surely founded
in itself? It coloured his unhappiness with a kind of
ecstasy, the joyful wounds which you'd think to meet in
saints and not in mere lovers. Yet one touch of humour
would have saved him from such dreadful comprehensive
suffering. It is easy to criticise, I know. I know.

*   *   *   *   *

In the great quietness of these winter evenings there is
one clock: the sea. Its dim momentum in the mind is the
fugue upon which this writing is made. Empty cadences
of sea-water, licking its own wounds, sulking along the
mouths of the delta, boiling upon those deserted beaches
—empty, forever empty under the gulls: white scrib-
ble on the grey, munched by clouds. If there are ever sails
here they die before the land shadows them. Wreckage
washed up on the pediments of islands, the last crust,
eroded by the weather, stuck in the blue maw of water . . .
gone!

*   *   *   *   *

Apart from the wrinkled old peasant who comes from
the village on her mule each day to clean the house, the
child and I are quite alone. It is happy and active amid
unfamiliar surroundings. I have not named it yet. Of
course it will be Justine—who else?

As for me I am neither happy nor unhappy; I lie
suspended like a hair or a feather in the cloudy mixtures
of memory. I spoke of the uselessness of art but added

nothing truthful about its consolations. The solace of such work as I do with brain and heart lies in this—that only *there*, in the silences of the painter or the writer can reality be reordered, reworked and made to show its significant side. Our common actions in reality are simply the sackcloth covering which hides the cloth-of-gold—the meaning of the pattern. For us artists there waits the joyous compromise through art with all that wounded or defeated us in daily life; in this way, not to evade destiny, as the ordinary people try to do, but to fulfil it in its true potential—the imagination. Otherwise why should we hurt one another? No, the remission I am seeking, and will be granted perhaps, is not one I shall ever see in the bright friendly eyes of Melissa or the sombre brow-dark gaze of Justine. We have all of us taken different paths now; but in this, the first great fragmentation of my maturity I feel the confines of my art and my living deepened immeasurably by the memory of them. In thought I achieve them anew; as if only here—this wooden table over the sea under an olive tree, only here can I enrich them as they deserve. So that the taste of this writing should have taken something from its living sub-jects—their breath, skin, voices—weaving them into the supple tissues of human memory. I want them to live again to the point where pain becomes art. . . . Perhaps this is a useless attempt, I cannot say. But I must try.

Today the child and I finished the hearth-stone of the house together, quietly talking as we worked. I talk to her as I would to myself if I were alone; she answers in an heroic language of her own invention. We buried the rings Cohen bought for Melissa in the ground under the hearth-stone, according to the custom of this island. This will ensure good luck to the inmates of the house.

❖   ❖   ❖   ❖   ❖

At the time when I met Justine I was almost a happy man. A door had suddenly opened upon an intimacy with Melissa—an intimacy not the less marvellous for being unexpected and totally undeserved. Like all egoists I can-not bear to live alone; and truly the last year of bachelorhood had sickened me—my domestic inadequancy, my hopelessness over clothes and food and money, had all reduced me to despair. I had sickened too of the cockroach-haunted rooms where I then lived, looked after by one-eyed Hamid, the Berber servant.

Melissa had penetrated my shabby defences not by any of the qualities one might enumerate in a lover—charm, exceptional beauty, intelligence—no, but by the force of what I can only call her charity, in the Greek sense of the word. I used to see her, I remember, pale, rather on the slender side, dressed in a shabby sealskin coat, leading her small dog about the winter streets. Her blue-veined phthisic hands, etc. Her eyebrows artificially pointed upwards to enhance those fine dauntlessly candid eyes. I saw her daily for many months on end, but her sullen aniline beauty awoke no response in me. Day after day I passed her on my way to the Café Al Aktar where Balthazar waited for me in his black hat to give me "instruction." I did not dream that I should ever become her lover.

I knew that she had once been a model at the Atelier—an unenviable job—and was now a dancer; more, that she was the mistress of an elderly furrier, a gross and vulgar commercial of the city. I simply make these few notes to record a block of my life which has fallen into the sea. Melissa! Melissa!

*   *   *   *   *

I am thinking back to the time when for the four of us the known world hardly existed; days became simply the spaces between dreams, spaces between the shifting floors of time, of acting, of living out the topical. . . . A tide of meaningless affairs nosing along the dead level of things, entering no climate, leading us nowhere, demanding of us nothing save the impossible—that we should be. Justine would say that we had been trapped in the projection of a will too powerful and too deliberate to be human—the gravitational field which Alexandria threw down about those it had chosen as its exemplars. . . .

*   *   *   *   *

Six o'clock. The shuffling of white-robed figures from the station yards. The shops filling and emptying like lungs in the Rue des Soeurs. The pale lengthening rays of the afternoon sun smear the long curves of the Esplanade, and the dazzled pigeons, like rings of scattered paper, climb above the minarets to take the last rays of the waning light on their wings. Ringing of silver on the money-changers' counters. The iron grille outside the bank still too hot to touch. Clip-clop of horse-drawn carriages carrying civil servants in red flowerpots towards the cafés on the sea-front. This is the hour least easy to bear, when from my balcony I catch an unexpected glimpse of her walking idly towards the town in her white sandals, still half asleep. Justine! The city unwrinkles like an old tortoise and peers about it. For a moment it relinquishes the torn rags of the flesh, while from some hidden alley by the slaughter-house, above the moans and screams of the cattle, comes the nasal chipping of a Damascus love-song; shrill quartertones, like a sinus being ground to powder.

Now tired men throw back the shutters of their balconies and step blinking into the pale hot light—etiolated flowers of afternoons spent in anguish, tossing upon ugly beds, bandaged by dreams. I have become one of these poor clerks of the conscience, a citizen of Alexandria. She passes below my window, smiling as if at some private satisfaction, softly fanning her cheeks with the little reed fan. It is a smile which I shall probably never see again for in company she only laughs, showing those magnificent white teeth. But this sad yet quick smile is full of a quality which ones does not think she owns—the power of mischief. You would have said that she was of a more tragic cast of character and lacked common humour. Only the obstinate memory of this smile is to make me doubt it in the days to come.

*   *   *   *   *

I have had many such glimpses of Justine at different times, and of course I knew her well by sight long before we met: our city does not permit anonymity to any with incomes of over two hundred pounds a year. I see her sit-

ting alone by the sea, reading a newspaper and eating an
apple; or in the vestibule of the Cecil Hotel, among the
dusty palms, dressed in a sheath of silver drops, holding
her magnificent fur at her back as a peasant holds his
coat—her long forefinger hooked through the tag. Nessim
has stopped at the door of the ballroom which is flooded
with light and music. He has missed her. Under the palms,
in a deep alcove, sit a couple of old men playing chess.
Justine has stopped to watch them. She knows nothing of
the game, but the aura of stillness and concentration
which brims the alcove fascinates her. She stands there
between the deaf players and the world of music for a
long time, as if uncertain into which to plunge. Finally
Nessim comes softly to take her arm and they stand
together for a while, she watching the players, he watching her. At last she goes softly, reluctantly, circumspectly
into the lighted world with a little sigh.

Then in other circumstances, less creditable no doubt to
herself, or to the rest of us: yet how touching, how
pliantly feminine this most masculine and resourceful of
women could be. She could not help but remind me of
that race of terrific queens which left behind them the ammoniac smell of their incestuous loves to hover like a
cloud over the Alexandrian subconscious. The giant man-
eating cats like Arsinoe were her true siblings. Yet behind
the acts of Justine lay something else, born of a later tragic
philosophy in which morals must be weighed in the
balance against rogue personality. She was the victim of
truly heroic doubts. Nevertheless I can still see a direct
connection between the picture of Justine bending over
the dirty sink with the foetus in it, and poor Sophia of
Valentinus who died for a love as perfect as it was wrong
headed.

*   *   *   *   *

At that epoch, Georges-Gaston Pombal, a minor consular official, shares a small flat with me in the Rue Nebi
Daniel. He is a rare figure among the diplomats in that he
appears to possess a vertebral column. For him the
tiresome treadmill of protocol and entertainment—so like
a surrealist nightmare—is full of exotic charm. He sees

diplomacy through the eyes of a Douanier Rousseau. He indulges himself with it but never allows it to engulf what remains of his intellect. I suppose the secret of his success is his tremendous idleness, which almost approaches the supernatural.

He sits at his desk in the Consulate-General covered by a perpetual confetti of pasteboard cards bearing the names of his colleagues. He is a pegamoid sloth of a man, a vast slow fellow given to prolonged afternoon siestas and Crebillon *fils*. His handkerchiefs smell wondrously of *Eau de Portugal*. His most favoured topic of conversation is women, and he must speak from experience for the succession of visitors to the little flat is endless, and rarely does one see the same face twice. "To a Frenchman the love here is interesting. They act before they reflect. When the time comes to doubt, to suffer remorse, it is too hot, nobody has the energy. It lacks *finesse*, this animalism, but it suits me. I've worn out my heart and head with love, and want to be left alone—above all, *mon cher*, from this Judeo-Coptic mania for *dissection*, for analysing the subject. I want to return to my farmhouse in Normandy heart-whole."

For long periods of the winter he is away on leave and I have the little dank flat to myself and sit up late, correcting exercise books, with only the snoring Hamid for company. In this last year I have reached a dead end in myself. I lack the will-power to do anything with my life, to better my position by hard work, to write: even to make love. I do not know what has come over me. This is the first time I have experienced a real failure of the will to survive. Occasionally I turn over a bundle of manuscript or an old proof-copy of a novel or book of poems with disgusted inattention; with sadness, like someone studying an old passport.

From time to time one of Georges' numerous girls strays into my net by calling at the flat when he is not there, and the incident serves for a while to sharpen my *taedium vitae*. Georges is thoughtful and generous in these matters for, before going away (knowing how poor I am) he often pays one of the Syrians from Golfo's tavern

in advance, and orders her to spend an occasional night in
the flat *en disponibilité*, as he puts it. Her duty is to cheer
me up, by no means an enviable task especially as on the
surface there is nothing to indicate lack of cheerfulness on
my part. Small talk has become a useful form of
automatism which goes on long after one has lost the need
to talk; if necessary I can even make love with relief, as
one does not sleep very well here: but without passion,
without attention.

Some of these encounters with poor exhausted creatures
driven to extremity by physical want are interesting, even
touching, but I have lost any interest in sorting my emotions so that they exist for me like dimensionless figures
flashed on a screen. "There are only three things to be
done with a woman," said Clea once. "You can love her,
suffer for her, or turn her into literature." I was experiencing a failure in all these domains of feeling.

I record this only to show the unpromising human
material upon which Melissa elected to work, to blow
some breath of life into my nostrils. It could not have been
easy for her to bear the double burden to her own poor
circumstances and illness. To add my burdens to hers
demanded real courage. Perhaps it was born of desperation, for she too had reached the dead level of things, as I
myself had. We were fellow-bankrupts.

For weeks her lover, the old furrier, followed me about
the streets with a pistol sagging in the pocket of his over-
coat. It was consoling to learn from one of Melissa's
friends that it was unloaded, but it was nevertheless
alarming to be haunted by this old man. Mentally we
must have shot each other down at every street corner of
the city. I for my part could not bear to look at that heavy
pock-marked face with its bestial saturnine cluster of tormented features smeared on it—could not bear to think of
his gross intimacies with her: those sweaty little hands
covered as thickly as a porcupine with black hair. For a
long time this went on and then after some months an extraordinary feeling of intimacy seemed to grow up between us. We nodded and smiled at each other when we
met. Once, encountering him at a bar, I stood for nearly

half an hour beside him; we were on the point of talking
to each other, yet somehow neither of us had the courage
to begin it. There was no common subject of conversation
save Melissa. As I was leaving I caught a glimpse of him
in one of the long mirrors, his head bowed as he stared into his wineglass. Something about his attitude—the clumsy
air of a trained seal grappling with human emotions—
struck me, and I realized for the first time that he probably loved Melissa as much as I did. I pitied his ugliness,
and the blank pained incomprehension with which he
faced emotions so new to him as jealousy, the deprivation
of a cherished mistress.

Afterwards when they were turning out his pockets I
saw among the litter of odds and ends a small empty
scent-bottle of the cheap kind that Melissa used; and I
took it back to the flat where it stayed on the mantelpiece
for some months before it was thrown away by Hamid in
the course of a spring-clean. I never told Melissa of this;
but often when I was alone at night while she was dancing, perhaps of necessity sleeping with her admirers, I
studied this small bottle, sadly and passionately reflecting
ing on this horrible old man's love and measuring it
against my own; and tasting too, vicariously, the desperation which makes one clutch at some small discarded
object which is still impregnated with the betrayer's
memory.

I found Melissa, washed up like a half-drowned bird, on
the dreary littorals of Alexandria, with her sex broken. . . .

* * * * *

Streets that run back from the docks with their tattered
rotten supercargo of houses, breathing into each others'
mouths, keeling over. Shuttered balconies swarming with
rats, and old women whose hair is full of the blood of
ticks. Peeling walls leaning drunkenly to east and west of
their true centre of gravity. The black ribbon of flies attaching itself to the lips and eyes of the children—the
moist beads of summer flies everywhere; the very weight
of their bodies snapping off ancient flypapers hanging in
the violet doors of booths and cafés. The smell of the

sweat-lathered Berberinis, like that of some decomposing
staircarpet. And then the street noises: shriek and clang
of the water-bearing Saidi, dashing his metal cups together as an advertisement, the unheeded shrieks which
pierce the hubbub from time to time, as of some small
delicately-organized animal being disembowelled. The
sores like ponds—the incubation of a human misery of
such proportions that one is aghast, and all one's human
feelings overflow into disgust and terror.

I wished I could imitate the self-confident directness
with which Justine threaded her way through these streets
toward the café where I waited for her: *El Bab*. The
doorway by the shattered arch where in all innocence we
sat and talked; but already our conversation had become
impregnated by understandings which we took for the
lucky omens of friendship merely. On that dun mud floor,
feeling the quickly cooling cylinder of the earth dip
towards the darkness, we were possessed only by a desire
to communicate ideas and experiences which overstepped
the range of thought normal to conversation among ordinary people. She talked like a man and I talked to her
like a man. I can only remember the pattern and weight
of these conversations, not their substance. And leaning
there on a forgotten elbow, drinking the cheap *arak* and
smiling at her, I inhaled the warm summer perfume of her
dress and skin—a perfume which was called, I don't know
why, *Jamais de la vie*.

*   *   *   *   *

These are the moments which possess the writer, not
the lover, and which live on perpetually. One can return
to them time and time again in memory, or use them as a
fund upon which to build the part of one's life which is
writing. One can debauch them with words, but one cannot spoil them. In this context too, I recover another such
moment, lying beside a sleeping woman in a cheap room
near the mosque. In that early spring dawn, with its dense
dew, sketched upon the silence which engulfs a whole city
before the birds awaken it, I caught the sweet voice of the
blind *muezzin* from the mosque reciting the *Ebed*—a

voice hanging like a hair in the palm-cooled upper airs of
Alexandria. "I praise the perfection of God, the Forever
existing" (this repeated thrice, ever more slowly, in a high
sweet register). "The perfection of God, the Desired, the
Existing, the Single, the Supreme: the perfection of God,
the One, the Sole: the perfection of Him who taketh unto
himself no male or female partner, nor any like Him, nor
any that is disobedient, nor any deputy, equal or off-
spring. His perfection be extolled."

The great prayer wound its way into my sleepy consciousness like a serpent, coil after shining coil of
words—the voice of the *muezzin* sinking from register to
register of gravity—until the whole morning seemed
dense with its marvellous healing powers, the intimations
of a grace undeserved and unexpected, impregnating that
shabby room where Melissa lay, breathing as lightly as a
gull, rocked upon the oceanic splendours of a language
she would never know.

* * * * *

Of Justine who can pretend that she did not have her
stupid side? The cult of pleasure, small vanities, concern
for the good opinion of her inferiors, arrogance. She could
be tiresomely exigent when she chose. Yes. Yes. But all
these weeds are watered by money. I will say only that in
many things she thought as a man, while in her actions
she enjoyed some of the free vertical independence of the
masculine outlook. Our intimacy was of a strange mental
order. Quite early on I discovered that she could mind-
read in an unerring fashion. Ideas came to us simultaneously. I remember once being made aware that she
was sharing in her mind a thought which had just
presented itself to mine, namely: "This intimacy *should
go no further*, for we have already exhausted all its
possibilities in our respective imaginations: and what we
shall end by discovering, behind the darkly woven colours
of sensuality, will be a friendship so profound that we
shall become bondsmen forever." It was, if you like, the
flirtation of minds prematurely exhausted by experience

which seemed so much more dangerous than a love founded in sexual attraction.

Knowing how much she loved Nessim and loving him so much myself, I could not contemplate this thought without terror. She lay beside me, breathing lightly, and staring at the cherub-haunted ceiling with her great eyes. I said: "It can come to nothing, this love-affair between a poor schoolteacher and an Alexandrian society woman. How bitter it would be to have it all end in a conventional scandal which would leave us alone together and give you the task of deciding how to dispose of me." Justine hated to hear the truth spoken. She turned upon one elbow and lowering those magnificent troubled eyes to mine she stared at me for a long moment. "There is no choice in this matter," she said in that hoarse voice I had come to love so much. "You talk as if there was a choice. We are not strong or evil enough to exercise choice. All this is part of an experiment arranged by something else, the city perhaps, or another part of ourselves. How do I know?"

I remember her sitting before the multiple mirrors at the dressmaker's, being fitted for a shark-skin costume, and saying: "Look! five different pictures of the same subject. Now if I wrote I would try for a multi-dimensional effect in character, a sort of prism-sightedness. Why should not people show more than one profile at a time?"

Now she yawned and lit a cigarette; and sitting up in bed clasped her slim ankles with her hands; reciting slowly, wryly, those marvellous lines of the old Greek poet about a love-affair long since past—they are lost in English. And hearing her speak his lines, touching every syllable of the thoughtful ironic Greek with tenderness, I felt once more the strange equivocal power of the city—its flat alluvial landscape and exhausted airs—and knew her for a true child of Alexandria; which is neither Greek, Syrian nor Egyptian, but a hybrid: a joint.

And with what feeling she reached the passage where the old man throws aside the ancient love-letter which had so moved him and exclaims: "I go sadly out on to the balcony; anything to change this train of thought, even if only to see some little movement in the city I love, in its

streets and shops!" Herself pushing open the shutters to
stand on the dark balcony above a city of coloured lights:
feeling the evening wind stir from the confines of Asia:
her body for an instant forgotten.

*   *   *   *   *

"Prince" Nessim is of course a joke; at any rate to the
shopkeepers and black-coated *commerçants* who saw him
drawn soundlessly down the Canopic way in the great silver Rolls with the daffodil hub-caps. To begin with he was
a Copt, not a Moslem. Yet somehow the nickname was
truly chosen for Nessim was princely in his detachment
from the common greed in which the recent instincts of
the Alexandrians—even the very rich ones—foundered.
Yet the factors which gave him a reputation for ec-
centricity were neither of them remarkable to those who
had lived outside the Levant. He did not care for money,
except to spend it—that was the first: the second was that
he did not own a *garçonnière*, and appeared to be quite
faithful to Justine—an unheard of state of affairs. As for
money, being so inordinately rich he was possessed by a
positive distaste for it, and would never carry it on his person. He spent in Arabian fashion and gave notes of hand
to shopkeepers; night-clubs and restaurants accepted his
signed cheques. Nevertheless his debts were punctually
honoured, and every morning Selim his secretary was sent
out with the car to trace the route of the previous day and
to pay any debts accumulated in the course of it.

This attitude was considered eccentric and highhanded
in the extreme by the inhabitants of the city whose coarse
and derived distinctions, menial preoccupations and faulty education gave them no clue to what style in the European sense was. But Nessim was born to this manner, not
merely educated to it; in this little world of studied carnal
moneymaking he could find no true province of operation
for a spirit essentially gentle and contemplative. The least
assertive of men he caused comment by acts which bore
the true stamp of his own personality. People were
inclined to attribute his manners to a foreign education,
but in fact Germany and England had done little but con-

fuse him and unfit him for the life of the city. The one had
implanted a taste for metaphysical speculation in what
was a natural Mediterranean mind, while Oxford had
tried to make him donnish and had only succeeded in
developing his philosophic bent to the point where he was
incapable of practising the art he most loved, painting. He
thought and suffered a good deal but he lacked the resolution to dare—the first requisite of a practitioner.

Nessim was at odds with the city, but since his enormous fortune brought him daily into touch with the
business men of the place they eased their constraint by
treating him with a humorous indulgence, a condescen-
sion such as one would bestow upon someone who was a
little soft in the head. It was perhaps not surprising if you
should walk in upon him at the office—that sarcophagus
of tubular steel and lighted glass—and find him seated
like an orphan at the great desk (covered in bells and
pulleys and patent lights)—eating brown bread and but-
ter and reading Vasari as he absently signed letters or
vouchers. He looked up at you with that pale almond
face, the expression shuttered, withdrawn, almost pleading. And yet somewhere through all this gentleness ran a
steel cord, for his staff was perpetually surprised to find
out that, inattentive as he appeared to be, there was no
detail of the business which he did not know; while hardly
a transaction he made did not turn out to be based on a
stroke of judgment. He was something of an oracle to his
own employees—and yet (they sighed and shrugged their
shoulders) he seemed not to care! Not to care about gain,
that is what Alexandria recognizes as madness.

I knew them by sight for many months before we actually met—as I knew everyone in the city. By sight and
no less by repute: for their emphatic, authoritative and
quite conventionless way of living had given them a certain notoriety among our provincial city-dwellers. She was
reputed to have had many lovers, and Nessim was
regarded as a *mari complaisant*. I had watched them
dancing together several times, he slender and with a
deep waist like a woman, and long arched beautiful
hands; Justine's lovely head—the deep bevel of that Ara-

bian nose and those translucent eyes, enlarged by belladonna. She gazed about her like a half-trained panther.

Then: once I had been persuaded to lecture upon the native poet of the city at the *Atelier des Beaux Arts*—a sort of club where gifted amateurs of the arts could meet, rent studios and so on. I had accepted because it meant a little money for Melissa's new coat, and autumn was on the way. But it was painful to me, feeling the old man all round me, so to speak, impregnating the gloomy streets around the lecture-room with the odour of those verses distilled from the shabby but rewarding loves he had experienced—loves perhaps bought with money, and lasting a few moments, yet living on now in his verse—so deliberately and tenderly had he captured the adventive minute and made all its colours fast. What an impertinence to lecture upon an ironist who so naturally, and with such fineness of instinct took his subject-matter from the streets and brothels of Alexandria! And to be talking, moreover, not to an audience of haberdashers' assistants and small clerks—his immortals—but to a dignified semicircle of society ladies for whom the culture he represented was a sort of blood-bank: they had come along for a transfusion. Many had actually foregone a bridge-party to do so, though they knew that instead of being uplifted they would be stupefied.

I remember saying only that I was haunted by his face—the horrifyingly sad gentle face of the last photograph; and when the solid burghers' wives had dribbled down the stone staircase into the wet streets where their lighted cars awaited them, leaving the gaunt room echoing with their perfumes, I noticed that they had left behind them one solitary student of the passions and the arts. She sat in a thoughtful way at the back of the hall, her legs crossed in a mannish attitude, puffing a cigarette. She did not look at me but crudely at the ground under her feet. I was flattered to think that perhaps one person had appreciated my difficulties. I gathered up my damp brief case and ancient mackintosh and made my way down to where a thin penetrating drizzle swept the streets

from the direction of the sea. I made for my lodgings
where by now Melissa would be awake, and would have
set out our evening meal on the newspaper-covered table,
having first sent Hamid out to the baker's to fetch the
roast—we had no oven of our own.

It was cold in the street and I crossed to the lighted
blaze of shops in Rue Fuad. In a grocer's window I saw a
small tin of olives with the name *Orvieto* on it, and overcome by a sudden longing to be on the right side of
the Mediterranean, entered the shop: bought it: had it
opened there and then: and sitting down at a marble
table in that gruesome light I began to eat Italy, its dark
scorched flesh, hand-modelled spring soil, dedicated
vines. I felt that Melissa would never understand this. I
should have to pretend I had lost the money.

I did not see at first the great car which she had abandoned in the street with its engine running. She came into
the shop with swift and resolute suddenness and said,
with the air of authority that Lesbians, or women with
money, assume with the obviously indigent: "What did
you mean by your remark about the antinomian nature of
irony?"—or some such sally which I have forgotten.

Unable to disentangle myself from Italy I looked up
boorishly and saw her leaning down at me from the mirrors on three sides of the room, her dark thrilling face full
of a troubled, arrogant reserve. I had of course forgotten
what I had said about irony or anything else for that matter, and I told her so with an indifference that was not
assumed. She heaved a short sigh, as if of natural relief,
and sitting down opposite me lit a French *caporal* and
with short decisive inspirations blew thin streamers of
blue smoke up into the harsh light. She looked to me a
trifle unbalanced, as she watched me with a candour I
found embarrassing—it was as if she were trying to
decide to what use I could be put. "I liked," she said, "the
way you quoted his lines about the city. Your Greek is
good. Doubtless you are a writer." I said: "Doubtless."
Not to be known always wounds. There seemed no point
in pursuing all this. I have always hated literary conversation. I offered her an olive which she ate swiftly, spitting

the pit into her gloved hand like a cat where she held it
absently, saying: "I want to take you to Nessim, my hus-
and. Will you come?"

A policeman had appeared in the doorway, obviously
troubled about the abandoned car. That was the first time
I saw the great house of Nessim with its statues and palm
loggias, its Courbets and Bonnards—and so on. It was
both beautiful and horrible. Justine hurried up the great
staircase, pausing only to transfer her olive-pit from the
pocket of her coat to a Chinese vase, calling all the time to
Nessim. We went from room to room, fracturing the
silences. He answered at last from the great studio on the
roof and racing to him like a gun-dog she metaphorically
dropped me at his feet and stood back, wagging her tail.
She had achieved me.

Nessim was sitting on the top of a ladder reading, and
he came slowly down to us, looking first at one and then at
the other. His shyness could not get any purchase of my
shabbiness, damp hair, tin of olives, and for my part I
could offer no explanation of my presence, since I did not
know for what purpose I had been brought here.

I took pity on him and offered him an olive; and sitting
down together we finished the tin, while Justine foraged
for drinks, talking, if I remember, of Orvieto where
neither of us had been. It is such a solace to think back to
that first meeting. Never have I been closer to them
both—closer, I mean, to their marriage; they seemed to me
then to be the magnificent two-headed animal a marriage
could be. Watching the benign warmth of the light in his
eye I realized, as I recalled all the scandalous rumours
about Justine, that whatever she had done had been done
in a sense *for him*—even what was evil or harmful in the
eyes of the world. Her love was like a skin in which he lay
sewn like the infant Heracles; and her efforts to achieve
herself had led her always towards, and not away from
him. The world has no use for this sort of paradox I know;
but it seemed to me then that Nessim knew and accepted
her in a way impossible to explain to someone for whom
love is still entangled with the qualities of possessiveness.
Once, much later, he told me: "What was I to do? Justine

was too strong for me in too many ways. I could only out-
love her—that was my long suit. I went ahead of her—I
anticipated every lapse; she found me already there, at
every point where she fell down, ready to help her to her
feet and show that it did not matter. After all she compromised the least part of me—my reputation."

This was much later: before the unlucky complex of
misfortunes had engulfed us we did not know each other
well enough to talk as freely as this. I also remember him
saying, once—this was at the summer villa near Bourg El
Arab: "It will puzzle you when I tell you that I thought
Justine great, in a sort of way. There are forms of
greatness, you know, which when not applied in art or
religion make havoc of ordinary life. Her gift was misap-
plied in being directed towards love. Certainly she was
bad in many ways, but they were all small ways. Nor can I
say that she harmed nobody. But those she harmed most
she made fruitful. She expelled people from their old
selves. It was bound to hurt, and many mistook the nature
of the pain she inflicted. Not I." And smiling his well-
known smile, in which sweetness was mixed with an inexpressible bitterness, he repeated softly under his breath
the words: "Not I."

*   *   *   *   *

Capodistria . . . how does he fit in? He is more of a
goblin than a man, you would think. The flat triangular
head of the snake with the huge frontal lobes; the hair
grows forward in a widow's peak. A whitish flickering
tongue is forever busy keeping his thin lips moist. He is
ineffably rich and does not have to lift a finger for himself.
He sits all day on the terrace of the Brokers' Club watching the women pass, with the restless eye of someone
endlessly shuffling through an old soiled pack of cards.
From time to time there is a flick, like a chameleon's
tongue striking—a signal almost invisible to the inattentive. Then a figure slips from the terrace to trail the
woman he has indicated. Sometimes his agents will quite
openly stop and importune women on the street in his
name, mentioning a sum of money. No one is offended by

the mention of money in our city. Some girls simply laugh. Some consent at once. You never see vexation on their features. Virtue with us is never feigned. Nor vice. Both are natural.

Capodistria sits remote from it all, in his immaculate shark-skin coat with the coloured silk handkerchief lolling at his breast. His narrow shoes gleam. His friends call him *Da Capo* because of a sexual prowess reputed to be as great as his fortune—or his ugliness. He is obscurely related to Justine who says of him: "I pity him. His heart has withered in him and he has been left with the five senses, like pieces of a broken wineglass." However a life of such striking monotony does not seem to depress him. His family is noted for the number of suicides in it, and his psychological inheritance is an unlucky one with its history of mental disturbance and illness. He is un-perturbed however and says, touching his temples with a long forefinger: "All my ancestors went wrong here in the head. My father also. He was a great womanizer. When he was very old he had a model of the perfect woman built in rubber—life-size. She could be filled with hot water in the winter. She was strikingly beautiful. He called her Sabina after his mother, and took her everywhere. He had a passion for travelling on ocean liners and actually lived on one for the last two years of his life, travelling backwards and forwards to New York. Sabina had a wonderful wardrobe. It was a sight to see them come into the dining-saloon, dressed for dinner. He travelled with his keeper, a manservant called Kelly. Be-tween them, held on either side like a beautiful drunkard, walked Sabina in her marvellous evening clothes. The night he died he said to Kelly: 'Send Demetrius a telegram and tell him that Sabina died in my arms tonight without any pain.' She was buried with him off Naples." His laughter is the most natural and unfeigned of any I have ever heard.

Later when I was half mad with worry and heavily in Capodistria's debt, I found him less accommodating a companion; and one night, there was Melissa sitting half drunk on the footstool by the fire holding in those long

reflective fingers the I.O.U. which I had made out to him
with the curt word *"discharged"* written across it in green
ink. . . . These memories wound. Melissa said: "Justine
would have paid your debt from her immense fortune. I
did not want to see her increase her hold over you.
Besides, even though you no longer care for me I still
wanted to do something for you—and this was the least of
sacrifices. I did not think that it would hurt you so much
for me to sleep with him. Have you not done the same for
me—I mean did you not borrow the money from Justine
to send me away for the X-ray business? Though you lied
about it I knew. I won't lie, I never do. Here, take it and
destroy it: but don't gamble with him any more. He is not
of your kind." And turning her head she made the Arab
motion of spitting.

*   *   *   *   *

Of Nessim's outer life—those immense and boring
receptions, at first devoted to business colleagues but later
to become devoted to obscure political ends—I do not
wish to write. As I slunk through the great hall and up the
stairs to the studio I would pause to study the great
leather shield on the mantelpiece with its plan of the
table—to see who had been placed on Justine's right and
left. For a short while they made a kindly attempt to
include me in these gatherings but I rapidly tired of them
and pleaded illness, though I was glad to have the run of
the studio and the immense library. And afterwards we
would meet like conspirators and Justine would throw off
the gay, bored, petulant affectations which she wore in
her social life. They would kick off their shoes and play pi-
quet by candlelight. Later, going to bed, she would catch
sight of herself in the mirror on the first landing and say
to her reflection: "Tiresome pretentious hysterical Jewess
that you are!"

*   *   *   *   *

Mnemjian's Babylonian barber's shop was on the corner of Fuad I and Nebi Daniel and here every morning
Pombal lay down beside me in the mirrors. We were lifted
simultaneously and swung smoothly down into the

ground wrapped like dead Pharaohs, only to reappear at
the same instant on the ceiling, spread out like specimens.
White cloths had been spread over us by a small black
boy while in a great Victorian moustache-cup the barber
thwacked up his dense and sweet-smelling lather before
applying it in direct considered brush-strokes to our
cheeks. The first covering complete, he surrendered his
task to an assistant while he went to the great strop hanging among the flypapers on the end wall of the shop and
began to sweeten the edge of an English razor.

Little Mnemjian is a dwarf with a violet eye that has
never lost its childhood. He is the Memory man, the archives of the city. If you should wish to know the ancestry
or income of the most casual passer-by you have only to
ask him; he will recite the details in a sing-song voice as he
strops his razor and tries it upon the coarse black hair of
his forearm. What he does not know he can find out in a
matter of moments. Moreover he is as well briefed in the
living as in the dead; I mean this in the literal sense, for
the Greek Hospital employs him to shave and lay out its
victims before they are committed to the undertakers—a
task which he performs with relish tinged by racial unc-
tion. His ancient trade embraces the two worlds, and
some of his best observations begin with the phrase: "As
so-and-so said to me with his *last breath*." He is rumoured
to be fantastically attractive to women and he is said to
have put away a small fortune earned for him by his admirers. But he also has several elderly Egyptian ladies, the
wives and widows of pashas, as permanent clients upon
whom he calls at regular intervals to set their hair. They
have, as he says slyly, "got beyond everything"—and
reaching up over his back to touch the unsightly hump
which crowns it he adds with pride: "*This* excites them."
Among other things, he has a gold cigarette case given to
him by one of these admirers in which he keeps a stock
of loose cigarette-paper. His Greek is defective but ad-
venturous and vivid and Pombal refuses to permit him
to talk French, which he does much better.

He does a little mild procuring for my friend, and I am
always astonished by the sudden flights of poetry of which

he is capable in describing his *protégées*. Leaning over
Pombal's moonlike face he will say, for example, in a
discreet undertone, as the razor begins to whisper: "I
have something for you—*something special.*" Pombal
catches my eye in the mirror and looks hastily away lest
we infect one another by a smile. He gives a cautious
grunt. Mnemjian leans lightly on the balls of his feet, his
eyes squinting slightly. The small wheedling voice puts a
husk of double meaning round everything he says, and his
speech is not the less remarkable for being punctuated by
small world-weary sighs. For a while nothing more is said
I can see the top of Mnemjian's head in the mirror—that
obscene outcrop of black hair which he had trained into a
spitcurl at each temple, hoping no doubt to draw attention away from that crooked *papier mâché* back of his.
While he works with a razor his eyes dim out and his
features become as expressionless as a bottle. His fingers
travel as coolly upon our live faces as they do upon those
of the fastidious and (yes, lucky) dead. "This time," says
Mnemjian, "you will be delighted from every point of
view. She is young, cheap and clean. You will say to yourself, a young partridge, a honey-comb with all its honey
sealed in it, a dove. She is in difficulties over money. She
has recently come from the lunatic asylum in Helwan
where her husband tried to get her locked up as mad. I
have arranged for her to sit at the Rose Marie at the end
table on the pavement. Go and see her at one o'clock; if
you wish her to accompany you give her the card I will
prepare for you. But remember, you will pay only me. As
one gentleman to another it is the only condition I lay
down."

He says nothing more for the time. Pombal continues to
stare at himself in the mirror, his natural curiosity doing
battle with the forlorn apathy of the summer air. Later no
doubt he will bustle into the flat with some exhausted,
disoriented creature whose distorted smile can rouse no
feelings in him save those of pity. I cannot say that my
friend lacks kindness, for he is always trying to find work
of some sort for these girls; indeed most of the consulates
are staffed by ex-casuals desperately trying to look cor-

rect: whose jobs they owe to Georges' importunities
among his colleagues of the career. Nevertheless there is
no woman too humble, too battered, too old, to receive
those outward attentions—those little gallantries and *sor-
ties* of wit which I have come to associate with the Gallic
temperament; the heady meretricious French charm
which evaporates so easily into pride and mental in-
dolence—like French thought which flows so quickly into
sand-moulds, the original *esprit* hardening immediately
into deadening concepts. The light play of sex which
hovers over his thought and actions has, however, an air
of disinterestedness which makes it qualitatively different
from, say, the actions and thoughts of Capodistria, who
often joins us for a morning shave. Capodistria has the
purely involuntary knack of turning everything into a
woman; under his eyes chairs become painfully conscious
of their bare legs. He impregnates things. At table I have
seen a water-melon become conscious under his gaze so
that it felt the seeds inside it stirring with life! Women feel
like birds confronted by a viper when they gaze into that
narrow flat face with its tongue always moving across the
thin lips I think of Melissa once more: *hortus conclusus,
soror mea sponsor....*

*   *   *   *   *

"*Regard dérisoire,*" says Justine. "How is it you are so
much one of us and yet . . . you are not?" She is combing
that dark head in the mirror, her mouth and eyes drawn
up about a cigarette. "You are a mental refugee of course,
being Irish, but you miss our *angoisse.*" What she is groping after is really the distinctive quality which emanates
not from us but from the landscape—the metallic flavours
of exhaustion which impregnate the airs of Mareotis.

As she speaks I am thinking of the founders of the city,
of the soldier-God in his glass coffin, the youthful body
lapped in silver, riding down the river towards his tomb.
Or of that great square Negro head reverberating with a
concept of God conceived in the spirit of pure intellectual
play—Plotinus. It is as if the preoccupations of this
landscape were centred somewhere out of reach of the

average inhabitant—in a region where the flesh, stripped
by over-indulgence of its final reticences, must yield to a
preoccupation vastly more comprehensive: or perish in
the kind of exhaustion represented by the works of the
Mouseion, the guileless playing of hermaphrodites in the
green courtyards of art and science. Poetry as a clumsy attempt at the artificial insemination of the Muses; the
burning stupid metaphor of Berenice's hair glittering in
the night sky above Melissa's sleeping face. "Ah!" said
Justine once, "that there should be something free, something Polynesian about the licence in which we live." Or
even Mediterranean, she might have added, for the con-
notation of every kiss would be different in Italy or Spain;
here our bodies were chafed by the harsh desiccated
winds blowing up out of the deserts of Africa and for love
we were forced to substitute a wiser but crueller mental
tenderness which emphasized loneliness rather than ex-
purgated it.

Now even the city had two centres of gravity—the true
and magnetic north of its personality: and between them
the temperament of its inhabitants sparked harshly like a
leaky electric discharge. Its spiritual centre was the
forgotten site of the Soma where once the confused young
soldier's body lay in its borrowed Godhead; its temporal
site the Brokers' Club where like Caballi* the cotton
brokers sat to sip their coffee, puff rank cheroots and
watch Capodistria—as people upon a river-bank will
watch the progress of a fisherman or an artist. The one
symbolized for me the great conquests of man in the
realms of matter, space and time—which must inevitably
yield their harsh knowledge of defeat to the conqueror in
his coffin; the other was no symbol but the living limbo of
free-will in which my beloved Justine wandered, searching with such frightening singleness of mind for the integrating spark which might lift her into a new perspective of herself. In her, as an Alexandrian, licence was in a
curious way a form of self-abnegation, a travesty of
freedom; and if I saw her as an exemplar of the city it was
not of Alexandria or Plotinus that I was forced to think,
but of the sad thirtieth child of Valentinos who fell, "not

like Lucifer by rebelling against God, but by desiring too
ardently to be united to him."* Anything pressed too far
becomes a sin.

Broken from the divine harmony of herself he fell, says
the tragic philosopher, and became the manifestation of
matter; and the whole universe of her city, of the world,
was formed out of her agony and remorse. The tragic seed
from which her thoughts and actions grew was the seed of
a pessimistic gnosticism.

That this identification was a true one I know—for
much later when, with so many misgivings, she allowed
me to join the little circle which gathered every month
about Balthazar, it was always what he had to say about
gnosticism which most interested her. I remember her
asking one night, so anxiously, so pleadingly if she had in-
terpreted his thinking rightly: "I mean, that God neither
created us nor wished us to be created, but that we are the
work of an inferior deity, a Demiurge, who wrongly
believed himself to be God? Heavens, how probable it
seems; and this overweening *hubris* has been handed on
down to our children." And stopping me as we walked by
the expedient of standing in front of me and catching hold
of the lapels of my coat she gazed earnestly into my eyes
and said: "What do you believe? You never say anthing.
At the most you sometimes laugh." I did not know how to
reply for all ideas seem equally good to me; the fact of
their existence proves that someone is creating. Does it
matter whether they are objectively right or wrong? They
could never remain so for long. "But it matters," she cried
with a touching emphasis. "It matters deeply my darling,
deeply."

We are the children of our landscape; it dictates
behaviour and even thought in the measure to which we
are responsive to it. I can think of no better identification.
"Your doubt, for example, which contains so much anxiety
and such a thirst for an absolute truth, is so different from
the scepticism of the Greek, from the mental play of the
Mediterranean mind with its deliberate resort to sophistry
as part of the *game* of thought; for your thought is a
weapon, a theology."

"But how else can action be judged?" "It cannot be judged comprehensively until thought itself can be judged, for our thoughts themselves are acts. It is an attempt to make partial judgements upon either that leads to misgivings."

I liked so much the way she would suddenly sit down on a wall, or a broken pillar in that shattered backyard to Pompey's Pillar, and be plunged in an inextinguishable sorrow at some idea whose impact had only just made itself felt in her mind. "You really believe so?" she would say with such sorrow that one was touched and amused at the same time. "And why do you smile? You always smile at the most serious things. Ah! surely you should be sad?" If she ever knew me at all she must later have discovered that for those of us who feel deeply and who are at all conscious of the inextricable tangle of human thought there is only one response to be made—ironic tenderness and silence.

In a night so brilliant with stars where the glow-worms in the shrill dry grass gave back their ghostly mauve lambence to the sky there was nothing else to do but sit by her side, stroking that dark head of beautiful hair and saying nothing. Underneath, like a dark river, the noble quotation which Balthazar had taken as a text and which he read in a voice that trembled partly with emotion and partly with the fatigue of so much abstract thought: "The day of the *corpora* is the night for the *spiritus*. When the bodies cease their labour the spirits in man begin their work. The waking of the body is the sleep of the spirit and the spirit's sleep a waking for the body." And later, like a thunderclap: *"Evil is good perverted."**

* * * * *

That Nessim had her watched I for a long time doubted; after all, she seemed as free as a bat to flit about the town at night, and never did I hear her called upon to give an account of her movements. It could not have been easy to spy upon someone so protean, in touch with the life of the town at so many points. Nevertheless it is possible that she was watched lest she should come to harm.

One night an incident brought this home to me, for I had been asked to dine at the old house. When they were alone we dined in a little pavilion at the end of the garden where the summer coolness could mingle with the whisper of water from the four lions' heads bordering the fountain. Justine was late on this particular occasion and Nessim sat alone, with the curtains drawn back towards the west, reflectively polishing a yellow jade from his collection in those long gentle fingers.

It was already forty minutes past the hour and he had already given the signal for dinner to begin when the little black telephone extension gave a small needle-like sound. He crossed to the table and picked it up with a sigh, and I heard him say, "yes" impatiently; then he spoke for a while in a low voice, the language changing abruptly to Arabic, and for a moment I had the sudden intuitive feeling that it was Mnemjian talking to him over the wire. I do not know why I should feel this. He scribbled something rapidly on an envelope and putting down the receiver stood for a second memorizing what he had written. Then he turned to me, and it was all of a sudden a different Nessim who said: "Justine may need our help. Will you come with me?" And without waiting for an answer he ran down the steps, past the lily-pond in the direction of the garage. I followed as well as I could and it could only have been a matter of minutes before he swung the little sports car through the heavy gates into Rue Fuad and began to weave his way down to the sea through the network of streets which slide down towards Ras El Tin. Though it was not late there were few people about and we raced away along the curving flanks of the Esplanade towards the Yacht Club grimly overtaking the few horse-drawn cabs ("carriages of love") which dawdled up and down by the sea.

At the fort we doubled back and entered the huddled slums which lie behind Tatwig Street, our blond headlights picking out the ant-hill cafés and crowded squares with an unaccustomed radiance; from somewhere behind the immediate skyline of smashed and unlimbered houses came the piercing shrieks and ululations of a burial

procession, whose professional mourners made the night
hideous with their plaints for the dead. We abandoned
the car in a narrow street by the mosque and Nessim entered the shadowy doorway of some great tenement
house, half of which consisted of shuttered and barred
offices with blurred nameplates. A solitary *boab* (the *con-
cierge* of Egypt) sat on his perch wrapped in clouts, for
all the world like some discarded material object (an old
motor tyre, say)—smoking a short-stemmed hubble-
bubble. Nessim spoke to him sharply, and almost before
the man could reply passed through the back of the building into a sort of dark backyard flanked by a series of
dilapidated houses built of earth-brick and scaly plaster.
He stopped only to light his cigarette-lighter, and by its
feeble light we began to quest along the doors. At the
fourth door he clicked the machine shut and knocked with
his fist. Receiving no answer he pushed it open.

A dark corridor led to a small shadowy room lit by the
feeble light of rush-lamps. This was apparently our
destination.

The scene upon which we intruded was ferociously
original, if for no other reason than that the light, pushing
up from the mud floor, touched out the eyebrows and lips
and cheek-bones of the participants while it left great
patches of shadow on their faces—so that they looked as if
they had been half-eaten by the rats which one could hear
scrambling among the rafters of this wretched tenement.
It was a house of child prostitutes, and there in the
dimness, clad in ludicrous biblical nightshirts, with
rouged lips, arch bead fringes and cheap rings, stood a
dozen fuzzy-haired girls who could not have been much
above ten years of age; the peculiar innocence of childhood which shone out from under the fancy-dress was in
startling contrast to the barbaric adult figure of the
French sailor who stood in the centre of the room on flexed
calves, his ravaged and tormented face thrust out from
the neck towards Justine who stood with her half-profile
turned towards us. What he had just shouted had expired
on the silence but the force with which the words had
been uttered was still visible in the jut of the chin and the

black corded muscles which held his head upon his shoulders. As for Justine, her face was lit by a sort of painful academic precision. She held a bottle raised in one hand, and it was clear that she had never thrown one before, for she held it the wrong way.

On a rotting sofa in one corner of the room, magnetically lit by the warm shadow reflected from the walls, lay one of the children horribly shrunk up in its nightshirt in an attitude which suggested death. The wall above the sofa was covered in the blue imprints of juvenile hands—the talisman which in this part of the world guards a house against the evil eye. It was the only decoration in the room: indeed the commonest decoration of the whole Arab quarter of the city.

We stood there, Nessim and I, for a good half-second, astonished by the scene which had a sort of horrifying beauty—like some hideous colored engraving for a Victorian penny bible, say, whose subject matter had somehow become distorted and displaced. Justine was breathing harshly in a manner which suggested that she was on the point of tears.

We pounced on her, I suppose, and dragged her out into the street; at any rate I can only remember the three of us reached the sea and driving the whole length of the Corniche in clean bronze moonlight, Nessim's sad and silent face reflected in the driving-mirror, and the figure of his silent wife seated beside him, gazing out at the crashing silver waves and smoking the cigarette which she had burrowed from the pockets of his jacket. Later in the garage, before we left the car, she kissed Nessim tenderly on the eyes.

* * * * *

All this I have come to regard as a sort of overture to that first real meeting face to face, when such understanding as we had enjoyed until then—a gaiety and friendship founded in tastes which were common to the three of us—disintegrated into something which was not love—how could it have been?—but into a sort of mental possession in which the bonds of a ravenous sexuality played the least part. How did we let it come about—matched

as we were so well in experience, weathered and sea-
soned by the disappointments of love in other places?

In autumn the female bays turn to uneasy phosphorus
and after the long chafing days of dust one feels the first
palpitations of the autumn, like the wings of a butterfly
fluttering to unwrap themselves. Mareotis turns lemon-
mauve and its muddy flanks are starred by sheets of ra-
diant anemones, growing through the quickened plaster-
mud of the shore. One day while Nessim was away in
Cairo I called at the house to borrow some books and to
my surprise found Justine alone in the studio, darning an
old pullover. She had taken the night train back to Alexandria, leaving Nessim to attend some business con-
ference. We had tea together and then, on a sudden impulse took our bathing things and drove out through the
rusty slag-heaps of Mex towards the sand-beaches off
Bourg El Arab, glittering in the mauve-lemon light of the
fast-fading afternoon. Here the open sea boomed upon
the carpets of fresh sand the colour of oxidized mercury;
its deep melodious percussion was the background to such
conversation as we had. We walked ankle deep in the
spurge of those shallow dimpled pools, choked here and
there with sponges torn up by the roots and flung ashore.
We passed no one on the road I remember save a gaunt
Bedouin youth carrying on his head a wire crate full of
wild birds caught with lime-twigs. Dazed quail.

We lay for a long time, side by side in our wet bathing
costumes to take the last pale rays of the sun upon our
skins in the delicious evening coolness. I lay with half-shut
eyes while Justine (how clearly I see her!) was up on one
elbow, shading her eyes with the palm of one hand and
watching my face. Whenever I was talking she had the
habit of gazing at my lips with a curious half-mocking, an
almost impertinent intentness, as if she were waiting for
me to mispronounce a word. If indeed it all began at this
point I have forgotten the context, but I remember the
hoarse troubled voice saying something like: "And if it
should happen to us—what would you say?" But before I
could say anything she leaned down and kissed me—I
should say derisively, antagonistically, on the mouth. This

seemed so much out of character that I turned with some
sort of half-formulated reproach on my lips—but from
here on her kisses were like tremendous soft breathless
stabs punctuating the savage laughter which seemed to
well up in her—a jeering unstable laughter. It struck me
then that she was like someone who had had a bad fright.
If I said now: "It must not happen to us," she must have
replied: "But let us *suppose*. What if it did?" Then—and
this I remember clearly—the mania for self-justification
seized her (we spoke French: language creates national
character) and between those breathless half-seconds
when I felt her strong mouth on my own and those
worldly brown arms closing upon mine: "I would not
mistake it for gluttony or self-indulgence. We are too
worldly for that: simply we have something to learn from
each other. What is it?"

What was it? "And is this the way?" I remember asking
as I saw the tall toppling figure of Nessim upon the evening sky. "I do not know," she said, with a savage,
obstinate, desperate expression of humility upon her face,
"I do not know"; and she pressed herself upon me like
someone pressing upon a bruise. It was as if she wished to
expunge the very thought of me, and yet in the fragile
quivering context of every kiss found a sort of painful surcease—like cold water on a sprain. How well I recognized
her now as a child of the city, which decrees that its
women shall be the voluptuaries not of pleasure but of
pain, doomed to hunt for what they least dare to find!

She got up now and walked away down the long curving perspective of the beach crossing the pools of lava
slowly, her head bent; and I thought of Nessim's
handsome face smiling at her from every mirror in the
room. The whole of the scene which we had just enacted
was invested in my mind with a dream-like improbability.
It was curious in an objective sort of way to notice how
my hands trembled as I lit a cigarette and rose to follow
her.

But when I overtook her and halted her the face she
turned to me was that of a sick demon. She was in a
towering rage. "You thought I simply wanted to make

love? God! haven't we had enough of that? How is it that
you do not *know* what I feel for once? How is it?" She
stamped her foot in the wet sand. It was not merely that a
geological fault had opened in the ground upon which we
had been treading with such self-confidence. It was as if
some long-disused mineshaft in my own character had
suddenly fallen in. I recognized that this barren traffic in
ideas and feelings had driven a path through towards the
denser jungles of the heart; and that here we became
bondsmen in the body, possessors of an enigmatic
knowledge which could only be passed on—received,
deciphered, understood—by those rare complementaries
of ours in the world. (How few they were, how seldom
one found them!) "After all," I remember her saying,
"this has nothing to do with sex," which tempted me to
laugh though I recognized in the phrase her desperate attempt to dissociate the flesh from the message it carried. I
suppose this sort of thing always happens to bankrupts
when they fall in love. I saw then what I should have seen
long before: namely that our friendship had ripened to a
point when we had already become in a way part-owners
of each other.

I think we were both horrified by the thought; for exhausted as we were we could not help but quail before
such a relationship. We did not say any more but walked
back along the beach to where we had left our clothes,
speechless and hand in hand. Justine looked utterly exhausted. We were both dying to get away from each
other, in order to examine our own feelings. We did not
speak to each other again. We drove into the city and she
dropped me at the usual corner near my flat. I snapped
the door of the car closed and she drove off without a
word or a glance in my direction.

As I opened the door of my room I could still see the
imprint of Justine's foot in the wet sand. Melissa was
reading, and looking up at me she said with characteristic
calm foreknowledge: "Something has happened—what is
it?" I could not tell her since I did not myself know. I took
her face in my hands and examined it silently, with a care
and attention, with a sadness and hunger I don't ever

remember feeling before. She said: "It is not me you are seeing, it is someone else." But in truth I was seeing Melissa for the first time. In some paradoxical way it was Justine who was now permitting me to see Melissa as she really was—and to recognize my love for her. Melissa smilingly reached for a cigarette and said: "You are falling in love with Justine"; and I answered as sincerely, as honestly, as painfully as I could: "No, Melissa, it is worse than that"—though I could not for the life of me have explained how or why.

When I thought of Justine I thought of some great freehand composition, a cartoon of a woman representing someone released from bondage in the male. "Where the carrion is," she once quoted proudly from Boehme, speaking of her native city, "there the eagles will gather." Truly she looked and seemed an eagle at this moment. But Melissa was a sad painting from a winter landscape contained by dark sky; a window-box with a few flowering geraniums lying forgotten on the window-sill of a cement-factory.

There is a passage in one of Justine's diaries which comes to mind here. I translate it here because though it must have referred to incidents long preceding those which I have recounted yet nevertheless it almost exactly expresses the curiously ingrown quality of a love which I have come to recognize as peculiar to the city rather than to ourselves. "Idle," she writes, "to imagine falling in love as a correspondence of minds, of thoughts; it is a simultaneous firing of two spirits engaged in the autonomous act of growing up. And the sensation is of something having noiselessly exploded inside each of them. Around this event, dazed and preoccupied, the lover moves examining his or her own experience; her gratitude alone, stretching away towards a mistaken donor, creates the illusion that she communicates with her fellow, but this is false. The loved object is simply one that has shared an experience at the same moment of time, narcissistically; and the desire to be near the beloved object is at first not due to the idea of possessing it, but simply to let the two experiences compare themselves, like reflections in different mirrors. All

this may precede the first look, kiss, or touch; precede am-
bition, pride, or envy; precede the first declarations which
mark the turning point—for from here love degenerates
into habit, possession, and back to loneliness." How
characteristic and how humourless a delineation of the
magical gift: and yet how true ... of Justine!

"Every man," she writes elsewhere, and here I can hear
the hoarse and sorrowful accents of her voice repeating
the words as she writes them: "Every man is made of clay
and daimon, and no woman can nourish both."

That afternoon she went home to find that Nessim had
arrived by the afternoon plane. She complained of feeling
feverish and went early to bed. When he came to sit by
her side and take her temperature she said something
which struck him as interesting enough to remember—for
long afterwards he repeated it to me: "This is nothing of
medical interest—a small chill. Diseases are not interested
in those who want to die." And then with one of those
characteristic swerves of association, like a swallow turning in mid-air she added, "Oh! Nessim, I have always
been so strong. Has it prevented me from being truly
loved?"

*   *   *   *   *

It was through Nessim that I first began to move with
any freedom in the great cobweb of Alexandrian society;
my own exiguous earnings did not even permit me to visit
the night-club where Melissa danced. At first I was a trifle
ashamed of being forever on the receiving end of Nessim's
hospitality, but we were soon such fast friends that I went
everywhere with them and never gave the matter a
thought. Melissa unearthed an ancient dinner-jacket from
one of my trunks and refurbished it. It was in their company that I first visited the club where she danced. It was
strange to sit between Justine and Nessim and watch the
flaky white light suddenly blaze down upon a Melissa I
could no longer recognize under a layer of paint which
gave her gentle face an air of gross and precocious
unimaginativeness. I was horrified too at the banality of
her dancing, which was bad beyond measure; yet watching her make those gentle and ineffectual movements of

her slim hands and feet (the air of a gazelle harnessed to a water-wheel) I was filled with tenderness at her mediocrity, at the dazed and self-deprecating way she bowed to the lukewarm applause. Afterwards she was made to carry a tray round and take up a collection for the orchestra, and this she did with a hopeless timidity, coming to the table where I sat with lowered eyes under those ghastly false lashes, and with trembling hands. My friends did not know at that time of our relationship; but I noticed Justine's curious and mocking glance as I turned out my pockets and found a few notes to thrust into the tray with hands that shook not less than Melissa's—so keenly did I feel her embarrassment.

Afterwards when I got back to the flat a little tipsy and exhilarated from dancing with Justine I found her still awake, boiling a kettle of water over the electric ring: "Oh why," she said, "did you put all that money into the collecting tray? A whole week's wages: are you mad? What will we eat tomorrow?"

We were both hopelessly improvident in money matters, yet somehow we managed better together than apart. At night, walking back late from the night-club, she would pause in the alley outside the house and if she saw my light still burning give a low whistle: and I, hearing the signal, would put down the book I was reading and creep quietly down the staircase, seeing in my mind's eye her lips pursed about that low liquid sound, as if to take the soft imprint of a brush. At the time of which I write she was still being followed about and importuned by the old man or his agents. Without exchanging a word we would join hands and hurry down the maze of alleys by the Polish Consulate, pausing from time to time in a dark doorway to see if there was anyone on our trail. At last, far down where the shops tailed away into the blue we would step out into the sea-gleaming milk-white Alexandrian midnight—our preoccupations sliding from us in that fine warm air; and we would walk towards the morning star which lay throbbing above the dark velvet breast of Montaza, touched by the wind and the waves.

In these days Melissa's absorbed and provoking

gentleness had all the qualities of a rediscovered youth.
Her long uncertain fingers—I used to feel them moving
over my face when she thought I slept, as if to memorize
the happiness we had shared. In her there was a pliancy, a
resilience which was Oriental—a passion to serve. My
shabby clothes—the way she picked up a dirty shirt
seemed to engulf it with an overflowing solicitude; in the
morning I found my razor beautifully cleaned and even
the toothpaste laid upon the brush in readiness. Her care
for me was a goad, provoking me to give my life some sort
of shape and style that might match the simplicity of hers.
Of her experiences in love she would never speak, turning
from them with a weariness and distaste which suggested
that they had been born of necessity rather than desire.
She paid me the compliment of saying: "For the first time
I am not afraid to be light-headed or foolish with a man."

Being poor was also a deep bond. For the most part our
excursions were the simple excursions that all provincials
make in a sea-side town. The little tin tram bore us with
the clicking of its wheels to the sand-beaches of Sidi Bishr,
or we spent Shem El Nessim in the gardens of Nouzha,
camped on the grass under the oleanders among some
dozens of humble Egyptian families. The inconvenience
of crowds brought us both distraction and great intimacy.
By the rotting canal watching the children dive for coins
in the ooze, or eating a fragment of watermelon from a
stall we wandered among the other idlers of the city,
anonymously happy. The very names of the tram stops
echoed the poetry of these journeys: Chatby, Camp de
César, Laurens, Mazarita, Glymenopoulos, Sidi Bishr. . . .

Then there was the other side: coming back late at
night to find her asleep with her red slippers kicked off
and the little hashish-pipe beside her on the pillow . . . I
would know that one of her depressions had set in. At
such times there was nothing to be done with her; she
would become pale, melancholy, exhausted-looking, and
would be unable to rouse herself from her lethargy for
days at a time. She talked much to herself, and would
spend hours listening to the radio and yawning, or going
negligently through a bundle of old film magazines. At

such times when the *cafard* of the city seized her I was at
my wits' end to devise a means of rousing her. She would
lie with far-seeing eyes like a sibyl, stroking my face and
repeating over and over again: "If you knew how I have
lived you would leave me. I am not the woman for you,
for any man. I am exhausted. Your kindness is wasted." If
I protested that it was not kindness but love she might say
with a grimace: "If it were love you would poison me
rather than let me go on like this." Then she would begin
to cough with her uncollapsed lung and, unable to bear
the sound, I would go for a walk in the dark Arab-
smudged street, or visit the British Council library to consult reference books; and here, where the general impression of British culture suggested parsimony, in-
digence, intellectual strap-hanging—here I would pass
the evening alone, glad of the studious rustle and babble
around me.

But there were other times too: those sun-tormented afternoons—"honey-sweating," as Pombal called them—
when we lay together bemused by the silence, watching
the yellow curtains breathing tenderly against the light—
the quiet respirations of the wind off Mareotis which
matched our own. Then she might rise and consult the
clock after giving it a shake and listening to it intently: sit
naked at the dressing-table to light a cigarette—looking so
young and pretty, with her slender arm raised to show the
cheap bracelet I had given her. ("Yes, I am looking at
myself, but it helps me to think about you.") And turning
aside from this fragile mirror-worship she would swiftly
cross to the ugly scullery which was my only bath-room,
and standing at the dirty iron sink would wash herself
with deft swift movements, gasping at the coldness of the
water, while I lay inhaling the warmth and sweetness of
the pillow upon which her dark head had been resting:
watching the long bereft Greek face, with its sane pointed
nose and candid eyes, the satiny skin that is given only to
the thymus-dominated, the mole upon the slender stalk of
the neck. These are the moments which are not calculable,
and cannot be assessed in words; they live on in the solution of memory, like wonderful creatures, unique of their

kind, dredged up from the floors of some unexplored ocean.

* * * * *

Thinking of that summer when Pombal decided to let his flat to Pursewarden, much to my annoyance. I disliked this literary figure for the contrast he offered to his own work—poetry and prose of real grace. I did not know him well but he was financially successful as a novelist which made me envious, and through years of becoming social practice had developed a sort of *savoir faire* which I felt should never become part of my own equipment. He was little, fattish and blond and gave the impression of a young man lying becalmed in his mother. I cannot say that he was not kind or good, for he was both—but the inconvenience of living in the flat with someone I did not like was galling. However it would have involved greater inconvenience to move so I accepted the boxroom at the end of the corridor at a reduced rent, and did my washing in the grimy little scullery.

Pursewarden could afford to be convivial and about twice a week I was kept up by the noise of drinking and laughter from the flat. One night quite late there came a knock at the door. In the corridor stood Pursewarden, looking pale and rather perky—as if he had just been fired out of a gun into a net. Beside him stood a stout naval stoker of unprepossessing ugliness—looking like all naval stokers; as if he had been sold into slavery as a child. "I say," said Pursewarden shrilly, "Pombal told me you were a doctor; would you come and take a look at somebody who is ill?" I had once told Georges of the year I spent as a medical student with the result that for him I had become a fully-fledged doctor. He not only confided all his own indispositions to my care—which included frequent infestations of body-crabs—but he once went so far as to try and persuade me to perform an abortion for him on the dining-room table. I hastened to tell Pursewarden that I was certainly not a doctor, and advised him to telephone for one: but the phone was out of order, and the *boab* could not be roused from his sleep: so more in the spirit of disinterested curiosity than anything I put on a

mackintosh over my pyjamas and made my way along the
corridor. This is how we met!

Opening the door I was immediately blinded by the
glare and smoke. The party did not seem to be of the
usual kind, for the guests consisted of three or four
maimed-looking naval cadets, and a prostitute from Golfo's tavern, smelling of briny paws and *taphia.** Im-
probably enough, too, she was bending over a figure
seated on the end of a couch—the figure which I now
recognize as Melissa, but which then seemed like a
catastrophic Greek comic mask. Melissa appeared to be
raving, but soundlessly for her voice had gone—so that
she looked like a film of herself without a sound-track.
Her features were a cave. The older woman appeared to
be panic-stricken, and was boxing her ears and pulling her
hair; while one of the naval cadets was splashing water
rather inexpertly upon her from a heavily decorated
chamber-pot which was one of Pombal's dearest treasures
and which bore the royal arms of France on its underside.
Somewhere out of sight someone was being slowly,
unctuously sick. Pursewarden stood beside me surveying
the scene, looking rather ashamed of himself.

Melissa was pouring with sweat, and her hair was glued
to her temples; as we broke the circle of her tormentors
she sank back into an expressionless quivering silence,
with this permanently engraved shriek on her face. It
would have been wise to try and find out where she had
been and what she had been eating and drinking, but a
glance at the maudlin, jabbering group around me
showed that it would be impossible to get any sense out of
them. Nevertheless, seizing the boy nearest me I started to
interrogate him when the hag from Golfo's, who was herself in a state of hysterics, and was only restrained by a
naval stoker (who had her pinioned from behind), began
to shout in a hoarse chewed voice, "Spanish fly. He gave it
to her." And darting out of the arms of her captor like a
rat she seized her handbag and fetched one of the sailors a
resounding crack over the head. The bag must have been
full of nails for he went down swimming and came up
with fragments of shattered crockery in his hair.

She now began to sob in a voice which wore a beard
and call for the police. Three sailors converged upon her
with blunt fingers extended advising, exhorting, imploring
her to desist. Nobody wanted a brush with the naval
police. But neither did anyone relish a crack from that
Promethean handbag, bulging with french letters and
belladonna bottles. She retreated carefully step by step.
(Meanwhile I took Melissa's pulse, and ripping off her
blouse listened to her heart. I began to be alarmed for her,
and indeed for Pursewarden who had taken up a strategic
position behind an armchair and was making eloquent
gestures at everyone.) By now the fun had started, for the
sailors had the roaring girl cornered—but unfortunately
against the decorative Sheraton cupboard which housed
Pombal's cherished collection of pottery. Reaching behind
her for support her hands encountered an almost inexhaustible supply of ammunition, and letting go her
handbag with a hoarse cry of triumph she began to throw
china with a single-mindedness and accuracy I have never
seen equalled. The air was all at once full of Egyptian and
Greek tear-bottles, Ushabti, and Sevres. It could not be
long now before there came the familiar and much-
dreaded banging of hob-nailed boots against the door-
lintels, as lights were beginning to go on all round us in
the building. Pursewarden's alarm was very marked indeed; as a resident and moreover a famous one he could
hardly afford the sort of scandal which the Egyptian press
might make out of an affray like this. He was relieved
when I motioned to him and started to wrap the by now
almost insensible figure of Melissa in the soft Bokhara rug.
Together we staggered with her down the corridor and into the blessed privacy of my box-room where, like Cleopa-
tra, we unrolled her and placed her on the bed.

I had remembered the existence of an old doctor, a
Greek, who lived down the street, and it was not long
before I managed to fetch him up the dark staircase,
stumbling and swearing in a transpontine demotic, dropping catheters and stethoscopes all the way. He pronounced Melissa very ill indeed but his diagnosis was am-
ple and vague—in the tradition of the city. "It is every-

thing," he said, "malnutrition, hysteria, alcohol, hashish, tuberculosis, Spanish fly . . . help yourself," and he made the gesture of putting his hand in his pocket and fetching it out full of imaginary diseases which he offered us to choose from. But he was also practical, and proposed to have a bed ready for her in the Greek Hospital next day. Meanwhile she was not to be moved.

I spent that night and the next on the couch at the foot of the bed. While I was out at work she was confided to the care of one-eyed Hamid, the gentlest of Berberines. For the first twelve hours she was very ill indeed, delirious at times, and suffered agonizing attacks of blindness—agonizing because they made her so afraid. But by being gently rough with her we managed between us to give her courage enough to surmount the worst, and by the afternoon of the second day she was well enough to talk in whispers. The Greek doctor pronounced himself satisfied with her progress. He asked her where she came from and a haunted expression came into her face as she replied "Smyrna"; nor would she give the name and address of her parents, and when he pressed her she turned her face to the wall and tears of exhaustion welled slowly out of her eyes. The doctor took up her hand and examined the wedding-finger. "You see," he said to me with a clinical detachment, pointing out the absence of a ring. "That is why. Her family has disowned her and turned her out of doors. It is so often these days . . ." and he shook a shaggy commiserating head over her. Melissa said nothing, but when the ambulance came and the stretcher was being prepared to take her away she thanked me warmly for my help, pressed Hamid's hand to her cheek, and surprised me by a gallantry to which my life had unaccustomed me: "If you have no girl when I come out, think of me. If you call me I will come to you."* I do not know how to reduce the gallant candour of the Greek to English.

So I had lost sight of her for a month or more; and indeed I did not think of her, having many other preoccupations at this time. Then, one hot blank afternoon, when I was sitting at my window watching the city unwrinkle

from sleep I saw a different Melissa walk down the street
and turn into the shadowy doorway of the house. She
tapped at my door and walked in with her arms full of
flowers, and all at once I found myself separated from
that forgotten evening by centuries. She had in her something of the same diffidence with which I later saw her
take up a collection for the orchestra in the night-club.
She looked like a statue of pride hanging its head.

A nerve-racking politeness beset me. I offered her a
chair and she sat upon the edge of it. The flowers were for
me, yes, but she had not the courage to thrust the bouquet
into my arms, and I could see her gazing distractedly
around for a vase into which she might put them. There
was only an enamel washbasin full of half-peeled pota-
toes. I began to wish she had not come. I would have liked
to offer her some tea but my electric ring was broken and
I had no money to take her out—at this time I was sliding
ever more steeply into debt. Besides, I had sent Hamid
out to have my only summer suit ironed and was clad in a
torn dressing-gown. She for her part looked wonderfully,
intimidatingly smart, with a new summer frock of a crisp
vine-leaf pattern and a straw hat like a great gold bell. I
began to pray passionately that Hamid would come back
and create a diversion. I would have offered her a
cigarette but my packet was empty and I was forced to
accept one of her own from the little filigree cigarette-case
she always carried. This I smoked with what I hoped was
an air of composure and told her that I had accepted a
new job near Sidi Gabr, which would mean a little extra
money. She said she was going back to work; her contract
had been renewed: but they were giving her less money.
After a few minutes of this sort of thing she said that she
must be leaving as she had a tea-appointment. I showed
her out on the landing and asked her to come again
whenever she wished. She thanked me, still clutching the
flowers which she was too timid to thrust upon me and
walked slowly downstairs. After she had gone I sat on the
bed and uttered every foul swear-word I could remember
in four languages—though it was not clear to me whom I
was addressing. By the time one-eyed Hamid came

shuffling in I was still in a fury and turned my anger upon him. This startled him considerably: it was a long time since I had lost my temper with him, and he retired into the scullery muttering and shaking his head and invoking the spirits to help him.

After I had dressed and managed to borrow some money from Pursewarden—while I was on my way to post a letter—I saw Melissa again sitting in the corner of a coffee shop, alone, with her hands supporting her chin. Her hat and handbag lay beside her and she was staring into her cup with a wry reflective air of amusement. Impulsively I entered the place and sat down beside her. I had come, I said, to apologize for receiving her so badly, but . . . and I began to describe the circumstances which had preoccupied me, leaving nothing out. The broken electric-ring, the absence of Hamid, my summer suit. As I began to enumerate the evils by which I was beset they began to seem to me slightly funny, and altering my angle of approach I began to recount them with a lugubrious exasperation which coaxed from her one of the most delightful laughs I have ever heard. On the subjects of my debts I frankly exaggerated, though it was certainly a fact that since the night of the affray Pursewarden was always ready to lend me small sums of money without hesitation. And then to cap it all, I said, she had appeared while I was still barely cured of a minor but irritating venereal infection—the fruit of Pombal's solicitude—contracted no doubt from one of the Syrians he had thoughtfully left behind him. This was a lie but I felt impelled to relate it in spite of myself. I had been terrified I said at the thought of having to make love again before I was quite well. At this she put out her hand and placed it on mine while she laughed, wrinkling up her nose: laughing with such candour, so lightly and effortlessly, that there and then I decided to love her.

We idled arm in arm by the sea that afternoon, our conversations full of the débris of lives lived without forethought, without architecture. We had not a taste in common. Our characters and predispositions were wholly different, and yet in the magical ease of this friendship we

felt something promised us. I like, also, to remember that
first kiss by the sea, the wind blowing up a flake of hair at
each white temple—a kiss broken off by the laughter
which beset her as she remembered my account of the
trials I was enduring. It symbolized the passion we enjoyed, its humour and lack of intenseness: its charity.

* * * * *

Two subjects upon which it was fruitless to question
Justine too closely: her age, her origins. Nobody—
possibly not even, I believe, Nessim himself—knew
all about her with any certainty. Even the city's
oracle Mnemjian seemed for once at a loss, though he was
knowledgeable about her recent love affairs. Yet the violet
eyes narrowed as he spoke of her and hesitantly he volun-
teered the information that she came from the dense At-
tarine Quarter, and had been born of a poor Jewish family
which had since emigrated to Salonika. The diaries are
not very helpful either since they lack clues—names,
dates, places—and consist for the most part of wild flights
of fancy punctuated by bitter little anecdotes and sharp
line-drawings of people whose identity is masked by a letter of the alphabet. The French she writes in is not very
correct, but spirited and highly-flavoured; and carries the
matchless quality of that husky speaking-voice. Look:
"Clea speaking of her childhood: thinking of mine, passionately thinking. The childhood of my race, my time. . . .
Blows first in the hovel behind the Stadium; the clock-
mender's shop. I see myself now caught in the passionate
concentration of watching a lover's sleeping face as I so
often saw him bent over a broken timepiece with the
harsh light pouring down noiselessly over him. Blows and
curses, and printed everywhere on the red mud walls (like
the blows struck by conscience) the imprint of blue
hands, fingers outstretched, that guarded us against the
evil eye. With these blows we grew up, aching heads,
flinching eyes. A house with an earthen floor alive with
rats, dim with wicks floating upon oil. The old money-
lender drunk and snoring, drawing in with every breath
the compost-odours, soil, excrement, the droppings of bats;

gutters choked with leaves and breadcrumbs softened by piss; yellow wreaths of jasmine, heady, meretricious. And then add screams in the night behind other shutters in that crooked street: the *bey* beating his wives because he was impotent. The old herb-woman selling herself every night on the flat ground among the razed houses—a sulky mysterious whining. The soft *pelm* noise of bare black feet passing on the baked mud street, late at night. Our room bulging with darkness and pestilence, and we Europeans in such disharmony with the fearful animal health of the blacks around us. The copulations of boabs shaking the house like a palm-tree. Black tigers with gleaming teeth. And everywhere the veils, the screaming, the mad giggle under the peppertrees, the insanity and the lepers. Such things as children see and store up to fortify or disorient their lives. A camel has collapsed from exhaustion in the street outside the house. It is too heavy to transport to the slaughter-house so a couple of men come with axes and cut it up there and then in the open street, alive. They hack through the white flesh—the poor creature looking ever more pained, more aristocratic, more puzzled as its legs are hacked off. Finally there is the head still alive, the eyes open, looking round. Not a scream of protest, not a struggle. The animal submits like a palmtree. But for days afterwards the mud street is soaked in its blood and our bare feet are printed by the moisture.

"Money falling into the tin bowls of beggars. Fragments of every language—Armenian, Greek, Amharic, Moroccan Arabic; Jews from Asia Minor, Pontus, Georgia: mothers born in Greek settlements on the Black Sea; communities cut down like the branches of trees, lacking a parent body, dreaming of Eden. These are the poor quarters of the white city; they bear no resemblance to those lovely streets built and decorated by foreigners where the brokers sit and sip their morning papers. Even the harbour does not exist for us here. In the winter, sometimes, rarely, you can hear the thunder of a siren—but it is another country. Ah! the misery of har-

bours and the names they conjure when you are going
nowhere. It is like a death—a death of the self uttered in
every repetition of the word *Alexandria, Alexandria.*"

                    *   *   *   *   *

Rue Bab-el-Mandeb, Rue Abou-el-Dardar, Minet-el-
Bassal (streets slippery with discarded fluff from the cotton marts), Nouzha (the rose-garden, some remembered
kisses) or bus stops with haunted names like Saba Pacha,
Mazloum, Zizinia Bacos, Schutz, Gianaclis. A city
becomes a world when one loves one of its inhabitants.

                    *   *   *   *   *

One of the consequences of frequenting the great house
was that I began to be noticed and to receive the attention
of those who considered Nessim influential and presumed
that if he spent his time with me I must also in some un-
discovered fashion, be either rich or distinguished. Pombal came to my room one afternoon while I was dozing
and sat on my bed: "Look here," he said, "you are beginning to be noticed. Of course a *cicisbeo* is a normal
enough figure in Alexandrian life, but things are going to
become socially very boring for you if you go out with
those two so much. Look!" And he handed me a large and
florid piece of pasteboard with a printed invitation on it
for cocktails at the French Consulate. I read it un-
comprehendingly. Pombal said: "This is very silly. My
chief, the consul-general, is impassionated by Justine. All
attempts to meet her have failed so far. His spies tell him
that you have an entrée into the family circle, indeed that
you are . . . I know, I know. But he is hoping to displace
you in her affections." He laughed heavily. Nothing
sounded more preposterous to me at this time. "Tell the
consul-general," I said . . . and uttered a forcible remark
or two which caused Pombal to click his tongue reprov-
ingly and shake his head. "I would love to," he said. "But
mom cher there is a Pecking Order among diplomats as
there is among poultry. I depend upon him for my little
cross."

Heaving his bulk round he next produced from his

pocket a battered little yellow-covered novelette and placed it on my knees. "Here is something to interest you. Justine was married when she was very young to a French national, Albanian by descent, a writer. This little book is about her—post-mortem on her; it is quite decently done." I turned the novel over in my hands. It was entitled *Moeurs* and it was by a certain Jacob Arnauti. The flyleaf showed it to have enjoyed numerous reprintings in the early thirties. "How do you know this?" I asked, and Georges winked a large, heavy-lidded reptilian eye as he replied. "We have been making enquiries. The Consul can think of nothing but Justine, and the whole staff has been busy for weeks collecting information about her. *Vive la France!*"

When he had gone I started turning the pages of *Moeurs*, still half-dazed by sleep. It was very well written indeed, in the first person singular, and was a diary of Alexandrian life as seen by a foreigner in the middle thirties. The author of the diary is engaged on research for a novel he proposes to do—and the day to day account of his life in Alexandria is accurate and penetrating; but what arrested me was the portrait of a young Jewess he meets and marries: takes to Europe: divorces. The foundering of this marriage on their return to Egypt is done with a savage insight that throws into relief the character of Claudia, his wife. And what astonished and interested me was to see in her a sketch of Justine I recognized without knowing: a younger, a more disoriented Justine, to be sure. But unmistakable. Indeed whenever I read the book, and this was often, I was in the habit of restoring her name to the text. It fitted with an appalling verisimilitude.

They met, where I had first seen her, in the gaunt vestibule of the Cecil, in a mirror. "In the vestibule of this moribund hotel the palms splinter and refract their motionless fronds in the gilt-edged mirrors. Only the rich can afford to stay permanently—those who live on in the guilt-edged security of a pensionable old age. I am looking for cheaper lodgings. In the lobby tonight a small circle of Syrians, heavy in their dark suits, and yellow in their scarlet *tarbushes*, solemnly sit. Their hippopotamus-

like womenfolk, lightly moustached, have jingled off to
bed in their jewelry. The men's curious soft oval faces and
effeminate voices are busy upon jewel-boxes—for each of
these brokers carries his choicest jewels with him in a
casket; and after dinner the talk has turned to male
jewelry. It is all the Mediterranean world has left to talk
about; a self-interest, a narcissism which comes from sexual exhaustion expressing itself in the possessive symbol:
so that meeting a man you are at once informed what he is
worth, and meeting his wife you are told in the same
breathless whisper what her dowry was. They croon like
eunuchs over the jewels, turning them this way and that
in the light to appraise them. They flash their sweet white
teeth in little feminine smiles. They sigh. A white-robed
waiter with a polished ebony face brings coffee. A silver
hinge flies open upon heavy white (like the thighs of
Egyptian women) cigarettes each with its few flecks of
hashish. A few grains of drunkenness before bedtime. I
have been thinking about the girl I met last night in the
mirror: dark on marble-ivory white: glossy black hair:
deep suspiring eyes in which one's glances sink because
they are nervous, curious, turned to sexual curiosity. She
pretends to be a Greek, but she must be Jewish. It takes a
Jew to smell out a Jew; and neither of us has the courage
to confess our true race. I have told her I am French.
Sooner or later we shall find one another out.

"The women of the foreign communities here are more
beautiful than elsewhere. Fear, insecurity dominates
them. They have the illusion of foundering in the ocean of
blackness all around. This city has been built like a dyke
to hold back the flood of African darkness; but the soft-
footed blacks have already started leaking into the European quarters: a sort of racial osmosis is going on. To be
happy one would have to be a Moslem, an Egyptian
woman—absorbent, soft, lax, overblown; given to
veneers; their waxen skins turn citron-yellow or melon-
green in the naphtha-flares. Hard bodies like boxes.
Breasts apple-green and hard—a reptilian coldness of the
outer flesh with its bony outposts of toes and fingers.
Their feelings are buried in the pre-conscious. In love they

give out nothing of themselves, having no self to give, but enclose themselves around you in an agonized reflection—an agony of unexpressed yearning that is at the opposite pole from tenderness, pleasure. For centuries now they have been shut in a stall with the oxen, masked, circumcised. Fed in darkness on jams and scented fats they have become tuns of pleasure, rolling on paper-white blue-veined legs.

"Walking through the Egyptian quarter the smell of flesh changes—ammoniac, sandal-wood, saltpetre, spice, fish. She would not let me take her home—no doubt because she was ashamed of her house in these slums. Nevertheless she spoke wonderfully about her childhood. I have taken a few notes; returning home to find her father breaking walnuts with a little hammer on the table by the light of an oil-lamp. I can see him. He is no Greek but a Jew from Odessa in fur cap with greasy ringlets. Also the kiss of the Berberin, the enormous rigid penis like an obsidian of the ice age; leaning to take her underlip between beautiful unfiled teeth. We have left Europe behind here and are moving towards a new spiritual latitude. She gave herself to me with such contempt that I was for the first time in my life surprised at the quality of her anxiety; it was as if she were desperate, swollen with disaster. And yet these women belonging to these lost communities have a desperate bravery very different to ours. They have explored the flesh to a degree which makes them true foreigners to us. How am I to write about all this? Will she come, or has she disappeared forever? The Syrians are going to bed with little cries, like migrating birds."

She comes. They talk. ("Under the apparent provincial sophistication and mental hardness I thought I detected an inexperience, not of the world to be sure but of society. I was interesting, I realized, as a foreigner with good manners—and she turned upon me now the shy-wise regard of an owl from those enormous brown eyes whose faintly bluish eyeballs and long lashes threw into relief the splendour of the pupils, glittering and candid.")

It may be imagined with what breathless, painful anx-

iety I first read this account of a love-affair with Justine;
and truly after many re-readings the book, which I now
know almost by heart, has always remained for me a
document full of personal pain and astonishment. "Our
love," he writes in another place, much later, "was like a
syllogism to which the true premises were missing: I
mean regard. It was a sort of mental possession which
trapped us both and set us to drift upon the shallow tepid
waters of Mareotis like spawning frogs, a prey to instincts
based in lassitude and heat. . . . No, that is not the way to
put it. It is not very just. Let me try again with these
infirm and unstable tools to sketch Claudia. Where shall
we begin?

"Well: her talent for situations had served her well for
twenty years of an erratic and unpunctual life. Of her
origins I learned little, save that she had been very poor.
She gave me the impression of someone engaged in giving
a series of savage caricatures of herself—but this is common to most lonely people who feel that their true self can
find no correspondence in another. The speed with which
she moved from one milieu to another, from one man,
place, date to another, was staggering. But her instability
had a magnificence that was truly arresting. The more I
knew her the less predictable she seemed; the only con-
stant was this frantic struggle to break through the barrier
of her autism. And every action ended in error, guilt,
repentance. How often I remember—'Darling, this time it
will be different. I promise you.'

"Later, when we went abroad: at the Adlon, the pollen
of the spotlights playing upon the Spanish dancers fuming
in the smoke of a thousand cigarettes; by the dark waters
of Buda, her tears dropping hotly among the quietly flowing dead leaves; riding on the gaunt Spanish plains, the
silence pock-marked by the sound of our horses' hooves:
by the Mediterranean lying on some forgotten reef. It was
never her betrayals that upset me—for with Justine the
question of male pride in possession became somehow
secondary. I was bewitched by the illusion that I could
really come to know her; but I see now that she was not
really a woman but the incarnation of Woman admitting

no ties in the society we inhabited. 'I hunt everywhere for
a life that is worth living. Perhaps if I could die or go mad
it would provide a focus for all the feelings I have which
find no proper outlet. The doctor I loved told me I was
a nymphomaniac—but there is no gluttony or self-indulgence in my pleasure, Jacob. It is purely wasted from
that point of view. The waste, my dear, the waste! You
speak of taking pleasure sadly, like the puritans do. Even
there you are unjust to me. I take it tragically, and if my
medical friends want a compound word to describe the
heartless creature I seem, why they will have to admit
that what I lack of heart I make up in soul. That is where
the trouble lies.' These are not, you see, the sort of distinctions of which women are usually capable. It was as if
somehow her world lacked a dimension, and love had
become turned inwards into a kind of idolatry. At first I
mistook   this   for   a   devastating   and   self-consuming
egotism, for she seemed so ignorant of the little prescribed
loyalties which constitute the foundations of affection between men and women. This sounds pompous, but never
mind. But now, remembering the panics and exaltations
which she endured, I wonder whether I was right. I am
thinking of those tiresome dramas—scenes in furnished
bedrooms, with Justine turning on the taps to drown the
noise of her own crying. Walking up and down, hugging
her arms in her armpits, muttering to herself, she seemed
to smoulder like a tar-barrel on the point of explosion. My
indifferent health and poor nerves—but above all my
European sense of humour—seemed at such times to goad
her beyond endurance. Suffering, let us say, from some
imagined slight at a dinner-party she would patrol the
strip of carpet at the foot of the bed like a panther. If I fell
asleep she might become enraged and shake me by the
shoulders, crying: 'Get up, Jacob. I am suffering, can't you
see?' When I declined to take a part in this charade she
would perhaps break something upon the dressing-table
in order to have an excuse to ring the bell. How many
fearful faces of nightmaids have I not seen confronted by
this wild figure saying with a terrifying politeness: 'Oblige
me by clearing up the dressing-table. I have clumsily

broken something.' Then she would sit smoking cigarette
after cigarette. 'I know exactly what this is,' I told her
once. 'I expect that every time you are unfaithful to me
and consumed by guilt you would like to provoke me to
beat you up and give a sort of remission for your sins. My
dear, I simply refuse to pander to your satisfactions. You
must carry your own burdens. You are trying hard to get
me to use a stockwhip on you. But I only pity you.' This, I
must confess, made her very thoughtful for a moment and
involuntarily her hands strayed to touch the smooth surface of the legs she had so carefully shaved that afternoon. . . .

"Latterly, too, when I began to weary of her, I found
this sort of abuse of the emotions so tiresome that I took to
insulting her and laughing at her. One night I called her a
tiresome hysterical Jewess. Bursting into those terrible
hoarse sobs which I so often heard that even now in
memory the thought of them (their richness, their
melodious density) hurts me, she flung herself down to
her own bed to lie, limbs loose and flaccid, played upon
by the currents of her hysteria like jets from a hose.

"Did this sort of thing happen so often or is it that my
memory has multiplied it? Perhaps it was only once, and
the echoes have misled me. At any rate I seem to hear so
often the noise she made unstopping the bottle of
sleeping-tablets, and the small sound of the tablets falling
into the glass. Even when I was dozing I would count, to
see that she did not take too many. All this was much
later, of course; in the early days I would ask her to come
into my bed and self-conscious, sullen, cold, she would
obey me. I was foolish enough to think that I could thaw
her out and give her the physical peace upon which—I
thought—mental peace must depend. I was wrong. There
was some unresolved inner knot which she wished to untie
and which was quite beyond my skill as a lover or a
friend. Of course. Of course. I knew as much as could be
known of the psychopathology of hysteria at that time.
But there was some other quality which I thought I could
detect behind all this. In a way she was not looking for life,

but for some integrating revelation which would give it
point.

"I have already described how we met—in the long
mirror of the Cecil, before the open door of the ballroom,
on a night of carnival. The first words we spoke were
spoken, symbolically enough, in the mirror. She was there
with a man who resembled a cuttle-fish and who waited
while she examined her dark face attentively. I stopped to
adjust an unfamiliar bow-tie. She had a hungry natural
candour which seemed proof against any suggestion of
forwardness as she smiled and said: 'There is never
enough light.' To which I responded without thought:
'For women perhaps. We men are less exigent.' We smiled
and I passed her on my way to the ballroom, ready to
walk out of her mirror-life forever, without a thought.
Later the hazards of one of those awful English dances,
called the Paul Jones I believe, left me facing her for a
waltz. We spoke a few disjointed words—I dance badly;
and here I must confess that her beauty made no impression on me. It was only later when she began her trick
of drawing hasty ill-defined designs round my character,
throwing my critical faculties into disorder by her sharp
penetrating stabs: ascribing to me qualities which she invented on the spur of the moment out of that remorseless
desire to capture my attention. Women must attack
writers—and from the moment she learned I was a writer
she felt disposed to make herself interesting by dissecting
me. All this would have been most flattering to my *amour
propre* had some of her observations been further from
the mark. But she was acute, and I was too feeble to resist
this sort of game—the mental ambuscades which constitute the opening gambits of a flirtation.

"From here I remember nothing more until that
night—that marvellous summer night on the moon-
drenched balcony above the sea with Justine pressing a
warm hand on my mouth to stop me talking and saying
something like: 'Quick. *Engorge-moi.* From desire to
revulsion—let's get it over.' She had, it seemed, already
exhausted me in her own imagination. But the words were

spoken with such weariness and humility—who could forbear to love her?

"It is idle to go over all this in a medium as unstable as words. I remember the edges and corners of so many meetings, and I see a sort of composite Justine, concealing a ravenous hunger for information, for power through self-knowledge, under a pretence of feeling. Sadly I am driven to wonder whether I ever really moved her—or existed simply as a laboratory in which she could work. She learned much from me: to read and reflect. She had achieved neither before. I even persuaded her to keep a diary in order to clarify her far from commonplace thoughts. And perhaps what I took to be love was merely a gratitude. Among the thousand discarded people, impressions, subjects of study—somewhere I see myself drifting, floating, reaching out arms. Strangely enough it was never in the *lover* that I really met her but in the *writer*. Here we clasped hands—in that amoral world of suspended judgements where curiosity and wonder seem greater than order—the syllogistic order imposed by the mind. This is where one waits in silence, holding one's breath, lest the pane should cloud over. I watched over her like this. I was mad about her.

"She had of course many secrets being a true child of the Mouseion, and I had to guard myself desperately against jealousy or the desire to intrude upon the hidden side of her life. I was almost successful in this and if I spied upon her it was really from curiosity to know what she might be doing or thinking when she was not with me. There was, for example, a woman of the town whom she visited frequently, and whose influence on her was profound enough to make me suspect an illicit relationship; there was also a man to whom she wrote long letters, though as far I could see he lived in the city. Perhaps he was bedridden? I made inquiries, but my spies always brought me back uninteresting information. The woman was a fortune-teller, elderly, a widow. The man to whom she wrote—her pen shrilling across the cheap notepaper—turned out to be a doctor who held a small part-time post on a local consulate. He was not bedrid-

den; but he was a homosexual, and dabbled in hermetic
philosophy which is now so much in vogue. Once she left
a particularly clear impression on my blotting-pad and in
the mirror (the mirror again!) I was able to read:—'my
life there is a sort of Unhealed Place as you call it which I
try to keep full of people, accidents, diseases, anything
that comes to hand. You are right when you say it is an
apology for better living, wiser living. But while I respect
your disciplines and your knowledge I feel that if I am
ever going to come to terms with myself I must work
through the dross in my own character and burn it up.
Anyone could solve my problem artificially by placing it
in the lap of a priest. We Alexandrians have more pride
than that—and more respect for religion. It would not be
fair to God, my dear sir, and whoever else I fail (I see you
smile) I am determined not to fail Him whoever He is.'

"It seemed to me then that if this was part of a love-
letter it was the kind of love-letter one could only address
to a saint; and again I was struck, despite the clumsiness
and incorrectness of the writing, by the fluency with which
she could dissociate between ideas of different categories.
I began to see her in an altered light; as somebody who
might well destroy herself in an excess of wrong-headed
courage and forfeit the happiness which she, in common
with all the rest of us, desired and lived only to achieve.
These thoughts had the effect of qualifying my love for
her, and I found myself filled sometimes by disgust for
her. But what made me afraid was that after quite a short
time I found to my horror that I could not live without
her. I tried. I took short journeys away from her. But
without her I found life full of consuming boredom which
was quite insupportable. I had fallen *in love*. The very
thought filled me with an inexplicable despair and
disgust. It was as if I unconsciously realized that in her I
had met my evil genius. To come to Alexandria heart-
whole and to discover an *amor fati*—it was a stroke of ill-
luck which neither my health nor my nerves felt capable
of supporting. Looking in the mirror I reminded myself
that I had turned forty and already there was a white hair
or two at my temples! I thought once of trying to end this

attachment, but in every smile and kiss of Justine I felt my
resolutions founder. Yet with her one felt all around the
companionship of shadows which invaded life and filled it
with a new resonance. Feeling so rich in ambiguities
could not be resolved by a sudden act of the will. I had at
times the impression of a woman whose every kiss was a
blow struck on the side of death. When I discovered, for
example (what I knew) that she had been repeatedly unfaithful to me, and at times when I had felt myself to be
closest to her, I felt nothing very sharp in outline: rather a
sinking numbness such as one might feel on leaving a
friend in hospital, to enter a lift and fall six floors in
silence, standing beside a uniformed automaton whose
breathing one could hear. The silence of my room
deafened me. And then, thinking about it, gathering my
whole mind about the fact I realized that what she had
done bore no relation to myself: it was an attempt to free
herself for me: to give me what she knew belonged to me.
I cannot say that this sounded any better to my ears than
a sophistry. Nevertheless my heart seemed to know the
truth of this and dictated a tactful silence to me to which
she responded with a new warmth, a new ardour, of
gratitude added to love. This again disgusted me
somewhat.

"Ah! but if you had seen her then as I did in her
humbler, gentler moments, remembering that she was
only a child, you would not have reproached me for
cowardice. In the early morning, sleeping in my arms, her
hair blown across that smiling mouth, she looked like no
other woman I could remember: indeed like no woman at
all, but some marvellous creature caught in the
Pleistocene stage of her development. And later again,
thinking about her as I did and have done these past few
years I was surprised to find that though I loved her
wholly and knew that I should never love anyone else
—yet I shrank from the thought that she might return.
The two ideas co-existed in my mind without displacing
one another. I thought to myself with relief, 'Good. I *have*
really loved at last. That is something achieved'; and to
this my alter ego added: 'Spare me the pangs of love *re-*

quited with Justine.' This enigmatic polarity of feeling
was something I found completely unexpected. If this was
love then it was a variety of the plant which I have never
seen before. ('Damn the word,' said Justine once, 'I
would like to spell it backwards as you say the Elizabethans did God. Call it *evol* and make it a part of "evolu-
tion" or "revolt." Never use the word to me.')"

*   *   *   *   *

These later extracts I have taken from the section of the
diary which is called *Posthumous Life* and is an attempt
the author makes to sum up and evaluate these episodes.
Pombal finds much of this banal and even dull; but who,
knowing Justine, could fail to be moved by it? Nor can it
be said that the author's intentions are not full of interest.
He maintains for example that real people can only exist
in the imagination of an artist strong enough to contain
them and give them form. "Life, the raw material, is only
lived *in potentia* until the artist deploys it in his work.
Would that I could do this service of love for poor
Justine." (I mean, of course, "Claudia.") "I dream of a
book powerful enough to contain the elements of
her—but it is not the sort of book to which we are ac-
customed these days. For example, on the first page a
synopsis of the plot in a few lines. Thus we might dispense
with the narrative articulation. What follows would be
drama freed from the bruden of form. *I would set my own
book free to dream.*"

But of course one cannot escape so easily from the pattern which he regards as imposed but which in fact grows
up organically within the work and appropriates it. What
is missing in his work—but this is a criticism of all works
which do not reach the front rank—is a sense of *play*. He
bears down so hard upon his subject-matter; so hard that
it infects his style with some of the unbalanced ferocity of
Claudia herself. Then, too, everything which is a fund of
emotion becomes of equal importance to him: a sign uttered by Claudia among the oleanders of Noussha, the
fireplace where she burnt the manuscript of his novel
about her ("For days she looked at me as if she were

trying to read my book in me"), the little room in the Rue
Lepsius. . . . He says of his characters: "All bound by time
in a dimension which is not reality *as we would wish it to
be*—but is created by the needs of the work. For all drama
creates bondage, and the actor is only significant to the
degree that he is bound."

But setting these reservations aside, how graceful and
accurate a portrait of Alexandria he manages to convey;
Alexandria and its women. There are sketches here of
Leonie, Gaby, Delphine—the pale rose-coloured one, the
gold, the bitumen. Some one can identify quite easily
from his pages. Clea, who still lives in that high studio, a
swallow's nest made of cobwebs and old cloth—he has
her unmistakably. But for the most part these Alexandrian
girls are distinguished from women in other places only
by a terrifying honesty and world-weariness. He is enough
of a writer to have isolated these true qualities in the city
of the Soma. One could not expect more from an intruder
of gifts who almost by mistake pierced the hard banausic
shell of Alexandria and discovered himself.

As for Justine herself, there are few if indeed any
references to Arnauti in the heavily armoured pages of her
diary. Here and there I have traced the letter A, but
usually in passages abounding with the purest introspection. Here is one where the identification might seem
plausible:

"What first attracted me in A was his room. There always seemed to me some sort of ferment going on there
behind the heavy shutters. Books lay everywhere with
their jackets turned inside out or covered in white draw-
ing-paper—as if to hide their titles. A huge litter of
newspapers with holes in them, as if a horde of mice had
been feasting in them—A's cuttings from 'real life' as he
called it, the abstraction which he felt to be so remote
from his own. He would sit down to his newspapers as if
to a meal in a patched dressing-gown and velvet slippers,
snipping away with a pair of blunt nail-scissors. He puzzled over 'reality' in the world outside his work like a
child: it was presumably a place where people could be
happy, laugh, bear children."

A few such sketches comprise the whole portrait of the author of *Moeurs;* it seems a meagre and disappointing reward for so much painstaking and loving observation; nor can I trace one word about their separation after this brief and fruitless marriage. But it was interesting to see from his book how he had made the same judgements upon her character as we were later to make, Nessim and I. The compliance she extorted from us all was the astonishing thing about her. It was as if men knew at once that they were in the presence of someone who could not be judged according to the standards they had hitherto employed in thinking about women. Clea once said of her (and her judgements were seldom if ever charitable): "The true whore is man's real darling—like Justine; she alone has the capacity to wound men. But of course our friend is only a shallow twentieth-century reproduction of the great *Hetairae* of the past, the type to which she belongs without knowing it, Lais, Charis and the rest. . . . Justine's role has been taken from her and on her shoulders society has placed the burden of guilt to add to her troubles. It is a pity. For she is truly Alexandrian."

For Clea too the little book of Arnauti upon Justine seemed shallow and infected by the desire to explain everything. "It is our disease," she said, "to want to contain everything within the frame of reference of a psychology or a philosophy. After all Justine cannot be justified or excused. She simply and magnificently *is*; we have to put up with her, like original sin. But to call her a nymphomaniac or to try and Freudianise her, my dear, takes away all her mythical substance—the only thing she really is. Like all amoral people she verges on the Goddess. If our world were a world there would be temples to accommodate her where she would find the peace she was seeking. Temples where one could outgrow the sort of inheritance she has: not these damn monasteries full of pimply Catholic youths who have made a bicycle saddle of their sexual organs."

She was thinking of the chapters which Arnauti has entitled *The Check*, and in which he thinks he has found the clue to Justine's instability of heart. They may be, as Clea

thinks, shallow, but since everything is susceptible of
more than one explanation they are worth consideration. I
myself do not feel that they explain Justine, but to a
degree they do illuminate her actions—those immense
journeys they undertook together across the length and
breadth of Europe. "In the very heart of passion," he
writes, adding in parentheses, "(passion which to her
seemed the most facile of gifts) there was a check—some
great impediment of feeling which I became aware of
only after many months. It rose up between us like a
shadow and I recognized, or thought I did, the true
enemy of the happiness which we longed to share and
from which we felt ourselves somehow excluded. What
was it?

"She told me one night as we lay in that ugly great bed
in a rented room—a gaunt rectangular room of a vaguely
French-Levantine shape and flavour: a stucco ceiling covered with decomposing cherubs and posies of vine-leaves.
She told me and left me raging with a jealousy I struggled
to hide—but a jealousy of an entirely novel sort. Its object
was a man who though still alive, *no longer existed*. It is
perhaps what the Freudians would call a screen-memory
of incidents in her earliest youth. She had (and there was
no mistaking the force of this confession for it was accompanied by floods of tears, and I have never seen her
weep like that before or since): she had been raped by
one of her relations. One cannot help smiling at the com-
monplaceness of the thought. It was impossible to judge
at what age. Nevertheless—and here I thought I had
penetrated to the heart of The Check: from this time forward she could obtain no satisfaction in love unless she
mentally re-created these incidents and re-enacted them.
For her we, her lovers, had become only mental
substitutes for this first childish act—so that love, as a sort
of masturbation, took on all the colours of neurasthenia;
she was suffering from an imagination dying of anaemia,
for she could possess no one thoroughly in the flesh. She
could not appropriate to herself the love she felt she
needed, for her satisfactions derived from the crepuscular
corners of a life she was no longer living. This was pas-

sionately interesting. But what was even more amusing
was that I felt this blow to my *amour propre* as a man exactly as if she had confessed to an act of deliberate un-
faithfulness. What! Every time she lay in my arms she
could find no satisfaction save through this memory? In a
way, then, I could not possess her: had never done so. I
was merely a dummy. Even now as I write I cannot help
smiling to remember the strangled voice in which I asked
who the man was, and where he was. (What did I hope to
do? Challenge him to a duel?) Nevertheless there he was,
standing squarely between Justine and me; between
Justine and the light of the sun.

"But here too I was sufficiently detached to observe
how much love feeds upon jealousy, for as a woman out of
my reach yet in my arms, she became ten times more
desirable, more necessary. It was a heartbreaking predicament for a man who had no intention of falling in love,
and for a woman who only wished to be delivered of an
obsession and set free to love. From this something else
followed: if I could break The Check I could possess her
truly, as no man had possessed her. I could step into the
place of the shadow and receive her kisses truly; now they
fell upon a corpse. It seemed to me that I understood
everything now.

"This explains the grand tour we took, hand in hand so
to speak, in order to overcome this succubus together with
help of science. Together we visited the book-lined cell of
Czechnia, where the famous mandarin of psychology sat,
gloating pallidly over his specimens. Basle, Zurich, Baden,
Paris—the flickering of steel rails over the arterial systems
of Europe's body: steel ganglia meeting and dividing
away across mountains and valleys. Confronting one's
face in the pimpled mirrors of the Orient Express. We carried her disease backwards and forwards over Europe like
a baby in a cradle until I began to despair, and even to
imagine that perhaps Justine did not wish to be cured of
it. For to the involuntary check of the psyche she added
another—of the will. Why this should be I cannot understand; but she would tell no one his name, the shadow's
name. A name which by now could mean everything or

nothing to her. After all, somewhere in the world he must be now, his hair thinning and greying from business worries or excesses, wearing a black patch over one eye as he did always after an attack of ophthalmia. (If I can describe him to you it is because once I actually saw him.) 'Why should I tell people his name?' Justine used to cry. 'He is nothing to me now—has never been. He has completely forgotten these incidents. Don't you see he is dead? When I see him . . .' This was like being stung by a serpent. 'So you do see him?' She immediately withdrew to a safer position. 'Every few years, passing in the street. We just nod.'

"So this creature, this pattern of ordinariness, was still breathing, still alive! How fantastic and ignoble jealousy is. But jealousy for a figment of a lover's imagination borders on the ludicrous.

"Then once, in the heart of Cairo, during a traffic jam, in the breathless heat of a midsummer night, a taxi drew up beside ours and something in Justine's expression drew my gaze in the direction of hers. In that palpitant moist heat, dense from the rising damps of the river and aching with the stink of rotten fruit, jasmine and sweating black bodies, I caught sight of the very ordinary man in the taxi next to us. Apart from the black patch over one eye there was nothing to distinguish him from the thousand other warped and seedy business men of this horrible city. His hair was thinning, his profile sharp, his eye beady: he was wearing a grey summer suit. Justine's expression of suspense and anguish was so marked however that involuntarily I cried: 'What is it?'; and as the traffic block lifted and the cab moved off she replied with a queer flushed light in her eye, an air almost of drunken daring: 'The man you have all been hunting for.' But before the words were out of her mouth I had understood and as if in a bad dream stopped our own taxi and leaped out into the road. I saw the red tail light of his taxi turning into Suleiman Pacha, too far away for me even to be able to distinguish its colour or number. To give chase was impossible for the traffic behind us was dense once more. I got back into the taxi trembling and speechless. So this was the man for whose name Freud had hunted with all the great might of his loving detachment. For this innocent middle-aged man Justine had lain suspended, every nerve tense as if in the act of levitation, while the thin steely voice of Magnani had repeated over and over again: 'Tell me his name; you must tell me his name'; while from the forgotten prospects where her memory lay confined her voice repeated like an oracle of the machine-age: 'I cannot remember. I cannot remember.'

"It seemed to me clear then that in some perverted way she did not wish to conquer The Check, and certainly all the power of the physicians could not persuade her. This was the bare case without orchestration, and here lay the so-called nymphomania with which these reverend gentlemen assured me that she was afflicted. At times I felt convinced that they were right; at others I doubted. Nevertheless it was tempting to see in her behaviour the excuse that every man held out for her the promise of a release in her passional self, release from this suffocating self-enclosure where sex could only be fed by the fat flames of fantasy.

"Perhaps we did wrong in speaking of it openly, of treating it as a problem, for this only invested her with a feeling of self-importance and moreover contributed a nervous hesitation to her which until then had been missing. In her passional life she was direct—like an axe falling. She took kisses like so many coats of paint. I am puzzled indeed to remember how long and how vainly I searched for excuses which might make her amorality if not palatable at least understandable. I realize now how much time I wasted in this way; instead of enjoying her and turning aside from these preoccupations with the thought, 'She is untrustworthy as she is beautiful. She takes love as plants do water, lightly, thoughtlessly.' Then I could have walked arm in arm with her by the rotting canal, or sailed on sundrenched Mareotis, enjoying her as she was, taking her as she was. What a marvellous capacity for unhappiness we writers have! I only know that this long and painful examination of Justine succeeded not only in making her less sure of herself, but also

more consciously dishonest; worst of all, she began to look
upon me as an enemy who watched for the least
misconstruction, the least word or gesture which might
give her away. She was doubly on her guard, and indeed
began to accuse me of an insupportable jealousy. Perhaps
she was right. I remember her saying: 'You live now
among my imaginary intimacies. I was a fool to tell you
everything, to be so honest. Look at the way you question
me now. Several days running the same questions. And at
the slightest discrepancy you are on me. You know I never
tell a story the same way twice. Does that mean that I am
lying?"

"I was not warned by this but redoubled my efforts to
penetrate the curtain behind which I thought my ad-
versary stood, a black patch over one eye. I was still in
correspondence with Magnani and tried to collect as
much evidence as possible which might help him
elucidate the mystery, but in vain. In the thorny jungle of
guilty impulses which constitute the human psyche who
can find a way—even when the subject wishes to co-
operate? The time we wasted upon futile researches into
her likes and dislikes! If Justine had been blessed with a
sense of humour what fun she could have had with us. I
remember a whole correspondence based upon the confession that she could not read the words 'Washington
D.C.' on a letter without a pang of disgust! It is a matter
of deep regret to me now that I wasted this time when I
should have been loving her as she deserved. Some of
these doubts must also have afflicted old Magnani for I
recall him writing: 'and my dear boy we must never
forget that this infant science we are working at, which
seems so full of miracles and promises, is at best founded
on much that is as shaky as astrology. After all, these important *names* we give to things! Nymphomania may be
considered another form of virginity if you wish; and as
for Justine, she may never have been in love. Perhaps one
day she will meet a man before whom all these tiresome
chimeras will fade into innocence again. You must not
rule this thought out.' He was not, of course, trying to hurt
me—for this was a thought I did not care to admit to

myself. But it penetrated me when I read it in this wise
old man's letter."

*   *   *   *   *

I had not read these pages of Arnauti before the afternoon at Bourg El Arab when the future of our relationship
was compromised by the introduction of a new ele-
ment—I do not dare to use the word love, for fear of
hearing that harsh sweet laugh in my imagination: a
laugh which would somewhere be echoed by the diarist.
Indeed so fascinating did I find his analysis of his subject,
and so closely did our relationship echo the relationship
he had enjoyed with Justine that at times I too felt like
some paper character out of *Moeurs*. Moreover, here I
am, attempting to do the same sort of thing with her in
words—though I lack his ability and have no pretensions
to being an artist. I want to put things down simply and
crudely, without style—the plaster and whitewash; for the
portrait of Justine should be rough-cast, with the honest
stonework of the predicament showing through.

After the episode of the beach we did not meet for some
small time, both of us infected by a vertiginous uncertainty—or at least I was. Nessim was called away to Cairo on
business but though Justine was, as far as I knew, at home
alone, I could not bring myself to visit the studio. Once as
I passed I heard the Bluthner and was tempted to ring the
bell—so sharply defined was the image of her at the black
piano. Then once passing the garden at night I saw someone—it must have been she—walking by the lily-pond,
shading a candle in the palm of one hand. I stood for a
moment uncertainly before the great doors wondering
whether to ring or not. Melissa at this time also had taken
the occasion to visit a friend in Upper Egypt. Summer was
growing apace, and the town was sweltering. I bathed as
often as my work permitted, travelling to the crowded
beaches in the little tin tram.

Then one day while I was lying in bed with a temperature brought on by an overdose of the sun Justine
walked into the dank calm of the little flat, dressed in a
white frock and shoes, and carrying a rolled towel under
one arm with her handbag. The magnificence of her dark

skin and hair glowed out of all this whiteness with an arresting quickness. When she spoke her voice was harsh
and unsteady, and it sounded for a moment as if she had
been drinking—perhaps she had. She put one hand out
and leaned upon the mantelshelf as she said: "I want to
put an end to all this as soon as possible. I feel as if we've
gone too far to go back." As for me I was consumed by a
terrible sort of desirelessness, a luxurious anguish of body
and mind which prevented me from saying anything,
thinking anything. I could not visualize the act of love
with her, for somehow the emotional web we had woven
about each other stood between us: an invisible cobweb
of loyalties, ideas, hesitations which I had not the courage
to brush aside. As she took a step forward I said feebly:
"This bed is so awful and smelly. I have been drinking. I
tried to make love to myself but it was no good—I kept
thinking about you." I felt myself turning pale as I lay
silent upon my pillows, all at once conscious of the silence
of the little flat which was torn in one corner by the drip-
ping of a leaky tap. A taxi brayed once in the distance,
and from the harbour, like the stifled roar of a minotaur,
came a single dark whiff of sound from a siren. Now it
seemed we were completely alone together.

The whole room belonged to Melissa—the pitiful dressing-table full of empty powder-boxes and photos: the
graceful curtain breathing softly in that breathless afternoon air like the sail of a ship. How often had we not lain
in one another's arms watching the slow intake and recoil
of that transparent piece of bright linen? Across all this, as
across the image of someone dearly loved, held in the
magnification of a gigantic tear moved the brown harsh
body of Justine naked. It would have been blind of me not
to notice how deeply her resolution was mixed with
sadness. We lay eye to eye for a long time, our bodies
touching, hardly communicating more than the animal
lassitude of that vanishing afternoon. I could not help
thinking then as I held her lightly in the crook of an arm
how little we own our bodies. I thought of the words of
Arnauti when he says: "It dawned on me then that in
some fearful way this girl had shorn me of all my *force*

morale. I felt as if I had had my head shaved." But
the French, I thought, with their endless gravitation between *bonheur* and *chagrin* must inevitably suffer when
they come up against something which does not admit
of the *préjugés;* born for tactics and virtuosity, not for
staying-power, they lack the little touch of crassness
which armours the Anglo-Saxon mind. And I thought:
"Good. Let her lead me where she will. She will find me a
match for her. And there'll be no talk of *chagrin* at the
end." Then I thought of Nessim, who was watching us
(though I did not know) as if through the wrong end of
an enormous telescope: seeing our small figures away on
the skyline of his own hopes and plans. I was anxious that
he should not be hurt.

But she had closed her eyes—so soft and lustrous now,
as if polished by the silence which lay so densely all
around us. Her trembling fingers had become steady and
at ease upon my shoulder. We turned to each other, closing like the two leaves of a door upon the past, shutting
out everything, and I felt her happy spontaneous kisses
begin to compose the darkness around us like successive
washes of a colour. When we had made love and lay once
more awake she said: "I am always so bad the first time,
why is it?"

"Nerves perhaps. So am I."

"You are a little afraid of me."

Then rising on an elbow as if I had suddenly woken up
I said: "But Justine, what on earth are we going to make
of all this? If this is to be—" But she became absolutely
terrified now and put her hand over my mouth, saying:
"For Godsake no justifications! Then I shall know we are
wrong! For nothing can justify it, nothing. And yet it has
got to be like this." And getting out of bed she walked
over to the dressing-table with its row of photos and
powder-boxes and with a single blow like that of a
leopard's paw swept it clean. *"That,"* she said, "is what I
am doing to Nessim and you to Melissa! It would be ignoble to try and pretend otherwise." This was more in the
tradition that Arnauti had led me to expect and I said
nothing. She turned now and started kissing me with such

a hungry agony that my burnt shoulders began to throb
until tears came into my eyes. "Ah!" she said softly and
sadly: "You are crying. I wish I could. I have lost the
knack."

I remember thinking to myself as I held her, tasting the
warmth and sweetness of her body, salt from the sea—her
ear-lobes tasted of salt—I remember thinking: "Every kiss
will take her near Nessim, but separates me further from
Melissa." But strangely enough I experienced no sense of
despondency or anguish; and for her part she must have
been thinking along the same lines for she suddenly said:
"Balthazar says that the natural traitors—like you and
I—are really Caballi. He says we are dead and live this
life as a sort of limbo. Yet the living can't do without us.
We infect them with a desire to experience more, to
grow."

I tried to tell myself how stupid all this was—a banal
story of an adultery which was among the cheapest commonplaces of the city: and how it did not deserve romantic
or literary trappings. And yet somewhere else, at a deeper
level, I seemed to recognize that the experience upon
which I had embarked would have the deathless finality
of a lesson learned. "You are too serious," I said, with a
certain resentment, for I was vain and did not like the sensation of being carried out of my depth. Justine turned her
great eyes on me. "O no!" she said softly, as if to herself:
"It would be silly to spread so much harm as I have done
and not to realize that it is my role. Only in this way, by
knowing what I am doing, can I ever outgrow myself. It
isn't easy to be me. I *so much* want to be responsible for
myself. Please never doubt that."

We slept, and I was only woken by the dry click of
Hamid's key turning in the lock and by his usual evening
performance. For a pious man, whose little prayer mat lay
rolled and ready to hand on the kitchen balcony, he was
extraordinarily superstitious. He was as Pombal said,
"djinn-ridden," and there seemed to be a djinn in every
corner of the flat. How tired I had become of hearing his
muttered "*Destoor, destoor,*" as he poured slops down the
kitchen sink—for here dwelt a powerful djinn and its par-

don had to be invoked. The bathroom too was haunted by them, and I could always tell when Hamid used the outside lavatory (which he had been forbidden to do) because whenever he sat on the watercloset a hoarse involuntary invocation escaped his lips ("Permission O ye blessed ones!") which neutralized the djinn which might otherwise have dragged him down into the sewage system. Now I heard him shuffling round the kitchen in his old felt slippers like a boa-constrictor muttering softly.

I woke Justine from a troubled doze and explored her mouth and eyes and fine hair with the anguished curiosity which for me has always been the largest part of sensuality. "We must be going," I said. "Pombal will be coming back from the Consulate in a little while."

I recall the furtive languour with which we dressed and silent as accomplices made our way down the gloomy staircase into the street. We did not dare to link arms, but our hands kept meeting involuntarily as we walked, as if they had not shaken off the spell of the afternoon and could not bear to be separated. We parted speechlessly too, in the little square with its dying trees burnt to the colour of coffee by the sun; parted with only one look—as if we wished to take up emplacements in each other's minds forever.

It was as if the whole city had crashed about my ears; I walked about in it aimlessly as survivors must walk about the streets of their native city after an earthquake, amazed to find how much that had been familiar was changed. I felt in some curious way deafened and remember nothing more except that much later I ran into Pursewarden and Pombal in a bar, and that the former recited some lines from the old poet's famous "The City" which struck me with a new force—as if the poetry had been newly minted: though I knew them well. And when Pombal said: "You are abstracted this evening. What is the matter?" I felt like answering him in the words of the dying Amr:* "I feel as if heaven lay close upon the earth and I between them both, breathing through the eye of a needle."

PART
two

To HAVE WRITTEN so much and to have said nothing about Balthazar is indeed an omission—for in a sense he is one of the keys to the City. The key: Yes, I took him very much as he was in those days and now in my memory I feel that he is in need of a new evaluation. There was much that I did not understand then, much that I have since learned. I remember chiefly those interminable evenings spent at the Café Al Aktar playing backgammon while he smoked his favourite Lakadif in a pipe with a long stem. If Mnemjian is the archives of the City, Balthazar is its Platonic *daimon*—the mediator between its Gods and its men. It sounds far-fetched, I know.

I see a tall man in a black hat with a narrow brim. Pombal christened him "the botanical goat." He is thin, stoops slightly, and has a deep croaking voice of great beauty, particularly when he quotes or recites. In speaking to you he never looks at you directly—a trait which I have noticed in many homosexuals. But in him this does not signify inversion of which he is not only not ashamed, but to which he is actually indifferent; his yellow goat-eyes are those of a hypnotist. In not looking at you he is sparing you from a regard so pitiless that it would discountenance you for an evening. It is a mystery how he can have, suspended from his trunk, hands of such monstrous ugliness. I would long since have cut them off and thrown them into the sea. Under his chin he has one dark spur of hair growing, such as one sometimes sees upon the hoof of a sculptured Pan.

Several times in the course of those long walks we took together, beside the sad velvet broth of the canal, I found myself wondering what was the quality in him which arrested me. This was before I knew anything about the Cabal. Though he reads widely Balthazar's conversation is not heavily loaded with the kind of material that might make one think him bookish: like Pursewarden. He loves poetry, parable, science and sophistry—but there is a lightness of touch and a judgement behind his thinking. Yet underneath the lightness there is something else—a resonance which gives his thinking density. His vein is aphoristic, and it sometimes gives him the touch of a minor oracle. I see now that he was one of those rare people who had found a philosophy for himself and whose life was occupied in trying to live it. I think this is the unanalysed quality which gives his talk cutting-edge.

As a doctor he spends much of his working-time in the government clinic for venereal disease. (He once said dryly: "I live at the centre of the city's life—its genitourinary system: it is a sobering sort of place.") Then, too, he is the only man whose paederasty is somehow no qualification of his innate masculinity of mind. He is neither a puritan nor its opposite. Often I have entered his little room in the Rue Lepsius—the one with the creaking cane chair—and found him asleep in bed with a sailor. He has neither excused himself at such a time nor even alluded to his bedfellow. While dressing he will sometimes turn and tenderly tuck the sheet round his partner's sleeping form. I take this naturalness as a compliment.

He is a strange mixture; at times I have heard his voice tremble with emotion as he alludes to some aspect of the Cabal which he has been trying to make comprehensible to the study-group. Yet once when I spoke enthusiastically of some remarks he had made he sighed and said, with that perfect Alexandrian scepticism which somehow underlay an unquestionable belief in and devotion to the Gnosis: "We are all hunting for rational reasons for believing in the absurd." At another time after a long and tiresome argument with Justine about heredity and environment he said: "Ah! my dear, after all the work of the philosophers on his soul and the doctors on his body, what can we say we really know about man? That he is, when all is said and done, just a passage for liquids and solids, a pipe of flesh."

He had been a fellow-student and close friend of the old poet, and of him he spoke with such warmth and penetration that what he had to say always moved me. "I sometimes think that I learned more from studying him than I did from studying philosophy. His exquisite balance of irony and tenderness would have put him among the saints had he been a religious man. He was by divine choice only a poet and often unhappy but with him one had the feeling that he was catching every minute as it flew and turning it upside down to expose its happy side. He was really using himself up, his inner self, in living. Most people lie and let life play upon them like the tepid discharges of a douche-bag. To the Cartesian proposition: 'I think therefore I am,' he opposed his own, which must have gone something like this: 'I imagine, therefore I belong and am free.' "

Of himself Balthazar once said wryly: "I am a Jew, with all the Jew's bloodthirsty interest in the ratiocinative faculty. It is the clue to many of the weaknesses in my thinking, and which I am learning to balance up with the rest of me—through the Cabal chiefly."

*   *   *   *   *

I remember meeting him, too, one bleak winter evening, walking along the rain-swept Corniche, dodging the sudden gushes of salt water from the conduits which lined it. Under the black hat a skull ringing with Smyrna, and the Sporades where his childhood lay. Under the black hat too the haunting illumination of a truth which he afterwards tried to convey me in an English not the less faultless for having been learned. We had met before, it is true, but glancingly: and would have perhaps passed each other with a nod had not his agitation made him stop me and take my arm. "Ah! you can help me!" he cried, taking me by the arm. "Please help me." His pale face with its gleaming goat-eyes lowered itself towards mine in the approaching dusk.

The first wet blank lamps had begun to stiffen the wet paper background of Alexandria. The sea-wall with its lines of cafés swallowed in the spray glowed with a smudged and trembling phosphorescence. The wind blew dead south. Mareotis crouched among her reeds, stiff as a crouching sphinx. He was looking, he said, for the key to his watch—the beautiful gold pocket-watch which had been made in Munich. I thought afterwards that behind the urgency of his expression he masked the symbolic meaning that this watch had for him: signifying the unbound time which flowed through his body and mine, marked off for so many years now by this historic timepiece. Munich, Zagreb, the Carpathians. . . . The watch had belonged to his father. A tall Jew, dressed in furs, riding in a sledge. He had crossed into Poland lying in his mother's arms, knowing only that the jewels she wore in that snowlit landscape were icy cold to the touch. The watch had ticked softly against his father's body as well as his own—like time fermenting in them. It was wound by a small key in the shape of an *ankh* which he kept attached to a strip of black ribbon on his key-ring. "Today is Saturday," he said hoarsely, "in Alexandria." He spoke as if a different sort of time obtained here, and he was not wrong. "If I don't find the key it will stop." In the last gleams of the wet dusk he tenderly drew the watch from its silk-lined waistcoat pocket. "I have until Monday evening. It will stop." Without the key it was useless to open the delicate golden leaf and expose the palpitating viscera of time itself stirring. "I have been over the ground three times. I must have dropped it between the café and the hospital." I would gladly have helped him, but night was falling fast; and after we had walked a short distance examining the interstices of the stones we were forced to give up the search. "Surely," I said, "you can have another key cut for it?" He answered impatiently, "Yes. Of course. But you don't understand. It belonged to this watch. It was part of it."

We went, I remember, to a café on the sea-front and sat despondently before a black coffee while he croaked on about this historic watch. It was during this conversa-

tion that he said: "I think you know Justine. She has
spoken to me warmly of you. She will bring you to the
Cabal." What is that?" I asked. "We study the Cabbala,"
he said almost shyly; "we are a sort of small lodge. She
said you knew something about it and would be interested." This astonished me for I had never, as far as I
knew, mentioned to Justine any line of study which I was
pursuing—in between long bouts of lethargy and self-
disgust. And as far as I knew the little suitcase containing
the Hermetica and other books of the kind had always
been kept under my bed locked. I said nothing however.
He spoke now of Nessim, saying: "Of all of us he is the
most happy in a way because he has no preconceived idea
of what he wants in return for his love. And to love in such
an unpremeditated way is something that most people
have to re-learn after fifty. Children have it. So has he. I
am serious."

"Did you know the writer Arnauti?"

"Yes. The author of *Moeurs*."

"Tell me about him."

"He intruded on us, but he did not see the spiritual city
underlying the temporal one. Gifted, sensitive, but very
French. He found Justine too young to be more than hurt
by her. It was ill luck. Had he found another a little older—all our women are Justines, you know, in different
styles—he might have—I will not say written better, for
his book is well written: but he might have found in it a
sort of resolution which would have made it more truly a
work of art."

He paused and took a long pull at his pipe before adding slowly: "You see in his book he avoided dealing with
a number of things which he knew to be true of Justine,
but which he ignored for purely artistic purposes—like
the incident of her child. I suppose he thought it smacked
of melodrama."

"What child was this?"

"Justine had a child, by whom I do not know. It was
kidnapped and disappeared one day. About six years old.
A girl. These things do happen quite frequently in Egypt
as you know. Later she heard that it had been seen or

recognized and began a frantic hunt for it through the
Arab quarter of every town, through every house of
ill-fame, since you know what happens to parentless children in Egypt. Arnauti never mentioned this, though he
often helped her follow up clues, and he must have seen
how much this loss contributed to her unhappiness."

"Who did Justine love before Arnauti?"

"I cannot remember. You know many of Justine's lovers
remained her friends; but more often I think you could
say that her truest friends were never lovers. The town is
always ready to gossip."

But I was thinking of a passage in *Moeurs* where
Justine comes to meet him with a man who is her lover.
Arnauti writes: "She embraced this man, her lover, so
warmly in front of me, kissing him on the mouth and eyes,
his cheeks, even his hands, that I was puzzled. Then it
shot through me with a thrill that it was really *me* she was
kissing in her imagination."

Balthazar said quietly: "Thank God I have been spared
an undue interest in love. At least the invert escapes this
fearful struggle to give oneself to another. Lying with
one's own kind, enjoying an experience, one can still keep
free the part of one's mind which dwells in Plato, or gar-
dening, or the differential calculus. Sex has left the body
and entered the imagination now; that is why Arnauti
suffered so much with Justine, because she preyed upon
all that he might have kept separate—his artist-hood if
you like. He is when all is said and done a sort of minor
Antony, and she a Cleo. You can read all about it in
Shakespeare. And then, as far as Alexandria is concerned,
you can understand why this is really a city of incest—I
mean that here the cult of Serapis was founded. For this
etiolation of the heart and reins in love-making must make
one turn inwards upon one's sister. The lover mirrors himself like Narcissus in his own family; there is no exit from
the predicament."

All this was not very comprehensible to me, yet vaguely
I felt a sort of correspondence between the associations he
employed; and certainly much of what he said seemed
to—not explain, but to offer a frame to the picture of

Justine—the dark, vehement creature in whose direct and energetic handwriting I had first read this quotation from Laforgue: "Je n'ai pas une jeune fille qui saurait me goûter. Ah! oui, une garde-malade! Une garde-malade pour l'amour de l'art, ne donnant ses baisers qu'à des mourants, des gens *in extremis*. . . ." Under this she wrote: "Often quoted by A. and at last discovered by accident in Laforgue."

"Have you fallen out of love with Melissa?" said Balthazar suddenly. "I do not know her. I have only seen her. Forgive me. I have hurt you."

It was at this time that I was becoming aware of how much Melissa was suffering. But not a word of reproach ever escaped her lips, nor did she ever speak of Justine. But she had taken on a lacklustre, unloved colour—her very flesh; and paradoxically enough though I could hardly make love to her without an effort, yet I felt myself at this time to be more deeply in love with her than ever. I was gnawed by a confusion of feelings and a sense of frustration which I had never experienced before; it made me sometimes angry with her.

It was so different from Justine, who was experiencing much the same confusion as myself between her ideas and her intentions, when she said: "Who invented the human heart, I wonder? Tell me, and then show me the place where he was hanged."

* * * * *

Of the Cabal itself, what is there to be said? Alexandria is a town of sects and gospels. And for every ascetic she has always thrown up one religious libertine—Carpocrates, Anthony—who was prepared to founder in the senses as deeply and truly as any desert father in the mind. "You speak slightingly of syncretism," said Balthazar once, "but you must understand that to work here at all—and I am speaking now as a religious maniac not a philosopher—one must try to reconcile two extremes of habit and behaviour which are not due to the intellectual disposition of the inhabitants, but to their soil, air, landscape. I mean extreme sensuality and intellectual asceticism. Historians always present syncretism as something which grew out of a mixture of warring intellectual principles; that hardly states the problem. It is not even a question of mixed races and tongues. It is the national peculiarity of the Alexandrians to seek a reconciliation between the two deepest psychological traits of which they are conscious. That is why we are hysterics and extremists. That is why we are the incomparable lovers we are."

This is not the place to try and write what I know of the Cabbala, even if I were disposed to try and define "The unpredicated ground of that Gnosis"; no aspiring hermetic could—for these fragments of revelation have their roots in the Mysteries. It is not that they are not to be revealed. They are raw experiences which only initiates can share.

I have dabbled in these matters before in Paris, conscious that in them I might find a pathway which could lead me to a deeper understanding of myself—the self which seemed to be only a huge, disorganised and shapeless society of lusts and impulses. I regarded this whole field of study as productive for my inner man, though a native and inborn scepticism kept me free from the toils of any denominational religion. For almost a year I had studied under Mustapha, a Sufi, sitting on the rickety wooden terrace of his house every evening listening to him talk in that soft cobweb voice. I had drunk sherbet with a wise Turkish Moslem. So it was with a sense of familiarity that I walked beside Justine through the twisted warren of streets which crown the fort of Kom El Dick, trying with one half of my mind to visualize how it must have looked when it was a Park sacred to Pan, the whole brown soft hillock carved into a pine-cone. Here the narrowness of the streets produced a sort of sense of intimacy, though they were lined only by verminous warrens and benighted little cafés lit by flickering rush-lamps. A strange sense of repose invested this little corner of the city giving it some of the atmosphere of a delta village. Below on the amorphous brown-violet *meidan* by the Railway Station, forlorn in the fading dusk little

crowds of Arabs gathered about groups of sportsmen
playing at single-stick, their shrill cries muffled in the fading dusk. Southward gleamed the tarnished platter of
Mareotis. Justine walked with her customary swiftness,
and in silence, impatient of my tendency to lag behind
and peer into the doorways on to those scenes of domestic
life which (lighted like toy theatres) seemed filled with a
tremendous dramatic significance.

The Cabal met at this time in what resembled a disused
curator's wooden hut, built against the red earth walls of
an embankment, very near to Pompey's Pillar. I suppose
the morbid sensitivity of the Egyptian Police to political
meetings dictated the choice of such a *venue*. One crossed
the wilderness of trenches and parapets thrown up by the
archaeologist and followed a muddy path through the
stone gate; then turning sharply at right angles one entered this large inelegant shack, one of whose walls was
the earth side of an embankment and whose floor was of
tamped earth. The interior was strongly lit by two petrol
lamps and furnished with chairs of wicker.

The gathering consisted of about twenty people drawn
from various parts of the city. I noticed with some surprise
the lean bored figure of Capodistria in one corner. Nessim
was there, of course, but there were very few represen-
tatives of the richer or more educated sections of the city.
There was, for example, an elderly clock-maker I knew
well by sight—a graceful silver-haired man whose austere
features had always seemed to me to demand a violin under them in order to set them off. A few nondescript elderly ladies. A chemist. Balthazar sat before them in a low
chair with his ugly hands lying in his lap. I recognized him
at once as if in an entirely new context as the habitué of
the Café Al Aktar with whom I had once played backgammon. A few desultory minutes passed in gossip
while the Cabal waited upon its later members; then the
old clock-maker stood up and suggested that Balthazar
should open proceedings, and my friend settled back in his
chair, closed his eyes and in that harsh croaking voice
which gradually gathered an extraordinary sweetness began to talk. He spoke, I remember, of the *fons signatus* of

the psyche and of its ability to perceive an inherent order
in the universe which underlay the apparent formlessness
and arbitrariness of phenomena. Disciplines of mind could
enable people to penetrate behind the veil of reality
and to discover harmonies in space and time which corresponded to the inner structure of their own psyches. But
the study of the Cabbala was both a science and a religion.
All this was of course familiar enough. But throughout Balthazar's expositions extraordinary fragments of thought
would emerge in the form of pregnant aphorisms which
teased the mind long after one had left his presence. I
remember him saying, for example, "None of the great
religions have done more than exclude, throw out a long
range of prohibitions. But prohibitions create the desire
they are intended to cure. We of this Cabal say: *indulge
but refine.* We are enlisting everything in order to make
man's wholeness match the wholeness of the universe—
even pleasure, the destructive granulation of the mind in
pleasure."

The constitution of the Cabal consisted of an inner
circle of initiates (Balthazar would have winced at the
word, but I do not know how else to express it) and an
outer circle of students to which Nessim and Justine
belonged. The inner circle consisted of twelve members
who were widely scattered over the Mediterranean—in
Beirut, Jaffa, Tunis and so on. In each place there was a
small academy of students who were learning to use the
strange mental-emotional calculus which the Cabbala has
erected about the idea of God. The members of the inner
Cabal corresponded frequently with one another, using
the curious old form of writing, known as the *boustrophedon;* that is to say a writing which is read from right to
left and from left to right in alternate lines. But the letters
used in their alphabet were ideograms for mental or spiritual states. I have said enough.

On that first evening Justine sat there between us, her
arms linked lightly in ours, listening with a humility and
concentration that were touching. At times the speaker's
eye rested on her for a moment with a glance of affectionate familiarity. Did I know then—or was it afterwards

I discovered—that Balthazar was perhaps her only friend
and certainly the only confidant she had in the city? I do
not remember. ("Balthazar is the only man to whom I can
tell everything. He only laughs. But somehow he helps me
to dispel the hollowness I feel in everything I do.") And it
was to Balthazar that she would always write those long
self-tortured letters which interested the curious mind of
Arnauti. In the diaries she recorded how one moonlight
night they gained access to the Museum and sat for an
hour among the statues "sightless as nightmares" listening
to him talk. He said many things which struck her then
but later when she came to try and write them down they
had vanished. Yet she did remember him saying in a quiet
reflective voice something about "those of us who are
bound to submit our bodies to the ogres," and the thought
penetrated her marrow as a reference to the sort of life she
was leading. As for Nessim, I remember him telling me
that once, when he was in a great agony of mind about
Justine, Balthazar remarked dryly to him: *"Omnis ar-
dentior amator propriae uxoris adulter est."* Adding as he
did so: "I speak now as a member of the Cabal, not as a
private person. Passionate love even for a man's own wife
is also adultery."

※   ※   ※   ※   ※

Alexandria Main Station: midnight. A deathly heavy
dew. The noise of wheels cracking the slime-slithering
pavements. Yellow pools of phosphorous light, and corridors of darkness like tears in the dull brick façade of a
stage set. Policemen in the shadows. Standing against an
insanitary brick wall to kiss her goodbye. She is going for
a week, but in the panic, half-asleep I can see that she
may never come back. The soft resolute kiss and the
bright eyes fill me with emptiness. From the dark platform comes the crunch of rifle-butts and the clicking of
Bengali. A detail of Indian troops on some routine
transfer to Cairo. It is only as the train begins to move,
and as the figure at the window, dark against the
darkness, lets go of my hand, that I feel Melissa is really
leaving; feel everything that is inexorably denied—the

long pull of the train into the silver light reminds me of
the sudden long pull of the vertebrae of her white back
turning in bed. "Melissa," I call out but the giant sniffing
of the engine blots out all sound. She begins to tilt, to
curve and slide; and quick as a scene-shifter the station
packs away advertisement after advertisement, stacking
them in the darkness. I stand as if marooned on an
iceberg. Beside me a tall Sikh shoulders the rifle he has
stopped with a rose. The shadowy figure is sliding away
down the steel rails into the darkness; a final lurch and the
train pours away down a tunnel, as if turned to liquid.

I walk about Moharrem-Bey that night, watching the
moon cloud over, preyed upon by an inexpressible anxiety.

Intense light behind cloud; by four o'clock a thin pure
drizzle like needles. The poinsettias in the Consulate garden stark with silver drops standing on their stamens. No
birds singing in the dawn. A light wind making the palm
trees sway their necks with a faint dry formal clicking.
The wonderful hushing of rain on Mareotis.

Five o'clock. Walking about in her room, studying
inanimate objects with intense concentration. The empty
powder-boxes. The depilatories from Sardis. The smell of
satin and leather. The horrible feeling of some great impending scandal. . . .

I write these lines in very different circumstances and
many months have elapsed since that night; here, under
this olive-tree, in the pool of light thrown by an oil lamp, I
write and relive that night which has taken its place in the
enormous fund of the city's memories. Somewhere else, in
a great study hung with tawny curtains Justine was copy-
ing into her diary the terrible aphorisms of Herakleitos.
The book lies beside me now. On one page she has written: "It is hard to fight with one's heart's desire; whatever
it wishes to get, it purchases at the cost of soul." And
lower down in the margin: "Night-walkers, Magians,
Bakchoi, Lenai and the *initiated*. . . ."

*   *   *   *   *

Was it about this time that Mnemjian startled me by

breathing into my ear the words: "Cohen is dying, you know?" The old furrier had drifted out of sight for some months past. Melissa had heard that he was in hospital suffering from uraemia. But the orbit we once described about the girl had changed; the kaleidoscope had tilted once more and he had sunk out of sight like a vanished chip of coloured glass. Now he was dying? I said nothing as I sat exploring the memories of those early days—the encounters at street-corners and bars. In the long silence that ensued Mnemjian scraped my hairline clean with a razor and began to spray my head with bay-rum. He gave a little sigh and said: "He has been asking for your Melissa. All night, all day."

"I will tell her," I said, and the little memory man nodded with a mossy conspiratorial look in his eyes. "What a horrible disease," he said under his breath, "he smells so. They scrape his tongue with a spatula. Pfui!" And he turned the spray upwards towards the roof as if to disinfect the memory: as if the smell had invaded the shop.

Melissa was lying on the sofa in her dressing-gown with her face turned to the wall. I thought at first she was asleep, but as I came in she turned and sat up. I told her Mnemjian's news. "I know," she said. "They sent me word from the hospital. But what can I do? I cannot go and see him. He is nothing to me, never was, never will be." Then getting up and walking the length of the room she added in a rage which hovered on the edge of tears. "He has a wife and children. What are they doing?" I sat down and once more confronted the memory of that tame seal staring sadly into a human wineglass. Melissa took my silence for criticism I suppose for she came to me and shook me gently by the shoulders, rousing me from my thoughts. "But if he is dying?" I said. The question was addressed as much to myself as to her. She cried out suddenly and kneeling down placed her head on my knees. "O it is so disgusting! Please do not make me go."

"Of course not."

"But if you think I should I will have to."

I said nothing. Cohen was in a sense already dead and buried. He had lost his place in our history, and an expenditure of emotional energy on him seemed to me useless. It had no relation to the real man who lay among the migrating fragments of his old body in a whitewashed ward. For us he had become merely an historic figure. And yet here he was, obstinately trying to insist on his identity, trying to walk back into our lives at another point in the circumference. What could Melissa give him now? What could she deny him?

"Would you like me to go?" I said. The sudden irrational thought had come into my mind that here, in the death of Cohen, I could study my own love and its death. That someone *in extremis*, calling for help to an old lover, could only elicit a cry of disgust—this terrified me. It was too late for the old man to awake compassion or even interest in my lover, who was already steeped in new misfortunes against the backcloth of which the old had faded, rotted. And in a little time perhaps, if she should call on me or I on her? Would we turn from each other with a cry of emptiness and disgust? I realized then the truth about all love: that it is an absolute which takes all or forfeits all. The other feelings, compassion, tenderness and so on, exist only on the periphery and belong to the constructions of society and habit. But she herself—austere and merciless Aphrodite—is a pagan. It is not our brains or instincts which she picks—but our very bones. It terrified me to think that this old man, at such a point in his life, had been unable to conjure up an instant's tenderness by the memory of anything he had said or done: tenderness from one who was at heart the most tender and gentle of mortals.

To be forgotten in this way was to die the death of a dog. "I shall go and see him for you," I said, though my heart quailed in disgust at the prospect; but Melissa had already fallen asleep with her dark head upon my knees. Whenever she was upset about anything she took refuge in the guileless world of sleep, slipping into it as smoothly and easily as a deer or a child. I put my hands inside the faded kimono and gently rubbed her shallow ribs and flanks. She stirred half-awake and murmured something inaudible as she allowed me to lift her and carry her

gently back to the sofa. I watched her sleeping for a long
time.

It was already dark and the city was drifting like a bed
of seaweed towards the lighted cafés of the upper town. I
went to Pastroudi and ordered a double whisky which I
drank slowly and thoughtfully. Then I took a taxi to the
hospital.

I followed a duty-nurse down the long anonymous
green corridors whose oil-painted walls exuded an atmosphere of damp. The white phosphorescent bulbs
which punctuated our progress wallowed in the gloom
like swollen glow-worms.

They had put him in the little ward with the single cur-
tained bed which was, as I afterwards learned from
Mnemjian, reserved for critical cases whose expectation of
life was short. He did not see me at first, for he was watching with an air of shocked exhaustion while a nurse disposed his pillows for him. I was amazed at the masterful,
thoughtful reserve of the face which stared up from
the mattress, for he had become so thin as almost to be
unrecognizable. The flesh had sunk down upon his cheek-
bones exposing the long slightly curved nose to its very
roots and throwing into relief the carved nostrils. This
gave the whole mouth and jaw a buoyancy, a spirit which
must have characterized his face in earliest youth. His
eyes looked bruised with fever and a dark stubble shaded
his neck and throat, but under this the exposed lines of
the face were as clean as those on the face of a man of
thirty. The images of him which I had so long held in my
memory—a sweaty porcupine, a tame seal—were immediately dissolved and replaced by this new face, this new
man who looked like—one of the beasts of the
Apocalypse. I stood for a long minute in astonishment
watching an unknown personage accepting the minis-
tration of the nurses with a dazed and regal exhaustion.
The duty-nurse was whispering in my ear: "It is good you
have come. Nobody will come and see him. He is delirious
at times. Then he wakes and asks for people. You are a
relation?"

"A business associate," I said.

"It will do him good to see a face he knows."

But would he recognize me, I wondered? If I had changed only half as much as he had we would be complete strangers to one another. He was lying back now, the breath whistling harshly through that long vulpine nose which lay resting against his face like the proud figurehead of an abandoned ship. Our whispers had disturbed him, for he turned upon me a vague but nevertheless pure and thoughtful eye which seemed to belong to some great bird of prey. Recognition did not come until I moved forward a few paces to the side of the bed. Then all at once his eyes were flooded with light—a strange mixture of humility, hurt pride, and innocent fear. He turned his face to the wall. I blurted out the whole of my message in one sentence. Melissa was away, I said, and I had telegraphed her to come as quickly as possible; meanwhile I had come to see if I could help him in any way. His shoulders shook, and I thought that an involuntary groan was about to burst from his lips; but presently in its place came the mockery of a laugh, harsh, mindless and unmusical. As if directed at the dead carcass of a joke so rotten and threadbare that it could compel nothing beyond this ghastly *rictus* gouged out in his taut cheeks.

"I know she is here," he said, and one of his hands came running over the counterpane like a frightened rat to grope for mine. "Thank you for your kindness." And with this he suddenly seemed to grow calm, though he kept his face turned away from me. "I wanted," he said slowly, as if he were collecting himself in order to give the phrase its exactest meaning, "I wanted to close my account honourably with her. I treated her badly, very badly. She did not notice, of course; she is too simple-minded, but good, such a good girl." It sounded strange to hear the phrase *"bonne copine"* on the lips of an Alexandrian, and moreover pronounced in the chipped trailing sing-song accent common to those educated here. Then he added, with considerable effort, and struggling against a formidable inner resistance. "I cheated her over her coat. It was really sealskin. Also the moths had been at it. I had it relined. Why should I do such a thing? When she was ill I

would not pay for her to see the doctor. Small things, but
they weigh heavy." Tears crowded up into his eyes and
his throat tightened as if choked by the enormity of such
thoughts. He swallowed harshly and said: "They were not
really in my character. Ask any business man who knows
me. Ask anyone."

But now confusion began to set in, and holding me
gently by the hand he led me into the dense jungle of his
illusions, walking among them with such surefootedness
and acknowledging them so calmly that I almost found
myself keeping company with them too. Unknown fronds
of trees arched over him, brushing his face, while cobbles
punctuated the rubber wheels of some dark ambulance
full of metal and other dark bodies, whose talk was of limbo—a repulsive yelping streaked with Arabic objurga-
tions. The pain, too, had begun to reach up at his reason
and lift down fantasies. The hard white edges of the bed
turned to boxes of coloured bricks, the white temperature
chart to a boatman's white face.

They were drifting, Melissa and he, across the shallow
blood-red waters of Mareotis, in each other's arms,
towards the rabble of mud-huts where once Rhakotis
stood. He reproduced their conversations so perfectly that
though my lover's share was inaudible I could nevertheless hear her cool voice, could deduce her questions
from the answers he gave her. She was desperately trying
to persuade him to marry her and he was temporizing, unwilling to lose the beauty of her person and equally
unwilling to commit himself. What interested me was the
extraordinary fidelity with which he reproduced this
whole conversation which obviously in his memory ranked
as one of the great experiences of his life. He did not know
then how much he loved her; it had remained for me to
teach him the lesson. And conversely how was it that
Melissa had never spoken to me of marriage, had never
betrayed to me the depth of her weakness and exhaustion
as she had to him? This was deeply wounding. My vanity
was gnawed by the thought that she had shown him a side
of her nature which she had kept hidden from me.

Now the scene changed again and he fell into a more

lucid vein. It was as if in the vast jungle of unreason we came upon clearings of sanity where he was emptied of his poetic illusions. Here he spoke of Melissa with feeling but coolly, like a husband of a king. It was as if now that the flesh was dying the whole funds of his inner life, so long dammed up behind the falsities of a life wrongly lived, burst through the dykes and flooded the foreground of his consciousness. It was not only Melissa either, for he spoke of his wife—and at times confused their names. There was also a third name, Rebecca, which he pronounced with a deeper reserve, a more passionate sorrow than either of the others. I took this to be his little daughter, for it is the children who deliver the final *coup de grâce* in all these terrible transactions of the heart.

Sitting there at his side, feeling our pulses ticking in unison and listening to him as he talked of my lover with a new magistral calm I could not help but see how much there was in the man which Melissa might have found to love. By what strange chance had she missed the real person? For far from being an object of contempt (as I had always taken him to be) he seemed to be now a dangerous rival whose powers I had been unaware of; and I was visited by a thought so ignoble that I am ashamed to write it down. I felt glad that Melissa had not come to see him die lest seeing him, as I saw him now, she might at a blow rediscover him. And by one of those paradoxes in which love delights I found myself more jealous of him in his dying than I had ever been during his life. These were horrible thoughts for one who had been so long a patient and attentive student of love, but I recognized once more in them the austere mindless primitive face of Aphrodite.

In a sense I recognized in him, in the very resonance of his voice when he spoke her name, a maturity which I lacked; for he had surmounted his love for her without damaging or hurting it, and allowed it to mature as all love should into a consuming and depersonalized friendship. So far from fearing to die, and importuning her for comfort, he wished only to offer her, from the inexhaustible treasury of his dying, a last gift.

The magnificent sable lay across a chair at the end of the bed wrapped in tissue paper; I could see at a glance that it was not the sort of gift for Melissa, for it would throw her scant and shabby wardrobe into confusion, out-shining everything. "I was always worried about money," he said felicitously, "while I was alive. But when you are dying you suddenly find yourself in funds." He was able for the first time in his life to be almost light-hearted. Only the sickness was there like some patient and cruel monitor.

He passed from time to time into a short confused sleep and the darkness hummed about my tired ears like a hive of bees. It was getting late and yet I could not bring myself to leave him. A duty-nurse brought me a cup of coffee and we talked in whispers. It was restful to hear her talk, for to her illness was simply a profession which she had mastered and her attitude to it was that of a jour-neyman. In her cold voice she said: "He deserted his wife and child for *une femme quelconque*. Now neither the wife nor the woman who is his mistress wants to see him. Well!" She shrugged her shoulders. These tangled loyal-ties evoked no feeling of compassion in her, for she saw them simply as despicable weaknesses. "Why doesn't the child come? Has he not asked for her?" She picked a front tooth with the nail of her little finger and said: "Yes. But he does not want to frighten her by letting her see him sick. It is you understand not pleasant for a child." She picked up an atomizer and languidly squirted some disin-fectant into the air above us, reminding me sharply of Mnemjian. "It is late," she added, "are you going to stay the night?"

I was about to make a move, but the sleeper awoke and clutched at my hand once more. "Don't go," he said in a deep fragmented but sane voice, as if he had overheard the last few phrases of our conversation. "Stay a little while. There is something else I have been thinking over and which I must reveal to you." Turning to the nurse he said quietly but distinctly, "Go!" She smoothed the bed and left us alone once more. He gave a great sigh which, if one had not been watching his face, might have seemed a

sigh of plenitude, happiness. "In the cupboard," he said,
"you will find my clothes." There were two dark suits
hanging up, and under his direction I detached a waistcoat from one of them, in the pockets of which I burrowed
until my fingers came upon two rings. "I had decided to
offer to marry Melissa *now* if she wished. That is why I
sent for her. After all what use am I? My name?" He
smiled vaguely at the ceiling. "And the rings—" he held
them lightly, reverently in his fingers like a communion
wafer. "These are rings she chose for herself long ago. So
now she must have them. Perhaps. . . ." He looked at me
for a long moment with pained, searching eyes, "But no,"
he said, "you will not marry her. Why should you? Never
mind. Take them for her, and the coat."

I put the rings into the shallow breast-pocket of my coat
and said nothing. He sighed once more and then to my
surprise, in a small gnome's tenor muffled almost to
inaudibility sang a few bars of a popular song which had
once been the rage of Alexandria, *Jamais de la vie*, and to
which Melissa still danced at the cabaret. "Listen to the
music!" he said, and I thought suddenly of the dying Antony in the poem of Cavafy—a poem he had never read,
would never read. Sirens whooped suddenly from the harbour like planets in pain. Then once more I heard this
gnome singing softly of *chagrin* and *bonheur*, and he was
singing not to Melissa but to Rebecca. How different from
the great heart-sundering choir that Antony heard—the
rich poignance of strings and voices which in the dark
street welled up—Alexandria's last bequest to those who
are her exemplars. Each man goes out to his own music, I
thought, and remembered with shame and pain the clumsy movements that Melissa made when she danced.

He had drifted now to the very borders of sleep and I
judged that it was time to leave him. I took the coat and
put it in the bottom drawer of the cupboard before tiptoe-
ing out and summoning the duty-nurse. "It is very late,"
she said.

"I will come in the morning," I said. I meant to.

Walking slowly home through the dark avenue of trees,
tasting the brackish harbour wind, I remembered Justine

saying harshly as she lay in bed: "We use each other like axes to cut down the ones we really love."

*   *   *   *   *

We have been told so often that history is indifferent, but we always take its parsimony or plenty as somehow planned; we never really listen. . . .

Now on this tenebrous peninsula shaped like a planeleaf, fingers outstretched (where the winter rain crackles like straw among the rocks), I walk stiffly sheathed in wind by a sealine choked with groaning sponges: hunting for the meaning to the pattern.

As a poet of the historic consciousness I suppose I am bound to see landscape as a field dominated by the human wish—tortured into farms and hamlets, ploughed into cities. A landscape scribbled with the signatures of men and epochs. Now, however, I am beginning to believe that the wish is inherited from the site; that man depends for the furniture of the will upon his location in place, tenant of fruitful acres or a perverted wood. It is not the impact of his freewill upon nature which I see (as I thought) but the irresistible growth, through him, of nature's own blind specified doctrines of variation and torment. She has chosen this poor forked thing as an exemplar. Then how idle it seems for any man to say, as I once heard Balthazar say: "The mission of the Cabal, if it has one, is so to ennoble function that even eating and excreting will be raised to the rank of arts." You will see in all this the flower of a perfect scepticism which undermines the will to survive. Only love can sustain one a little longer.

I think, too, that something of this sort must have been in Arnauti's mind when he wrote: "For the writer people as psychologies are finished. The contemporary psyche has exploded like a soap-bubble under the investigations of the mystagogues. What now remains to the writer?"

Perhaps it was the realization of this which made me select this empty place to live for the next few years—this sunburnt headland in the Cyclades. Surrounded by history on all sides, this empty island alone is free from every reference. It has never been mentioned in the annals of the race which owns it. Its historic past is refunded, not into time, but into place—no temples, groves, amphitheatres, to corrupt ideas with their false comparisons. A shelf of coloured boats, a harbour over the hills, and a little town denuded by neglect. That is all. Once a month a steamer touches on its way to Smyrna.

These winter evenings the sea-tempests climb the cliffs and invade the grove of giant untended planes where I walk, talking a sudden wild slang, slopping and tilting the schooner trees.

I walk here with those coveted intimations of a past which none can share with me; but which time itself cannot deprive me of. My hair is clenched back to my scalp and one hand guards the burning dottle of my pipe from the force of the wind. Above, the sky is set in a brilliant comb of stars. Antares guttering up there, buried in spray. . . . To have cheerfully laid down obedient books and friends, lighted rooms, fireplaces built for conversation—the whole parish of the civilized mind—is not something I regret but merely wonder at.

In this choice too I see something fortuitous, born of impulses which I am forced to regard as outside the range of my own nature. And yet, strangely enough, it is only here that I am at last able to re-enter, reinhabit the un-buried city with my friends; to frame them in the heavy steel webs of metaphors which will last half as long as the city itself—or so I hope. Here at least I am able to see their history and the city's as one and the same phenomenon.

But strangest of all: I owe this release to Purse-warden—the last person I should ever have considered a possible benefactor. That last meeting, for example, in the ugly and expensive hotel bedroom to which he always moved on Pombal's return from leave . . . I did not recognize the heavy musty odour of the room as the odour of his impending suicide—how should I? I knew he was unhappy; even had he not been he would have felt obliged to simulate unhappiness. All artists today are expected to cultivate a little fashionable unhappiness. And being Anglo-Saxon there was a touch of maudlin self-pity and weakness which made him drink a bit. That evening he was savage, silly and witty by turns; and listening to him I remember thinking suddenly: "Here is someone who in farming his talent has neglected his sensibility, not by accident, but deliberately, for its self-expression might have brought him into conflict with the world, or his loneliness threatened his reason. He could not bear to be refused admittance, while he lived, to the halls of fame and recognition. Underneath it all he has been steadily putting up with an almost insupportable consciousness of his own mental poltroonery. And now his career has reached an interesting stage: I mean beautiful women, whom he always felt to be out of reach as a timid provincial would, are now glad to be seen out with him. In his presence they wear the air of faintly distracted Muses suffering from constipation. In public they are flattered if he holds a gloved hand for an instant longer than form permits. At first all this must have been balm to a lonely man's vanity; but finally it has only furthered his sense of insecurity. His freedom, gained through a modest financial success, has begun to bore him. He has begun to feel more and more wanting in true greatness while his name has been daily swelling in size like some disgusting poster. He has realized that people are walking the street with a Reputation now and not a man. They see him no longer—and all his work was done in order to draw attention to the lonely, suffering figure he felt himself to be. His name has covered him like a tombstone. And now comes the terrifying thought: perhaps there *is* no one left to see? Who, after all, is he?"

I am not proud of these thoughts, for they betray the envy that every failure feels for every success; but spite may often see as clearly as charity. And indeed, running as it were upon a parallel track in my mind went the words which Clea once used about him and which, for some reason, I remembered and reflected upon: "He is unlovely somewhere. Part of the secret is his physical ungainliness. Being wizened his talent has a germ of shyness in it. Shyness has laws: you can only give yourself, tragically, to those who least understand. For to under-

stand one would be to admit pity for one's frailty. Hence
the women he loves, the letters he writes to the women he
loves, stand as ciphers in his mind for the women he
thinks he wants, or at any rate deserves—*cher ami.*"
Clea's sentences always broke in half and ended in that
magical smile of tenderness—"am I my brother's
keeper?". . .

(What I most need to do is to record experiences, not in
the order in which they took place—for that is
history—but in the order in which they first became
significant for me.)

What, then, could have been his motive in leaving me
five hundred pounds with the sole stipulation that I
should spend them with Melissa? I thought perhaps that
he may have loved her himself but after deep reflection I
have come to the conclusion that he loved, not her, but my
love for her. Of all my qualities he envied me only my
capacity to respond warmly to endearments whose value
he recognized, perhaps even desired, but from which he
would be forever barred by self-disgust. Indeed this itself
was a blow to my pride for I would have liked him to admire—if not the work I have done—at least the promise it
shows of what I have yet to do. How stupid, how limited
we are—mere vanities on legs!

We had not met for weeks, for we did not habitually
frequent each other, and when we did it was in the little
tin *pissotière* in the main square by the tram-station. It
was after dark and we would never have recognized each
other had not the headlights of a car occasionally drenched
the foetid cubicle in white light like spray. "Ah!" he
said in recognition: unsteadily, thoughtfully, for he was
drunk. (Some time, weeks before, he had left me five hundred pounds; in a sense he had summed me up, judged
me—though that judgement was only to reach me from
the other side of the grave.)

The rain cropped at the tin roof above us. I longed to go
home, for I had had a very tiring day, but I feebly
lingered, obstructed by the apologetic politeness I always
feel with people I do not really like. The slightly wavering
figure outlined itself upon the darkness before me. "Let

me," he said in a maudlin tone, "confide in you the secret
of my novelist's trade. I am a success, you a failure. The
answer, old man, is sex and plenty of it." He raised his
voice and his chin as he said, or rather declaimed, the
word "sex": tilting his scraggy neck like a chicken drinking and biting off the word with a half-yelp like a drill-
serjeant. "Lashings of sex," he repeated more normally,
"but remember," and he allowed his voice to sink to a
confidential mumble, "*stay buttoned up tight.* Eternal
grandma strong to save. You must stay buttoned up and
suffering. Try and look as if you had a stricture, a book society choice. What is not permissible is rude health, or-
dure, the natural and the funny. That was all right for
Chaucer and the Elizabethans but it won't make the
grade today—buttoned up tightly with stout Presbyterian
buttons." And in the very act of shaking himself off he
turned to me a face composed to resemble a fly-
button—tight, narrow and grotesque. I thanked him but
he waved aside the thanks in a royal manner. "It's all
free," he said, and leading me by the hand he piloted me
out into the dark street. We walked towards the lighted
centre of the town like bondsmen, fellow writers, heavy
with a sense of different failures. He talked confidentially
to himself of matters which interested him in a mumble
which I could not interpret. Once as we turned into the
Rue des Soeurs he stopped before the lighted door of a
house of ill fame and pronounced: "Baudelaire says that
copulation is the lyric of the mob. Not any more alas! For
sex is dying. In another century we shall lie with our
tongues in each other's mouths, silent and passionless as
sea-fruit. O yes! Indubitably so." And he quoted the
Arabic proverb which he uses as an epigraph to his
trilogy: "The world is like a cucumber—today it's in your
hand, tomorrow up your arse." We then resumed our
stitching, crab-like advance in the direction of his hotel,
he repeating the word "indubitably" with obvious pleasure at the soft plosive sound of it.

He was unshaven and haggard, but in comparatively
good spirits after the walk and we resorted to a bottle of
gin which he kept in the commode by his bed. I com-

mented on the two bulging suitcases which stood by the
dressing-table ready packed; over a chair lay his raincoat
stuffed with newspapers, pyjamas, toothpaste, and so on.
He was catching the night train for Gaza, he said. He
wanted to slack off and pay a visit to Petra. The
galleyproofs of his latest novel had already been cor-
rected, wrapped up and addressed. They lay dead upon
the marble top of the dressing-table. I recognized in his
sour and dejected attitude the exhaustion which pursues
the artist after he has brought a piece of work to completion. These are the low moments when the long flirtation
with suicide begins afresh.

Unfortunately, though I have searched my mind, I can
recall little of our actual conversation, though I have often
tried to do so. The fact that this was our last meeting has
invested it, in retrospect, with a significance which surely
it cannot have possessed. Nor, for the purposes of this
writing, has he ceased to exist; he has simply stepped into
the quicksilver of a mirror as we all must—to leave our
illnesses, our evil acts, the hornets' nest of our desires, still
operative for good or evil in the real world—which is the
memory of our friends. Yet the presence of death always
refreshes experience thus—that is its function: to help us
deliberate on the novelty of time. Yet at that moment we
were both situated at points equidistant from death—or
so I think. Perhaps some quiet premeditation blossomed
in him even then—no matter. I cannot tell. It is not
mysterious that any artist should desire to end a life which
he has exhausted—(a character in the last volume exclaims: "For years one has to put up with the feeling that
people do not care, really care, about one; then one day
with growing alarm, one realizes that it is God who does
not care: and not merely that he does not *care*, he does
not care *one way or the other*").

But this aside reminds me of one small fragment of that
drunken conversation. He spoke derisively of Balthazar,
of his preoccupation with religion, of the Cabal (of which
he had only heard). I listened without interrupting him
and gradually his voice ran down like a time-piece overcome by the weight of seconds. He stood up to pour him-

self a drink and said: "One needs a tremendous ignorance
to approach God. I have always known too much I suppose."

These are the sort of fragments which tease the waking
mind on evenings like these, walking about in the wintry
darkness; until at last I turn back to the crackling fire of
olive-wood in the old-fashioned arched hearth where
Justine lies asleep in her cot of sweet-smelling pine.

How much of him can I claim to know? I realize that
each person can only claim one aspect of our character as
part of his knowledge. To every one we turn a different
face of the prism. Over and over again I have found
myself surprised by observations which brought this home
to me. As for example when Justine said of Pombal, "one
of the great primates of sex." To me my friend had never
seemed predatory; only self-indulgent to a ludicrous
degree. I saw him as touching and amusing, faintly to be
cherished for an inherent ridiculousness. But she must
have seen in him the great soft-footed cat he was (to her).

And as for Pursewarden, I remember, too, that in the
very act of speaking thus about religious ignorance he
straightened himself and caught sight of his pale reflection in the mirror. The glass was raised to his lips, and
now, turning his head he squirted out upon his own glittering reflection a mouthful of the drink. That remains
clearly in my mind: a reflection liquefying in the mirror of
that shabby, expensive room which seems now so appropriate a place for the scene which must have followed
later that night.

❋   ❋   ❋   ❋   ❋

Place Zagloul—silverware and caged doves. A vaulted
cave lined with black barrels and choking with the smoke
from flying whitebait and the smell of *retzinnato*. A
message scribbled on the edge of a newspaper. Here I
spilt wine on her cloak, and while attempting to help her
repair the damage, accidentally touched her breasts. No
word was spoken. While Pursewarden spoke so brilliantly
of Alexandria and the burning library. In the room above
a poor wretch screaming with meningitis. . . .

Today, unexpectedly, comes a squinting spring shower, stiffening the dust and pollen of the city, flailing the glass roof of the studio where Nessim sits over his *croquis* for his wife's portrait. He has captured her sitting before the fire with a guitar in her hands, her throat snatched up by a spotted scarf, her singing head bent. The noise of her voice is jumbled in the back of his brain like the sound-track of an earthquake run backwards. Prodigious archery over the parks where the palm-trees have been dragged back taut; a mythology of yellow-maned waves attacking the Pharos. At night the city is full of new sounds, the pulls and stresses of the wind, until you feel it has become a ship, its old timbers groaning and creaking with every assault of the weather.

This is the weather Scobie loves. Lying in bed he will fondle his telescope lovingly, turning a wistful eye on the blank wall of rotting mud-brick which shuts off his view of the sea.

Scobie is getting on for seventy and still afraid to die; his one fear is that he will awake one morning and find himself lying dead—Lieutenant-Commander Scobie. Consequently it gives him a severe shock every morning when the water-carriers shriek under his window before dawn, waking him up. For a moment, he says, he dare not open his eyes. Keeping them fast shut (for fear that they might open on the heavenly host or the cherubims hymning) he gropes along the cake-stand beside his bed and grabs his pipe. It is always loaded from the night before and an open matchbox stands beside it. The first whiff of seaman's plug restores both his composure and his eyesight. He breathes deeply, grateful for the reassurance. He smiles. He gloats. Drawing the heavy sheepskin which serves him as a bedcover up to his ears he sings his little triumphal paean to the morning, his voice crackling like tinfoil. *"Taisez-vous, petit babouin: laissez parler votre mère."*

His pendulous trumpeter's cheeks become rosy with the effort. Taking stock of himself he discovers that he has the inevitable headache. His tongue is raw from last night's brandy. But against these trifling discomforts the prospect of another day in life weighs heavily. *"Taisez-vous, petit babouin,"* and so on, pausing to slip in his false teeth. He places his wrinkled fingers to his chest and is comforted by the sound of his heart at work, maintaining a tremulous circulation in that venous system whose deficiencies (real or imaginary I do not know) are only offset by brandy in daily and all-but lethal doses. He is rather proud of his heart. If you ever visit him when he is in bed he is almost sure to grasp your hand in a horny mandible and ask you to feel it: "Strong as a bullock, what? Ticking over nicely," is the way he puts it, in spite of the brandy. Swallowing a little you shove your hand inside his cheap night-jacket to experience those sad, blunt, far-away little bumps of life—like a foetal heart in the seventh month. He buttons up his pyjamas with a touching pride and gives his imitation roar of animal health. "Bounding from my bed like a lion"—that is another of his phrases. You have not experienced the full charm of the man until you have actually seen him, bent double with rheumatism, crawling out from between his coarse cotton sheets like a derelict. Only in the warmest months of the year do his bones thaw out sufficiently to enable him to stand fully erect. In the summer afternoons he walks the Park, his little cranium glowing like a minor sun, his briar canted to heaven, his jaw set in a violent grimace of lewd health.

No mythology of the city would be complete without its Scobie, and Alexandria will be the poorer for it when his sun-cured body wrapped in a Union Jack is finally lowered into the shallow grave which awaits him at the Roman Catholic cemetery by the tram-line.

His exiguous nautical pension is hardly enough to pay for the one cockroach-infested room which he inhabits in the slum-area behind Tatwig Street; he ekes it out with an equally exiguous salary from the Egyptian Government which carries with it the proud title of Bimbashi in the Police Force. Clea has painted a wonderful portrait of him in his police uniform with the scarlet tarbush on his head, and the great fly-whisk, as thick as a horse's tail, laid gracefully across his bony knees.

It is Clea who supplies him with tobacco and I with admiration, company, and weather permitting, brandy. We take it in turns to applaud his health, and to pick him up when he has struck himself too hard on the chest in enthusiastic demonstration of it. Origins he has none—his past proliferates through a dozen continents like a true subject of myth. And his presence is so rich with imaginary health that he needs nothing more—except perhaps an occasional trip to Cairo during Ramadan when his office is closed and when presumably all crime comes to a standstill because of the fast.

Youth is beardless, so is second childhood. Scobie tugs tenderly at the remains of a once handsome and bushy torpedo-beard—but very gently, caressingly, for fear of pulling it out altogether and leaving himself quite naked. He clings to life like a limpet, each year bringing its hardly visible sea-change. It is as if his body were being reduced, shrunk, by the passing of the winters; his cranium will soon be the size of a baby's. A year or two more and we will be able to squeeze it into a bottle and pickle it forever. The wrinkles become ever more heavily indented. Without his teeth his face is the face of an ancient ape; above the meagre beard his two cherry-red cheeks known affectionately as "port" and "starboard," glow warm in all weathers.

Physically he has drawn heavily on the replacement department; in nineteen ten a fall from the mizzen threw his jaw two points west by south-west, and smashed the frontal sinus. When he speaks his denture behaves like a moving staircase, travelling upwards and round inside his skull in a jerky spiral. His smile is capricious; it might appear from anywhere, like that of the Cheshire Cat. In ninety-eight, he made eyes at another man's wife (so he says) and lost one of them. No one except Clea is supposed to know about this, but the replacement in this case was rather a crude one. In repose it is not very noticeable, but the minute he becomes animated a disparity between his two eyes becomes obvious. There is also a small technical problem: his own eye is almost permanently bloodshot. On the very first occasion when he treated me to a reedy rendering of "Watchman, What of the Night?", while he stood in the corner of the room with an ancient chamber-pot in his hand, I noticed that his right eye moved a trifle slower than his left. It seemed then to be a larger imitation of the stuffed eagle's eye which lours so glumly from a niche in the public library. In winter, however, it is the false eye and not the true which throbs unbearably making him morose and foul-mouthed until he has applied a little brandy to his stomach.

Scobie is a sort of protozoic profile in fog and rain, for he carries with him a sort of English weather, and he is never happier than when he can sit over a microscopic wood-fire in winter and talk. One by one his memories leak through the faulty machinery of his mind until he no longer knows them for his own. Behind him I see the long grey rollers of the Atlantic at work, curling up over his memories, smothering them in spray, blinding him. When he speaks of the past it is in a series of short dim telegrams—as if already communications were poor, the weather inimical to transmission. In Dawson City the ten who went up the river were frozen to death. Winter came down like a hammer, beating them senseless: whisky, gold, murder—it was like a new crusade northward into the timberlands. At this time his brother fell over the falls in Uganda; in his dream he saw the tiny figure, like a fly, fall and at once get smoothed out by the yellow claw of water. No: that was later when he was already staring along the sights of a carbine into the very brain-box of a Boer. He tries to remember exactly *when* it must have been, dropping his polished head into his hands; but the grey rollers intervene, the long effortless tides patrol the barrier between himself and his memory. That is why the phrase came to me: a *sea-change* for the old pirate: his skull looks palped and sucked down until only the thinnest integument separates his smile from the smile of the hidden skeleton. Observe the brain-case with its heavy indentations: the twigs of bone inside his wax fingers: the rods of tallow which support his quivering shins. . . . Really, as Clea has remarked, old Scobie is like some little old experimental engine left over from the last century,

something as pathetic and friendly as Stephenson's first
Rocket.

He lives in his little sloping attic like an anchorite. "An
anchorite!" that is another favourite phrase; he will pop
his cheek vulgarly with his finger as he utters it, allowing
his rolling eye to insinuate all the feminine indulgences he
permits himself in secret. This is for Clea's benefit,
however; in the presence of "a perfect lady," he feels
obliged to assume a protective colouring which he sheds
the moment she leaves. The truth is somewhat sadder.
"I've done quite a bit of scout-mastering," he admits to
me *sotto voce*, "with the Hackney Troop. That was after I
was invalided out. But I had to keep out of England, old
boy. The strain was too much for me. Every week I expected to see a headline in the *News of the World*,
'Another youthful victim of scoutmaster's dirty wish.'
Down in Hackney things didn't matter so much. My kids
were experts in woodcraft. Proper young Etonians
I used to call them. The scoutmaster before me got twenty
years. It's enough to make one have Doubts. These things
made you think. Somehow I couldn't settle down in Hackney. Mind you, I'm a bit past everything now, but I do
like to have my peace of mind—just in case. And
somehow in England one doesn't feel free any more. Look
at the way they are pulling up clergymen, respected
churchmen and so on. I used to lie awake worrying. Finally I came abroad as a private tooter—Toby Mannering,
his father was an M.P., wanted an excuse to travel. They
said he had to have a tooter. He wanted to go into the
navy. That's how I fetched up here. I saw at once it was
nice and free-and-easy here. Got a job right off with the
Vice Squad under Nimrod Pasha. And here I am, dear boy.
And no complaints do you see? Looking from east to west
over this fertile Delta what do I see? Mile upon mile of
angelic little black bottoms."

The Egyptian Government, with the typical generous
quixotry the Levant lavishes on any foreigner who shows
a little warmth and friendliness, had offered him a means
to live on in Alexandria. It is said that after his appoint-
ment to the Vice Squad vice assumed such alarming pro-

portions that it was found necessary to upgrade and
transfer him; but he himself always maintained that his
transfer to the routine C.I.D. branch of the police had
been a deserved promotion—and I for my part have never
had the courage to tease him on the subject. His work is
not onerous. For a couple of hours every morning he
works in a ramshackle office in the upper quarter of the
town, with the fleas jumping out of the rotten woodwork
of his old-fashioned desk. He lunches modestly at the
Lutetia and, funds permitting, buys himself an apple and
a bottle of brandy for his evening meal there. The long
fierce summer afternoons are spent in sleep, in turning
over the newspapers which he borrows from a friendly
Greek newsvendor. (As he reads the pulse in the top of
his skull beats softly.) Ripeness is all.

The furnishing of his little room suggests a highly eclec-
tic spirit; the few objects which adorn the anchorite's life
have a severely personal flavour, as if together they composed the personality of their owner. That is why Clea's
portrait gives such a feeling of completeness, for she has
worked into the background the whole sum of the old
man's possessions. The shabby little crucifix on the wall
behind the bed, for example; it is some years since Scobie
accepted the consolations of the Holy Roman Church
against old age and those defects of character which had
by this time become second nature. Nearby hangs a small
coloured print of the Mona Lisa whose enigmatic smile
has always reminded Scobie of his mother. (For my part
the famous smile has always seemed to me to be the smile
of a woman who has just dined off her husband.)
However this too has somehow incorporated itself into the
existence of Scobie, established a special and private relationship. It is as if his Mona Lisa were like no other; it is a
deserter from Leonardo.

Then, of course, there is the ancient cake-stand which
serves as his commode, bookcase and escritoire in one.
Clea has accorded it the ungrudging treatment it
deserves, painting it with a microscopic fidelity. It has
four tiers, each fringed with a narrow but elegant bevel. It
cost him ninepence farthing in the Euston Road in 1911,

and it has travelled twice round the world with him. He
will help you admire it without a trace of humour or self-
consciousness. "Fetching little thing, what?" he will say
jauntily, as he takes a cloth and dusts it. The top tier, he
will explain carefully, was designed for buttered toast: the
middle for shortbreads: the bottom tier is for "two kinds
of cake." At the moment, however, it is fulfilling another
purpose. On the top shelf lies his telescope, compass and
Bible; on the middle tier lies his correspondence which
consists only of his pension envelope; on the bottom tier,
with tremendous gravity lies a chamber-pot which is always referred to as "the heirloom," and to which is attached a mysterious story which he will one day confide to
me.

The room is lit by one weak electric-light bulb and a
cluster of rush lights standing in a niche which also houses
an earthenware jar full of cool drinking water. The one
uncurtained window looks blindly out upon a sad peeling
wall of mud. Lying in bed with the smoky feeble glare of
the night-lights glinting in the glass of his compass—lying
in bed after midnight with the brandy throbbing in his
skull he reminds me of some ancient wedding-cake, waiting only for someone to lean forward and blow out the
candles!

His last remark at night, when one has seen him safely
to bed and tucked him in—apart from the vulgar "Kiss
Me Hardy" which is always accompanied by a leer and a
popped cheek—is more serious. "Tell me honestly." he
says. "Do I look my age?"

Frankly Scobie looks anybody's age; older than the
birth of tragedy, younger than the Athenian death.
Spawned in the Ark by a chance meeting and mating of
the bear and the ostrich; delivered before term by the
sickening grunt of the keel on Ararat. Scobie came forth
from the womb in a wheel chair with rubber tyres,
dressed in a deer-stalker and a red flannel binder. On his
prehensile toes the glossiest pair of elastic-sided boots. In
his hand a ravaged family Bible whose fly-leaf bore the
words "Joshua Samuel Scobie 1870. Honour thy father
and thy mother." To these possessions were added eyes

like dead moons, a distinct curvature of the pirate's spinal column, and a taste for quinqueremes. It was not blood which flowed in Scobie's veins but green salt water, deep-sea stuff. His walk is the slow rolling grinding trudge of a saint walking on Galilee. His talk is a green-water jargon swept up in five oceans—an antique shop of polite fable bristling with sextants, astrolabes, porpentines and isobars. When he sings, which he so often does, it is in the very accents of the Old Man of the Sea. Like a patron saint he has left little pieces of his flesh all over the world, in Zanzibar, Colombo, Togoland, Wu Fu: the little deciduous morsels which he has been shedding for so long now, old antlers, cuff-links, teeth, hair. . . . Now the retreating tide has left him high and dry above the speeding currents of time, Joshua the insolvent weather-man, the islander, the anchorite.

*   *   *   *   *

Clea, the gentle, lovable, unknowable Clea is Scobie's greatest friend, and spends much of her time with the old pirate; she deserts her cobweb studio to make him tea and to enjoy those interminable monologues about a life which has long since receded, lost its vital momentum, only to live on vicariously in the labyrinths of memory.

As for Clea herself: is it only my imagination which makes it seem so difficult to sketch her portrait? I think of her so much—and yet I see how in all this writing I have been shrinking from dealing directly with her. Perhaps the difficulty lies here: that there does not seem to be an easy correspondence between her habits and her true disposition. If I should describe the outward structure of her so much—and yet I see how in all this writing I have her life—so disarmingly simple, graceful, self-contained —there is a real danger that she might seem either a nun for whom the whole range of human passions had given place to an absorbing search for her subliminal self, or a disappointed and ingrown virgin who had deprived herself of the world because of some psychic instability, or some insurmountable early wound.

Everything about her person is honey-gold and warm in

tone; the fair, crisply-trimmed hair which she wears rather long at the back, knotting it simply at the downy nape of her neck. This focuses the candid face of a minor muse with its smiling grey-green eyes. The calmly disposed hands have a deftness and shapeliness which one only notices when one sees them at work, holding a paint-brush perhaps or setting the broken leg of a sparrow in splints made from match-ends.

I should say something like this: that she had been poured, while still warm, into the body of a young grace: that is to say, into a body born without instincts or desires.

To have great beauty; to have enough money to con-struct an independent life; to have a skill—these are the factors which persuade the envious, the dispirited to regard her as undeservedly lucky. But why, ask her critics and observers, has she denied herself marriage?

She lives in modest though not miserly style, inhabiting a comfortable attic-studio furnished with little beyond an iron bed and a few ragged beach chairs which in the sum-mer are transferred bodily to her little bathing cabin at Sidi Bishr. Her only luxury is a glittering tiled bathroom in the corner of which she has installed a minute stove to cope with whatever cooking she feels inclined to do for herself; and a bookcase whose crowded shelves indicate that she denies it nothing.

She lives without lovers or family ties, without malices or pets, concentrating with single-mindedness upon her painting which she takes seriously, but not too seriously. In her work, too, she is lucky; for these bold yet elegant canvases radiate clemency and humour. They are full of a sense of play—like children much-beloved.

But I see that I have foolishly spoken of her as "denying herself marriage." How this would anger her: for I remember her once saying: "If we are to be friends you must not think or speak about me as someone who is de-nying herself something in life. My solitude does not deprive me of anything, nor am I fitted to be other than I am. I want you to see how successful I am and not imagine me full of inner failings. As for love itself—*cher ami*—I told you already that love interested me only very briefly—and men more briefly still; the few, indeed the one, experience which marked me was an experience with a woman. I am still living in the happiness of that perfectly *achieved* relationship: any physical substitute would seem today horribly vulgar and hollow. But do not imagine me as suffering from any fashionable form of broken heart. No. In a funny sort of way I feel that our love has really gained by the passing of the love-object; it is as if the physical body somehow stood in the way of love's true growth, its self-realization. Does that sound calamitous?" She laughed.

We were walking, I remember, along the rainswept Corniche in autumn, under a darkening crescent of clouded sky; and as she spoke she put her arm affectionately through mine and smiled at me with such tenderness that a passer-by might have been forgiven for imagining that we ourselves were lovers.

"And then," she went on, "there is another thing which perhaps you will discover for yourself. There is something about love—I will not say defective for the defect lies in ourselves: but something we have mistaken about its nature. For example, the love you now feel for Justine is not a different love for a different object but the same love you feel for Melissa trying to work itself out through the medium of Justine. Love is horribly stable, and each of us is only allotted a certain portion of it, a ration. It is capable of appearing in an infinity of forms and attaching itself to an infinity of people. But it is limited in quantity, can be used up, become shop-worn and faded before it reaches its true object. For its destination lies somewhere in the deepest regions of the psyche where it will come to recognize itself as self-love, the ground upon which we build the sort of health of the psyche. I do not mean egoism or narcissism."

It was conversations like these: conversations lasting sometimes far into the night, which first brought me close to Clea, taught me that I could rely upon the strength which she had quarried out of self-knowledge and reflection. In our friendship we were able to share our private thoughts and ideas, to test them upon one another, in a way that would have been impossible had we been linked more closely by ties which, paradoxically enough, separate more profoundly than they join, though human illusion forbids us to believe this. "It is true," I remember her saying once, when I had mentioned this strange fact, "that in some senses I am closer to you than either Melissa or Justine. You see, Melissa's love is too confiding: it blinds her. While Justine's cowardly monomania sees one through an invented picture of one, and this forbids you to do anything except to be a demoniac like her. Do not look hurt. There is no malice in what I say."

But apart from Clea's own painting, I should not forget to mention the work she does for Balthazar. She is the clinic painter. For some reason or other my friend is not content with the normal slipshod method of recording medical anomalies by photographs. He is pursuing some private theory which makes him attach importance to the pigmentation of the skin in certain stages of his pet diseases. The ravages of syphilis, for example, in every degree of anomaly, Clea has recorded for him in large coloured drawings of terrifying lucidity and tenderness. In a sense these are truly works of art; the purely utilitarian object has freed the painter from any compulsion towards self-expression; she has set herself to record; and these tortured and benighted human members which Balthazar picks out daily from the long sad queue in the out-patients' ward (like a man picking rotten apples from a barrel) have all the values of depicted human faces—abdomens blown like fuses, skin surfaces shrunken and peeling like plaster, carcinomata bursting through the rubber membranes which retain them. . . . I remember the first time I saw her at work; I had called on Balthazar at the clinic to collect a certificate for some routine matter in connection with the school at which I worked. Through the glass doors of the surgery I caught a glimpse of Clea, whom I did not then know, sitting under the withered pear-tree in the shabby garden. She was dressed in a white medical smock, and her colours were laid out methodically beside her on a slab of fallen marble. Before her, seated half-crouching upon a wicker chair, was a big-

breasted sphinx-faced *fellah* girl, with her skirt drawn up
above her waist to expose some choice object of my
friend's study. It was a brilliant spring day, and in the
distance one could hear the scampering of the sea. Clea's
capable and innocent fingers moved back and forth upon
the white surface of the paper, surely, deftly, with wise
premeditation. Her face showed the rapt and concen-
trated pleasure of a specialist touching in the colours of
some rare tulip.

When Melissa was dying it was for Clea that she asked;
and it was Clea who spent whole nights at her bedside
telling her stories and tending her. As for Scobie—I do not
dare to say that their inversion constituted a hidden
bond—sunk like a submarine cable linking two continents—for that might do an injustice to both. Certainly
the old man is unaware of any such matter; and she for
her part is restrained by her perfect tact from showing
him how hollow are his boasts of love-making. They are
perfectly matched, and perfectly happy in their relationship, like a father and daughter. On the only occasion
when I heard him rally her upon not being married Clea's
lovely face became round and smooth as that of a
schoolgirl, and from the depths of an assumed seriousness
which completely disguised the twinkle of the imp in her
grey eyes, she replied that she was waiting for the right
man to come along: at which Scobie nodded profoundly,
and agreed that this was the right line of conduct.

It was from a litter of dusty canvases in one corner of
her studio that I unearthed a head of Justine one day—a
half profile, touched in impressionistically and obviously
not finished. Clea caught her breath and gazed at it with
all the compassion a mother might show for a child which
she recognized as ugly, but which was none the less
beautiful for her. "It is ages old," she said; and after much
reflection gave it to me for my birthday. It stands now on
the old arched mantelshelf to remind me of the breathless,
incisive beauty of that dark and beloved head. She has
just taken a cigarette from between her lips, and she is
about to say something which her mind has already for-

mulated but which has so far only reached the eyes. The
lips are parted, ready to utter it in words.

*   *   *   *   *

A mania for self-justification is common both to those
whose consciences are uneasy and to those who seek a
philosophic rationale for their actions: but in either case it
leads to strange forms of thinking. The idea is not spontaneous, but *voulue*. In the case of Justine this mania led
to a perpetual flow of ideas, speculations on past and present actions, which pressed upon her mind with the
weight of a massive current pressing upon the walls of a
dam. And for all the wretched expenditure of energy in
this direction, for all the passionate contrivance in her
self-examination, one could not help distrusting her con-
clusions, since they were always changing, were never at
rest. She shed theories about herself like so many petals.
"Do you not believe that love consists wholly of paradoxes?" she once asked Arnauti. I remember her asking me
much the same question in that turbid voice of hers which
somehow gave the question tenderness as well as a sort of
menace. "Supposing I were to tell you that I only allowed
myself to approach you to save myself from the danger
and ignominy of falling deeply in love with you? I felt I
was saving Nessim with every kiss I gave you." How
could this, for example, have constituted the true motive
for that extraordinary scene on the beach? No rest from
doubt, no rest from doubt. On another occasion she dealt
with the problem from another angle, not perhaps less
truthfully: "The moral is—what is the moral? We were
not simply gluttons, were we? And how completely this
love-affair has repaid all the promises it held out for
us—at least for me. We met and the worst befell us, but
the best part of us, our lovers. O! please do not laugh at
me."

For my part I remained always stupefied and mum-
chance at all the avenues opened up by these thoughts;
and afraid, so strange did it seem to talk about what we
were actually experiencing in such obituary terms. At
times I was almost provoked like Arnauti, on a similar oc-

casion, to shout: "For the love of God, stop this mania for unhappiness or it will bring us to disaster. You are exhausting our lives before we have a chance to live them." I knew of course the uselessness of such an exhortation. There are some characters in this world who are marked down for self-destruction, and to these no amount of rational argument can appeal. For my part Justine always reminded me of a somnambulist discovered treading the perilous leads of a high tower; any attempt to wake her with a shout might lead to disaster. One could only follow her silently in the hope of guiding her gradually away from the great shadowy drops which loomed up on every side.

But by some curious paradox it was these very defects of character—these vulgarities of the psyche—which constituted for me the greatest attraction of this weird kinetic personage. I suppose in some way they corresponded to weaknesses in my own character which I was lucky to be able to master more thoroughly than she could. I know that for us love-making was only a small part of the total picture projected by a mental intimacy which proliferated and ramified daily around us. How we talked! Night after night in shabby sea-front cafés (trying ineffectually to conceal from Nessim and other common friends an attachment for which we felt guilty). As we talked we insensibly drew nearer and nearer to each other until we were holding hands, or all but in each other's arms: not from the customary sensuality which afflicts lovers but as if the physical contact could ease the pain of self-exploration.

Of course this is the unhappiest love-relationship of which a human being is capable—weighed down by something as heartbreaking as the post-coital sadness which clings to every endearment, which lingers like a sediment in the clear waters of a kiss. "It is easy to write of kisses," says Arnauti, "but where passion should have been full of clues and keys it served only to slake our thoughts. It did not convey information as it usually does. There was so much else going on." And indeed in making love to her I too began to understand fully what he meant

in describing The Check as "the parching sense of lying
with some lovely statue which was unable to return the
kisses of the common flesh which it touches. There was
something exhausting and perverting about loving so well
and yet loving so little."

The bedroom for example with its bronze phosphorous
light, the pastels burning in the green Tibetan urn diffus-
ing a smell of roses to the whole room. By the bed the rich
poignant scent of her powder hanging heavy in the bed-
curtains. A dressing-table with its stoppered cream and
salves. Over the bed the Universe of Ptolemy! She has had
it drawn upon parchment and handsomely framed. It will
hang forever over her bed, over the eikons in their leather
cases, over the martial array of philosophers. Kant in his
nightcap feeling his way upstairs. Jupiter Tonans. There
is somehow a heavy futility in this array of great
ones—among whom she has permitted Pursewarden an
appearance. Four of his novels are to be seen though
whether she has put them there specially for the occasion
(we are all dining together) I cannot say. Justine surrounded by her philosophers is like an invalid surrounded
by medicines—empty capsules, bottles and syringes. "Kiss
her," says Arnauti, "and you are aware that her eyes do
not close but open more widely, with an increasing doubt
and madness. The mind is so awake that it makes any gift
of the body partial—a panic which will respond to nothing less than a *curette*. At night you can hear her brain
ticking like a cheap alarm-clock."

On the far wall there is an idol the eyes of which are lit
from within by electricity, and it is to this graven mentor
that Justine acts her private role. Imagine a torch thrust
through the throat of a skeleton to light up the vault of the
skull from which the eyeless sockets ponder. Shadows
thrown on the arch of the cranium flap there in imprison-
ment. When the electricity is out of order a stump of candle is soldered to the bracket: Justine then, standing
naked on tip-toes to push a lighted match into the eyeball
of the God. Immediately the furrows of the jaw spring into relief, the shaven frontal bone, the straight rod of the
nose. She has never been tranquil unless this visitant from

distant mythology is watching over her nightmares. Under it lie a few small inexpensive toys, a celluloid doll, a sailor, about which I have never had the courage to question her. It is to this idol that her most marvellous dialogues are composed. It is possible, she says, to talk in her sleep and be overheard by the wise and sympathetic mask which has come to represent what she calls her Noble Self—adding sadly, with a smile of misgiving, "It does exist you know."

The pages of Arnauti run through my mind as I watch her and talk to her. "A face famished by the inward light of her terrors. In the darkness long after I am asleep she wakes to ponder on something I have said about our relationship. I am always waking to find her busy with something, preoccupied; sitting before the mirror naked, smoking a cigarette, and tapping with her bare foot on the expensive carpet." It is strange that I should always see Justine in the context of this bedroom which she could never have known before Nessim gave it to her. It is always here that I see her undergoing those dreadful intimacies of which he writes. "There is no pain compared to that of loving a woman who makes her body accessible to one and yet who is incapable of delivering her true self—because she does not know where to find it." How often, lying beside her, I have debated these observations which, to the ordinary reader, might pass unnoticed in the general flux and reflux of ideas in *Moeurs*.

She does not slide from kisses into sleep—a door into a private garden—as Melissa does. In the warm bronze light her pale skin looks paler—the red estable flowers growing in the cheeks where the light sinks and is held fast. She will throw back her dress to unroll her stocking and show you the dark cicatrice above the knee, lodged between the twin dimples of the suspender. It is indescribable the feeling I have when I see this wound—like a character out of the book—and recall its singular origin. In the mirror the dark head, younger and more graceful now than the original it has outlived, gives back a vestigial image of a young Justine—like the calcimined imprint of a fern in chalk; the youth she believes she has lost.

I cannot believe that she existed so thoroughly in some
other room; that the idol hung elsewhere, in another setting. Somehow I always see her walking up the long staircase, crossing the gallery with its *putti* and ferns, and then
entering the low doorway into this most private of rooms.
Fatma, the black Ethiopian maid, follows her. Invariably
Justine sinks on to the bed and holds out her ringed
fingers; as with an air of mild hallucination the Negress
draws them off the long fingers and places them in a small
casket on the dressing-table. The night on which Pursewarden and I dined alone with her we were invited back
to the great house, and after examining the great cold
reception rooms Justine suddenly turned and led the way
upstairs, in search of an ambience which might persuade
my friend, whom she greatly admired and feared, to relax.

Pursewarden had been surly all evening, as he often
was, and had busied himself with the drinks to the exclu-
sion of anything else. The little ritual with Fatma seemed
to free Justine from constraint; she was free to be natural,
to move about with "that insolent unbalanced air, cursing
her frock for catching in the cupboard door," or pausing
to apostrophize herself in the great spade-shaped mirror.
She told us of the mask, adding sadly, "It sounds cheap
and rather theatrical, I know. I turn my face to the wall
and talk to it. I forgive myself my trespasses as I forgive
those who trespass against me. Sometimes I rave a little
and beat on the wall when I remember the follies which
must seem insignificant to others or to God—if there is a
God. I speak to the person I always imagine inhabiting a
green and quiet place like the Twenty-third Psalm." Then
coming to rest her head upon my shoulder and put her
arms round me, "That is why so often I ask you to be a little tender with me. The edifice feels as if it had cracked up
here. I need little strokes and endearments like you give
Melissa; I know it is she you love. Who could love me?"

Pursewarden was not, I think, proof against the
naturalness and charm of the tones in which she said this,
for he went to the corner of the room and gazed at her
bookshelf. The sight of his own books made him first pale
and then red, though whether with shame or anger I

could not tell. Turning back he seemed at first about to say something, but changed his mind. He turned back once more with an air of guilty chagrin to confront that tremendous shelf. Justine said: "If you wouldn't consider it an impertinence I should so like you to autograph one for me," but he did not reply. He stayed quite still, staring at the shelf, with his glass in his hand. Then he wheeled about and all of a sudden he appeared to have become completely drunk; he said in a fierce ringing tone: "The modern novel! The *grumus merdae* left behind by criminals upon the scene of their misdeeds." And quietly falling sideways, but taking care to place his glass upright on the floor he passed immediately into a magistral sleep.

The whole of the long colloquy which ensued took place over this prostrate body. I took him to be asleep, but in fact he must have been awake for he subsequently reproduced much of Justine's conversation in a cruel satirical short story, which for some reason amused Justine though it caused me great pain. He described her black eyes shining with unshed tears as she said (sitting at the mirror, the comb travelling through her hair, crackling and sputtering like her voice): "When I first met Nessim and knew that I was falling in love with him I tried to save us both. I deliberately took a lover—a dull brute of a Swede, hoping to wound him and force him to detach himself from his feeling for me. The Swede's wife had left him and I said (anything to stop him snivelling): 'Tell me how she behaves and I will imitate her. In the dark we are all meat and treacherous however our hair kinks or skin smells. Tell me, and I will give you the wedding-smile and fall into your arms like a mountain of silk.' And all the time I was thinking over and over again: 'Nessim. Nessim.'"

I remember in this context, too, a remark of Purse-warden's which summed up his attitude to our friends. "Alexandria!" he said (it was on one of those long moonlit walks), "Jews with their cafeteria mysticism! How could one deal with it in words? Place and people?" Perhaps then he was meditating this cruel short story and casting about for ways and means to deal with us. "Justine and

her city are alike in that they both have a strong flavour
without having any real character."

I am recalling now how during that last spring
(forever) we walked together at full moon, overcome by
the soft dazed air of the city, the quiet ablutions of water
and moonlight that polished it like a great casket. An
aerial lunacy among the deserted trees of the dark
squares, and the long dusty roads reaching away from
midnight to midnight, bluer than oxygen. The passing
faces had become gem-like, tranced—the baker at his machine making the staff of tomorrow's life, the lover hurrying back to his lodging, nailed into a silver helmet of
panic, the six-foot cinema posters borrowing a ghastly
magnificence from the moon which seemed laid across
the nerves like a bow.

We turn a corner and the world becomes a pattern of
arteries, splashed with silver and deckle-edged with
shadow. At this far end of Kom El Dick not a soul abroad
save an occasional obsessive policeman, lurking like a
guilty wish in the city's mind. Our footsteps run punctually as metronomes along the deserted pavements: two
men, in their own time and city, remote from the world,
walking as if they were treading one of the lugubrious
canals of the moon. Pursewarden is speaking of the book
which he has always wanted to write, and of the difficulty
which besets a city-man when he faces a work of art.

"If you think of yourself as a sleeping city for example
. . . what? You can sit quiet and hear the processes going
on, going about their business; volition, desire, will, cogni-
tion, passion, conation. I mean like the million legs of a
centipede carrying on with the body powerless to do anything about it. One gets exhausted trying to cir-
cumnavigate these huge fields of experience. We are
never free, we writers. I could explain it much more
clearly if it was dawn. I long to be musical in body and
mind. I want style, consort. Not the little mental squirts as
if through the ticker-tape of the mind. It is the age's disease, is it not? It explains the huge waves of occultism
lapping round us. The Cabal, now, and Balthazar. He will
never understand that it is with God we must be the most

careful; for He makes such a powerful appeal to what is
lowest in human nature—our feeling of insufficiency, fear
of the unknown, personal failings; above all our
monstrous egotism which sees in the martyr's crown an
athletic prize which is really hard to attain. God's real and
subtle nature must be clear of distinctions: a glass of
spring-water, tasteless, odourless, merely refreshing: and
surely its appeal would be to the few, the very few, real
contemplatives? As for the many it is already included in
the part of their nature which they least wish to admit or
examine. I do not believe that there is any system which
can do more than pervert the essential idea. And then, all
these attempts to circumscribe God in words or ideas. . . .
No one thing can explain everything: though everything
can illuminate something. God, I must be still drunk. If
God were anything He would be an art. Sculpture or
medicine. But the immense extension of knowledge in this
our age, the growth of new sciences, makes it almost impossible for us to digest the available flavours and put
them to use.

"Holding a candle in your hand, I mean, you can throw
the shadow of the retinal blood-vessels on the wall. It isn't
silent enough. It's never dead still in there: never quiet
enough for the trismegistus to be fed. All night long you
can hear the rush of blood in the cerebral arteries. The
loins of thinking. It starts you going back along the cogs of
historical action, cause and effect. You can't rest ever, you
can't give over and begin to scry. You climb through the
physical body, softly parting the muscle-schemes to admit
you—muscle striped and unstriped; you examine the coil
ignition of the guts in the abdomen, the sweetbreads, the
liver choked with refuse like a sink-filter, the bag of urine,
the red unbuckled belt of the intestines, the soft horny
corridor of the oesophagus, the glottis with its mucilage
softer than the pouch of a kangaroo. What do I mean?
You are searching for a coordinating scheme, the syntax of
a Will which might stabilize everything and take the
tragedy out of it. The sweat breaks out on your face, a
cold panic as you feel the soft contraction and expansion
of the viscera busy about their job, regardless of the man

watching them who is yourself. A whole city of processes,
a factory for the production of excrement, my goodness, a
daily sacrifice. An offering to the toilet for every one you
make to the altar. Where do they meet? Where is the correspondence? Outside in the darkness by the railway
bridge the lover of this man waits for him with the same
indescribable maggotry going on in her body and blood;
wine swilling the conduits, the pylorus disgorging like a
sucker, the incommensurable bacteriological world multiplying in every drop of semen, spittle, sputum, musk. He
takes a spinal column in his arms, the ducts flooded with
ammonia, the meninges exuding their pollen, the cornea
glowing in its little crucible. . . ."

He begins now that shocking boyish laughter, throwing
back his head until the moonlight plays upon his perfect
white teeth under the sad little blond moustache.

It was on such a night that our footsteps led us to Balthazar's door, and seeing his light on, we knocked. The
same night, on the old horn gramophone (with an emotion so deep that it was almost horror) I heard some
amateur's recording of the old poet reciting the lines
which begin:

> *Ideal voices and much beloved*
> *Of those who died, of those who are*
> *Now lost for us like the very dead;*
> *Sometimes within a dream they speak*
> *Or in the ticking brain a thought revives them. . . .*

These fugitive memories explain nothing, illuminate
nothing: yet they return again and again when I think of
my friends as if the very circumstances of our habits had
become impregnated with what he then felt, the parts we
then acted. The slither of tyres across the waves of the
desert under a sky blue and frost-bound in winter; or in
summer a fearful lunar bombardment which turned the
sea to phosphorus—bodies shining like tin, crushed in
electric bubbles; or walking to the last spit of sand near
Montaza, sneaking through the dense green darkness of
the King's gardens, past the drowsy sentry, to where the

force of the sea was suddenly crippled and the waves hobbled over the sand-bar. Or walking arm-in-arm down the long gallery, already gloomy with an unusual yellow winter fog. Her hand is cold so she has slipped it in my pocket. Today because she has no emotion whatsoever she tells me that she is in love with me—something she has always refused to do. At the long windows the rain hisses down suddenly. The dark eyes are cool and amused. A centre of blackness in things which trembles and changes shape. "I am afraid of Nessim these days. He has changed." We are standing before the Chinese paintings from the Louvre. "The meaning of space," she says with disgust. There is no form, no pigment, no lens any more—simply a gaping hole into which the infinite drains slowly into the room: a blue gulf where the tiger's body was, emptying itself into the preoccupied atmosphere of the studios. Afterwards we walk up the dark staircase to the top floor to see Sveva, to put on the gramophone and dance. The little model pretends that she is heartbroken because Pombal has cast her off after a "whirlwind romance" lasting nearly a month.

My friend himself is a little surprised at the force of an attachment which could make him think of one woman for so long a time. He has cut himself while shaving and his face looks grotesque with a moustache of surgical tape stuck to it. "It is a city of aberrations," he repeats angrily. "I very nearly married her. It is infuriating. Thank God that the veil lifted when it did. It was seeing her naked in front of the mirror. All of a sudden I was disgusted—though I mentally admitted a sort of Renaissance dignity in the fallen breasts, the waxy skin, the sunken belly and the little peasant paws. All of a sudden I sat up in bed and said to myself, 'My God! She is an elephant in need of a coat of whitewash!' "

Now Sveva is quietly sniffing into her handkerchief as she recounts the extravagant promises which Pombal has made her, and which will never be fulfilled. "It was a curious and dangerous attachment for an easy-going man" (I hear Pombal's voice explaining). "It felt as if her cool murderous charity had eaten away my locomotive centres, paralysed my nervous system. Thank God I am free to concentrate on my work once more."

He is troubled about his work. Rumours of his habits and general outlook have begun to get back to the Consulate. Lying in bed he plans a campaign which will get him crucified and promoted to a post with more scope. "I have decided that I simply must get my cross. I am going to give several skilfully graded parties. I shall count on you: I shall need a few shabby people at first in order to give my boss the feeling that he can patronize me socially. He is a complete *parvenu* of course and rose on his wife's fortune and judicious smarming of powerful people. Worst of all he has a distinct inferiority complex about my own birth and family background. He has still not quite decided whether to do me down or not; but he has been taking soundings at the Quai d'Orsay to see how well padded I am there. Since my uncle died, of course, and my godfather the bishop was involved in that huge scandal over the brothel in Reims, I find myself rather less steady on my feet. I shall have to make the brute feel protective, feel that I need encouraging and bringing out. Pouagh! First a rather shabby party with one celebrity only. O why did I join the service? Why have I not a small fortune of my own?"

Hearing all this in Sveva's artificial tears and then walking down the draughty staircase again arm in arm thinking not of Sveva, not of Pombal, but of the passage in Arnauti where he says of Justine: "Like women who think by biological precept and without the help of reason. To such women how fatal an error it is to give oneself; there is simply a small chewing noise, as when the cat reaches the backbone of the mouse."

The wet pavements are slick underfoot from the rain, and the air has become dense with the moisture so ardently longed for by the trees in the public gardens, the statues and other visitants. Justine is away upon another tack, walking slowly in her glorious silk frock with the dark lined cape, head hanging. She stops in front of a lighted shop-window and takes my arms so that I face her, looking into my eyes: "I am thinking about going away," she says in a quiet puzzled voice. "Something is happening to Nessim and I don't know what it is as yet." Then suddenly the tears come into her eyes and she says: "For the first time I am afraid, and I don't know why."

three

THAT second spring the khamseen was worse than I have ever known it before or since. Before sunrise the skies of the desert turned brown as buckram, and then slowly darkened, swelling like a bruise and at last releasing the outlines of cloud, giant octaves of ochre which massed up from the Delta like the drift of ashes under a volcano. The city has shuttered itself tightly, as if against a gale. A few gusts of air and a thin sour rain are the forerunners of the darkness which blots out the light of the sky. And now unseen in the darkness of shuttered rooms the sand is invading everything, appearing as if by magic in clothes long locked away, books, pictures and teaspoons. In the locks of doors, beneath fingernails. The harsh sobbing air dries the membranes of throats and noses, and makes eyes raw with the configurations of conjunctivitis. Clouds of dried blood walk the streets like prophecies; the sand is settling into the sea like powder into the curls of a stale wig. Choked fountain-pens, dry lips—and along the slats of the Venetian shutters thin white drifts as of young snow. The ghastly feluccas passing along the canal are crewed by ghouls with wrapped heads. From time to time a cracked wind arrives from directly above and stirs the whole city round and round so that one has the illusion that everything—trees, minarets, monuments and people—has been caught in the final eddy of some great whirlpool and will pour softly back at last into the desert from which they rose, reverting once more to the anonymous wave-sculptured floor of dunes. . . .

I cannot deny that by this time we had both been seized by an exhaustion of spirit which had made us desperate, reckless, impatient of discovery. Guilt always hurries towards its complement, punishment: only there does its satisfaction lie. A hidden desire for some sort of expiation dictated Justine's folly which was greater than mine; or perhaps we both dimly sensed that, bound as we were hand and foot to each other, only an upheaval of some sort could restore each to his vulgar right mind. These days were full of omens and warnings upon which our anxiety fed.

One-eyed Hamid told me one day of a mysterious caller who had told him that he must keep careful watch on his master as he was in great danger from some highly-placed personage. His description of the man might have been that of Selim, Nessim's secretary: but it also might have been any of the 150,000 inhabitants of the province. Meanwhile Nessim's own attitude to me had changed, or rather deepened into a solicitous and cloying sweetness. He shed his former reserve. When he spoke to me he used unfamiliar endearments and took me affectionately by the sleeve. At times as we spoke he would flush suddenly: or tears would come into his eyes and he would turn aside his head to hide them. Justine watched this with a concern which was painful to observe. But the very humiliation and self-reproach we felt at wounding him only drove us closer together as accomplices. At times she spoke of going away: at times I did the same. But neither of us could move. We were forced to await the outcome with a fatality and exhaustion that was truly fearful to experience.

Nor were our follies diminished by these warnings; rather did they multiply. A dreadful inadvertency reigned over our actions, an appalling thoughtlessness marked our behaviour. Nor did we (and here I realized that I had lost myself completely) even hope to avert whatever fate might be in store for us. We were only foolishly concerned lest we might not be able to share it—lest it might separate us! In this plain courting of martyrdom I realized that we showed our love at its hollowest, its most defective. "How disgusting I must seem to you," said Justine once, "with my obscene jumble of conflicting ideas: all this sickly preoccupation with God and a total inability to obey the smallest moral injunction from my inner nature like being faithful to a man one adores. I tremble for myself, my dear one, I tremble. If only I could escape from the tiresome classical Jewess of neurology. . . . If only I could peel it off."

During this period, while Melissa was away in Palestine on a cure (I had borrowed the money from Justine in order for her to go) we had several narrow escapes. For example, one day we were talking, Justine and I, in the great bedroom of the house. We had come in from bathing and had taken cold showers to get the salt off our skins. Justine sat on the bed naked under the bathroom towel which she had draped round her like a chiton. Nessim was away in Cairo where he was supposed to make a radio broadcast on behalf of some charity or other. Outside the window the trees nodded their dusty fronds in the damp summer air, while the faint huddle of traffic on Rue Fuad could be heard.

Nessim's quiet voice came to us from the little black radio by the bed, converted by the microphone into the voice of a man prematurely aged. The mentally empty phrases lived on in the silence they invaded until the air seemed packed with commonplaces. But the voice was beautiful, the voice of someone who had elaborately isolated himself from feeling. Behind Justine's back the door into the bathroom was open. Beyond it, a pane of clinical whiteness, lay another door leading to an iron fire-escape—for the house had been designed round a central well so that its bathrooms and kitchens could be connected by a cobweb of iron staircases such as span the engine-room of a ship. Suddenly, while the voice was still talking and while we listened to it, there came the light youthful patter of footsteps on the iron staircase outside the bathroom: a step unmistakably that of Nessim—or of any of the 150,000 inhabitants of the province. Looking over Justine's shoulder I saw developing on the glass panel of the frosted door, the head and shoulders of a tall slim man, with a soft felt hat pulled down over his eyes. He developed like a print in a photographer's developing-

bowl. The figure paused with outstretched hand upon the
knob of the door. Justine, seeing the direction of my
glance, turned her head. She put one naked arm round my
shoulders as both of us, with a feeling of complete calm
whose core, like a heart beating, was a feverish impotent
sexual excitement watched the dark figure standing there
between two worlds, depicted as if on an X-ray screen. He
would have found us absurdly posed, as if for a photograph, with an expression, not of fear but of guiltless relief upon our faces.

For a long time the figure stood there, as if in deep
thought, perhaps listening. Then it shook its head once,
slowly, and after a moment turned away with an air of
perplexity to dissolve slowly on the glass. As it turned it
seemed to slip something into the right-hand pocket of its
coat. We heard the steps slowly diminishing—a dull
descending scale of notes—on the iron ladder in the well.
We neither of us spoke, but turned as if with deepened
concentration to the little black radio from which the
voice of Nessim still flowed with uninterrupted urbanity
and gentleness. It seemed impossible that he could be in
two places at once. It was only when the announcer informed us that the speech had been recorded that we understood. Why did he not open the door?

I suppose the truth is that he had been seized by the
vertiginous uncertainty which, in a peaceable nature,
follows upon a decision to act. Something had been building itself up inside him all this time, grain by grain, until
the weight of it had become insupportable. He was aware
of a profound interior change in his nature which had at
last shaken off the long paralysis of impotent love which
had hitherto ruled his actions. The thought of some sudden concise action, some determining factor for good or
evil, presented itself to him as an intoxicating novelty.
He felt (so he told me later) like a gambler about to
stake the meagre remains of a lost fortune upon one desperate throw. But the nature of his action had not yet
been decided upon. What form should it take? A mass of
uneasy fantasies burst in.

Let us suppose that two major currents had reached

their confluence in this desire to act; on the one hand the
dossier which his agents had collected upon Justine had
reached such proportions that it could not be ignored; on
the other he was haunted by a new and fearful thought
which for some reason had not struck him before—namely
that Justine was really falling in love at last. The whole
temper of her personality seemed to be changing; for
the first time she had become reflective, thoughtful, and
full of the echoes of a sweetness which a woman can always afford to spend upon the man she does not love.
You see, he too had been dogging her steps through the
pages of Arnauti.

"Originally I believed that she must be allowed to
struggle towards me through the jungle of The Check.
Whenever the wounding thought of her infidelity came
upon me I reminded myself that she was not a pleasure-
seeker, but a hunter of pain in search of herself—and me.
I thought that if one man could release her from herself
she would then become accessible to all men, and so to me
who had most claim upon her. But when I began to see
her melting like a summer ice-cap, a horrible thought
came to me: namely that he who broke The Check must
keep her forever, since the peace he gave her was precisely that for which she was hunting so frantically
through our bodies and fortunes. For the first time my
jealousy, helped forward by my fear, mastered me."

He might have explained it thus. Yet it has always
seemed fantastic to me that even now he was jealous of
everyone except the true author of Justine's present concern—myself. Despite the overwhelming mass of evidence he hardly dared to allow himself to suspect me.
It is not love that is blind, but jealousy. It was a long time
before he could bring himself to trust the mass of
documentation his agents had piled up around us, around
our meetings, our behaviour. But by now the facts had ob-
truded themselves so clearly that there was no possibility
of error. The problem was how to dispose of me—"I do
not mean in the flesh so much: you had become merely an
image standing in my light. I saw you perhaps dying,

perhaps going away. I did not know. The very uncertainty
was itself exciting to the pitch of drunkenness."

But side by side with these preoccupations were
others—the posthumous problems which Arnauti had
been unable to solve and which Nessim had been following up with true Oriental curiosity over a period of years.
He was now near to the man with the black patch over
one eye—nearer than any of us had ever been. Here was
another piece of knowledge which as yet he could not
decide how best to use. If Justine was really ridding herself of him, however, what good would there be in reveng-
ing himself upon the true person of the mysterious being?
On the other hand if I was about to step into the place
vacated by the image? . . .

I asked Selim point-blank whether he had ever visited
my flat to warn one-eyed Hamid. He did not reply but
lowered his head and said under his breath, "My master is
not himself these days."

Meanwhile my own fortunes had taken an absurd and
unexpected turn. One night there came a banging on the
door and I opened it to admit the dapper figure of an
Egyptian Army officer clad in resplendent boots and tarbush, carrying under his arm a giant fly-whisk with an
ebony handle. Yussouf Bey spoke nearly perfect English,
allowing it to fall negligently from his lips, word by well-
chosen word, out of an earnest coal-black face fitted with
a dazzle of small perfect teeth like seed-pearls. He had
some of the endearing solemnity of a talking watermelon
just down from Cambridge. Hamid brought him habitual
coffee and a sticky liqueur, and over it he told me that a
great friend of mine in a high position very much wished
to see me. My thoughts at once turned to Nessim; but this
friend, the watermelon asserted, was an Englishman, an
official. More he could not say. His mission was confidential. Would I go with him and visit my friend?

I was full of misgivings. Alexandria, outwardly so
peaceful, was not really a safe place for Christians. Only
last week Pombal had come home with a story of the
Swedish vice-consul whose car had broken down on the
Matrugh road. He had left his wife alone in it while he

walked to the nearest telephone-point in order to ring up
the consulate and ask them to send out another car. He
had arrived back to find her body sitting normally on the
back seat—without a head. Police were summoned and
the whole district was combed. Some Bedouin encamped
nearby were among those interrogated. While they were
busy denying any knowledge of the accident, out of the
apron of one of the women rolled the missing head. They
had been trying to extract the gold teeth which had been
such an unpleasant feature of her party-smile. This sort of
incident was not sufficiently uncommon to give one
courage in visiting strange quarters of the town after dark,
so it was with no feeling of jauntiness that I followed the
soldier into the back of a staff-car behind a uniformed
driver and saw myself being whirled towards the seedier
quarters of the town. Yussouf Bey stroked his neat little
brush-stroke moustache with the anticipatory air of a
musician tuning an instrument. It was useless to question
him further: I did not wish to betray any of the anxiety I
felt. So I made a sort of inner surrender to the situation, lit
a cigarette, and watched the long dissolving strip of the
Corniche flow past us.

Presently the car dropped us and the soldier led me on
foot through a straggle of small streets and alleys near the
Rue des Soeurs. If the object here was to make me lose
myself it succeeded almost immediately. He walked with
a light self-confident step, humming under his breath.
Finally we debouched into a suburban street full of mer-
chants' stores and stopped before a great carved door
which he pushed open after having first rung a bell. A
courtyard with a stunted palm-tree; the path which
crossed it was punctuated by a couple of feeble lanterns
standing on the gravel. We crossed it and ascended some
stairs to where a frosted electric light bulb gleamed harshly above a tall white door. He knocked, entered and
saluted in one movement. I followed him into a large,
rather elegant and warmly-lighted room with neat polished floors enhanced by fine Arab carpets. In one corner
seated at a high inlaid desk with the air of a man riding a
penny-farthing sat Scobie, with a scowl of self-importance

overlapping the smile of welcome with which he greeted
me. "My God," I said. The old pirate gave a Drury Lane
chuckle and said: "At last, old man, at last." He did not
rise however but sat on in his uncomfortable high-backed
chair, tarbush on head, whisk on knee, with a vaguely im-
pressive air. I noticed an extra pip on his shoulder,
betokening heaven knows what increase of rank and
power. "Sit down, old man," he said with an awkward
sawing movement of the hand which bore a faint
resemblance to a Second Empire gesture. The soldier was
dismissed and departed grinning. It seemed to me that
Scobie did not look very much at ease in these opulent
surroundings. He had a slightly defensive air. "I asked
them to get hold of you," he said, sinking his voice to a
theatrical whisper, "for a very special reason." There were
a number of green files on his desk and a curiously dis-
embodied-looking tea-cosy. I sat down.

He now rose quickly and opened the door. There was
nobody outside. He opened the window. There was no
one standing on the sill. He placed the tea-cosy over the
desk telephone and reseated himself. Then, leaning forward and speaking carefully, he rolled his glass eye at me
as with a conspiratorial solemnity he said: "Not a word to
anyone, old man. Swear you won't say a word." I swore.
"They've made me head of the Secret Service." The words
fairly whistled in his dentures. I nodded in amazement.
He drew a deep sucking breath as if he had been
delivered of a weight and went on. "Old boy, there's
going to be a war. Inside information." He pointed a long
finger at his own temple. "There's going to be a war. The
enemy is working night and day, old boy, right here
among us." I could not dispute this. I could only marvel at
the new Scobie who confronted me like a bad magazine
illustration. "You can help us scupper them, old man," he
went on with a devastating air of authority. "We want to
take you on our strength." This sounded most agreeable. I
waited for details. "The most dangerous gang of all is
right here, in Alexandria," the old man creaked and
boomed, "and you are in the centre of it. All friends of
yours."

I saw through the knotted eyebrows and the rolling excited eye the sudden picture of Nessim, a brief flash, as of intuition, sitting at his huge desk in the cold steel-tube offices watching a telephone ring while the beads of sweat stood out on his forehead. He was expecting a message about Justine—one more twist of the knife. Scobie shook his head, "Not him so much," he said. "He's in it, of course. The leader is a man called Balthazar. Look what the censorship have been picking up."

He extracted a card from a file and passed it to me. Balthazar writes an exquisite hand and the writing was obviously his; but I could not help smiling when I saw that the reverse of the postcard contained only the little chessboard diagram of the *boustrophedon*. Greek letters filled up the little squares. "He's got so much damn cheek he sends them through the open post." I studied the diagram and tried to remember the little I had learned from my friend of the calculus. "It's a nine-power system. I can't read this one," I said. Scobie added breathlessly: "They have regular meetings, old man, to pool information. We know this for a fact." I held the postcard lightly in my fingers and seemed to hear the voice of Balthazar saying: "The thinker's job is to be suggestive: that of the saint to be silent about his discovery."

Scobie was leaning back in his chair now with unconcealed self-satisfaction. He had puffed himself out like a pouter-pigeon. He took his tarbush off his head, looked at it with an air of complaisant patronage, and placed it on the tea-cosy. Then he scratched his fissured skull with bony fingers and went on—"We simply can't break the code," he said. "we've got dozens of them"—he indicated a file full of photostatic reproductions of similar postcards. "They've been round the code-rooms: even to the Senior Wranglers in the Universities. No good, old man." This did not surprise me. I laid the postcard on the pile of photostats and returned to the contemplation of Scobie. "That is where you come in," he said with a grimace, "if you will come in, old man. We want you to break the code however long it takes you. We'll put you on a damn good screw, too. What do you say?"

What could I say? The idea was too delightful to be
allowed to melt. Besides during the last months my
schoolwork had fallen off so much that I was sure my contract was not going to be renewed at the end of the present term. I was always arriving late from some meeting
with Justine. I hardly bothered to correct papers any
more. I had become irritable and surly with my colleagues
and directors. Here was a chance to become my own man.
I heard Justine's voice in my head saying: "Our love has
become like some fearful misquotation in a popular saying," as I leaned forward once more and nodded my head.
Scobie expelled a breath of relieved pleasure and relaxed
once more into the pirate. He confided his office to an
anonymous Mustapha who apparently dwelt somewhere
in the black telephone—Scobie always looked into the
mouthpiece as he spoke, as if into a human eye. We left
the building together and allowed a staff car to take us
down towards the sea. Further details of my employment
could be discussed over the little bottle of brandy in the
bottom of the cake-stand by his bed.

We allowed ourselves to be dropped on the Corniche
and walked together the rest of the way by a brilliant
bullying moonlight, watching the old city dissolve and
reassemble in the graphs of evening mist, heavy with the
inertia of its surrounding desert, of the green alluvial Delta which soaked into its very bones, informing its values.
Scobie talked inconsequently of this and that. I remember
him bemoaning the fact that he had been left an orphan
at an early age. His parents had been killed together under dramatic circumstances which gave him much food
for reflection. "My father was an early pioneer of motor-
ing, old man. Early road races, flat out at twenty miles an
hour—all that sort of thing. He had his own landau. I can
see him now sitting behind the wheel with a big moustache. Colonel Scobie, M.C. A Lancer he was. My mother
sat beside him, old man. Never left his side, not even for
road races. She used to act as his mechanic. The newspapers always had pictures of them at the start, sitting up
there in bee-keeper's veils—God knows why the pioneers
always wore those huge veils. Dust, I suppose."

The veils had proved their undoing. Rounding a hairpin in the old London-Brighton road race his father's veil had been sucked into the front axle of the car they were driving. He had been dragged into the road, while his companion had careered on to smash headlong into a tree. "The only consolation is that that is just how he would have liked to go out. They were leading by quarter of a mile."

I have always been very fond of ludicrous deaths and had great difficulty in containing my laughter as Scobie described this misadventure to me with portentous rotations of his glass eye. Yet as he talked and I listened to this, half my thoughts were running upon a parallel track, busy about the new job I was to undertake, assessing it in terms of the freedom it offered me. Later that night Justine was to meet me near Montaza—the great car purring like a moth in the palm-cooled dusk of the road. What would she say to it? She would be delighted of course to see me freed from the shackles of my present work. But a part of her would groan inwardly at the thought that this relief would only create for us further chances to consort, to drive home our untruth, to reveal ourselves more fully than ever to our judges. Here was another paradox of love; that the very thing which brought us closer together—the *boustrophedon*—would, had we mastered the virtues which it illustrated, have separated us forever—I mean in the selves which preyed upon each other's infatuated images.

"Meanwhile," as Nessim was to say in those gentle tones so full of the shadowy sobriety which comes into the voice of those who have loved truly and failed to be loved in return, "meanwhile I was dwelling in the midst of a vertiginous excitement for which there was no relief except through an action the nature of which I could not discern. Tremendous bursts of self-confidence were succeeded by depressions so deep that it seemed I would never recover from them. With a vague feeling that I was preparing myself for a contest—as an athlete does—I began to take fencing lessons and learned to shoot with a pocket automatic. I studied the composition and effects of poisons from a manual of toxicology which I borrowed from Dr. Fuad Bey."

He had begun to harbour feelings which would not yield to analysis. The periods of intoxication were followed by others in which he felt, as if for the first time, the full weight of his loneliness: an inner agony of spirit for which, as yet, he could find no outward expression, either in paint or in action. He mused now incessantly upon his early years, full of a haunting sense of richness: his mother's shadowy house among the palms and poinsettias of Aboukir: the waters pulling and slithering among the old fort's emplacements, compiling the days of his early childhood in single condensed emotions born from visual memory. He clutched at these memories with a terror and clarity he had never experienced before. And all the time, behind the screen of nervous depression—for the incomplete action which he meditated lay within him like a *coitus interruptus*—there lived the germ of a wilful and uncontrolled exaltation. It was as if he were being egged on, to approach nearer and nearer . . . to what exactly? He could not tell; but here his ancient terror of madness stepped in and took possession of him, disturbing his physical balance, so that he suffered at times from attacks of vertigo which forced him to grope around himself like a blind man for something upon which to sit down—a chair or sofa. He would sit down, panting slightly and feeling the sweat beginning to start out on his forehead; but with relief that nothing of his interior struggle was visible to the casual onlooker. Now too he noticed that he involuntarily repeated phrases aloud to which his conscious mind refused to listen. "Good," she heard him tell one of his mirrors, "so you are falling into a neurasthenia!" And later as he was stepping out into the brilliant starlit air, dressed in his well-cut evening clothes, Selim, at the wheel of the car, heard him add: "I think this Jewish fox has eaten my life."

At times, too, he was sufficiently alarmed to seek, if not the help, at least the surcease of contact with other human beings: a doctor who left him with a phosphorous tonic and a regimen he did not follow. The sight of a column of

marching Carmelites, tonsured like mandrils, crossing
Nebi Daniel drove him to renew his lapsed friendship
with Father Paul who in the past had seemed so profoundly happy a man, folded into his religion like a razor
into its case. But now the kind of verbal consolations
offered him by this lucky, happy, unimaginative brute
only filled him with nausea.

One night he knelt down beside his bed—a thing he
had not done since his twelfth year—and deliberately set
himself to pray. He stayed there a long time, mentally
spellbound, tongue-tied, with no words or thoughts shap-
ing themselves in his mind. He was filled by some ghastly
inhibition like a mental stroke. He stayed like this until he
could stand it no longer—until he felt that he was on the
point of suffocating. Then he jumped into bed and drew
the sheets over his head murmuring broken fragments of
oaths and involuntary pleadings which he did not
recognize as emanating from any part of himself.

Outwardly however there were no signs of these strug-
gles to be seen; his speech remained dry and measured
despite the fever of the thoughts behind it. His doctor
complimented him on his excellent reflexes and assured
him that his urine was free from excess albumen. An occasional headache only proved him to be a victim of *petit
mal*—or some other such customary disease of the rich
and idle.

For his own part he was prepared to suffer thus as long
as the suffering remained within the control of his consciousness. What terrified him only was the sensation of
utter loneliness—a reality which he would never, he
realized, be able to communicate either to his friends or to
the doctors who might be called in to pronounce upon
anomalies of behaviour which they would regard only as
symptoms of disorder.

He tried feverishly to take up his painting again, but
without result. Self-consciousness like a poison seemed to
eat into the very paint, making it sluggish and dead. It
was hard even to manipulate the brush with an invisible
hand pulling at one's sleeve the whole time, hindering,

whispering, displacing all freedom and fluidity of movement.

Surrounded as he was by this menacing twilight of the feelings he turned once more, in a vain effort to restore his balance and composure, to the completion of the Summer Palace—as it was jokingly called; the little group of Arab huts and stables at Abu Sir. Long ago, in the course of a ride to Benghazi along the lonely shoreline, he had come upon a fold in the desert, less than a mile from the sea, where a fresh spring suddenly burst through the thick sand pelt and hobbled a little way down towards the desolate beaches before it was overtaken and smothered by the dunes. Here the Bedouin, overtaken by the involuntary hunger for greenness which lies at the heart of all desert-lovers, had planted a palm and a fig whose roots had taken a firm subterranean grip upon the sandstone from which the pure water ran. Resting with the horses in the shade of these young trees, Nessim's eye had dwelt with wonder upon the distant view of the old Arab fort, and the long-drawn white scar of the empty beach where the waves pounded night and day. The dunes had folded themselves hereabouts into a long shapely valley which his imagination had already begun to people with clicking palm-trees and the green figs which, as always near running water, offer a shade so deep as to be like a wet cloth pressed to the skull. For a year he had allowed the spot to mature in his imagination, riding out frequently to study it in every kind of weather, until he had mastered its properties. He had not spoken of it to anyone, but in the back of his mind had lurked the idea of building a summer pleasure house for Justine—a miniature oasis where she could stable her three Arab thoroughbreds and pass the hottest season of the year in her favourite amusements, bathing and riding.

The spring had been dug out, channelled and gathered into the marble cistern which formed the centrepiece to the little courtyard, paved with rough sandstone, around which the house and stables were to stand. As the water grew so the green grew with it; shade created the prongy abstract shapes of cactus and the bushy exuberance of In-

dian corn. In time even a melon-bed was achieved—like
some rare exile from Persia. A single severe stable in the
Arab style turned its back upon the winter sea-wind,
while in the form of an L grew up a cluster of store-rooms
and small living-rooms with grilled windows and shutters
of black iron.

Two or three small bedrooms, no larger than the cells of
medieval monks, gave directly into a pleasant oblong central room with a low ceiling, which was both living-and
dining-room; at one end a fireplace grew up massive and
white, and with decorated lintels suggested by the designs
of Arab ceramics. At the other end stood a stone table and
stone benches reminiscent of some priory refectory used
by desert fathers perhaps. The severity of the room was
discountenanced by rich Persian rugs and some tremendous carved chests with gilt ornamentation writhing over
their hooked clasps and leather-polished sides. It was all
of a controlled simplicity which is the best sort of
magnificence. On the severe white-washed walls, whose
few grilled windows offered sudden magnificent slotted
views of beach and desert, hung a few old trophies of
hunting or meditation, like: an Arab lance-pennon, a Bud-
dhist *mandala*, a few assegais in exile, a longbow still used
for hunting of hares, a yacht-burgee. There were no books
save an old Koran with ivory covers and tarnished metal
clasps, but several packs of cards lay about on the sills,
including the Grand Tarot for amateur divination and a
set of Happy Families. In one corner, too, there stood an
old samovar to do justice to the one addiction from which
they both suffered—tea-drinking.

The work went forward slowly and hesitantly, but
when at last, unable to contain his secret any longer, he
had taken Justine out to see it, she had been unable to
contain her tears as she walked about it, from window to
window of the graceful rooms, to snatch now a picture of
the emerald sea rolling on the sand, now a sudden whorled
picture of the dunes sliding eastward into the sky. Then
she had sat down abruptly before the thorn fire in
her habit and listened to the soft clear drumming of the
sea upon the long beaches mingled with the cough and

stamp of the horses in their new stalls beyond the courtyard. It was late autumn, then, and in the moist gathering darkness the fireflies had begun to snatch fitfully,
filling them both with pleasure to think that already their
oasis had begun to support other life than their own.

What Nessim had begun was now Justine's to complete.
The small terrace under the palm-tree was extended
towards the east and walled in to hold back the steady
sand-drift which, after a winter of wind, would move forward and cover the stones of the courtyard in six inches of
sand. A windbreak of junipers contributed a dull copper
humus of leaf-mould which in time would become firm
soil nourishing first bushes and later other and taller trees.

She was careful, too, to repay her husband's thought-
fulness by paying a tribute to what was then his ruling
passion—astronomy. At one corner of the L-shaped block
of buildings she laid down a small observatory which
housed a telescope of thirty magnifications. Here Nessim
would sit night after night in the winter, dressed in his old
rust-coloured *abba*, staring gravely at Betelgeuse, or
hovering over books of calculations for all the world like
some medieval soothsayer. Here too their friends could
look at the moon or by altering the angle of the barrel
catch sudden smoky glimpses of the clouds of pearl which
the city always seemed to exhale from afar.

All this, of course, began to stand in need of a guardian,
and it came as no surprise to them when Panayotis arrived
and took up his residence in a tiny room near the stables.
This old man with his spade beard and gimlet-eyes had
been for twenty years a secondary schoolteacher at
Damanhur. He had taken orders and spent nine years at
the monastery of St. Catherine in Sinai. What brought
him to the oasis it was impossible to tell for at some stage
in his apparently unadventurous life he had had his
tongue cut out of his head. From the signs he made in
response to questions it might seem that he had been making a pilgrimage on foot to the little shrine of St. Menas situated to the west when he had stumbled upon the oasis.
At any rate there seemed nothing fortuitous about his
decision to adopt it. He fitted it to perfection, and for a

small salary stayed there all the year round as watchman
and gardener. He was an able-bodied little old man, active
as a spider, and fearfully jealous of the green things which
owed their life to his industry and care. It was he who
coaxed the melon-bed into life and at last persuaded a
vine to start climbing beside the lintel of the central doorway. His laughter was an inarticulate clucking, and he
had a shy habit of hiding his face in the tattered sleeve of
his old beadle's soutane. His Greek loquacity, dammed up
behind his disability, had overflowed into his eyes where
it sparkled and danced at the slightest remark or question.
What more could anyone ask of life, he seemed to say,
than this oasis by the sea?

What more indeed? It was the question that Nessim
asked himself repeatedly as the car whimpered towards
the desert with hawk-featured Selim motionless at the
wheel. Some miles before the Arab fort the road fetches
away inland from the coast and to reach the oasis one
must swerve aside off the tarmac along an outcrop of stiff
flaky dune—like beaten white of egg, glittering and mica-
shafted. Here and there where the swaying car threatens
to sink its driving-wheels in the dune they always find
purchase again on the bed of friable sandstone which
forms the backbone to the whole promontory. It was ex-
hilarating to feather this sea of white crispness like a cut-
ter travelling before a following wind.

It had been in Nessim's mind for some time past—the
suggestion had originally been Pursewarden's—to repay
the devotion of old Panayotis with the only kind of gift
the old man would understand and find acceptable: and
he carried now in his polished brief-case a dispensation
from the Patriarch of Alexandria permitting him to build
and endow a small chapel to St. Arsenius in his house. The
choice of saint had been, as it always should be, fortuitous. Clea had found an eighteenth-century ikon of
him, in pleasing taste, lying among the lumber of a Muski
stall in Cairo. She had given it to Justine as a birthday
present.

These then were the treasures they unpacked before the
restless bargaining eye of the old man. It took them some

time to make him understand for he followed Arabic in-
differently and Nessim knew no Greek. But looking up at
last from the written dispensation he clasped both hands
and threw up his chin with a smile; he seemed about to
founder under the emotions which beset him. Everything
was understood. Now he knew why Nessim had spent
such hours considering the empty end-stable and sketch-
ing on paper. He shook his hands warmly and made inarticulate clucking-noises. Nessim's heart went out to
him with a kind of malicious envy to see how
wholehearted his pleasure was at this act of thought-
fulness. From deep inside the *camera obscura* of the
thoughts which filled his mind he studied the old beadle
carefully, as if by intense scrutiny to surprise the single-
heartedness which brought the old man happiness, peace
of mind.

Here at least, thought Nessim, building something with
my own hands will keep me stable and unreflective—and
he studied the horny old hands of the Greek with admir-
ing envy as he thought of the time they had killed for him,
of the thinking they had saved him. He read into them
years of healthy bodily activity which imprisoned
thought, neutralized reflection. And yet . . . who could
say? Those long years of school-teaching: the years in the
monastery: and now the long winter solitude which
closed in around the oasis, when only the boom and slither
of the sea and the whacking of palm-fronds were there to
accompany one's thoughts. . . . There is always time for
spiritual crises, he thought, as he doggedly mixed cement
and dry sand in a wooden mortar.

But even here he was not to be left alone for Justine,
with that maddening guilty solicitude which she had
come to feel for the man whom she loved, and yet was
trying to destroy, appeared with her trio of Arabs and
took up her summer quarters at the oasis. A restless,
moody, alert familiar. And then I, impelled by the fearful
pangs her absence created in me, smuggled a note to her
telling her either that she must return to the city or persuade Nessim to invite me out to the Summer Palace.
Selim duly arrived with the car and motored me out in a

sympathetic silence into which he did not dare to inject
the slightest trace of contempt.

For his part Nessim received me with a studied tenderness; in fact, he was glad to see us again at close quarters, to detach us from the fictitious framework of his
agents' reports and to judge for himself if we were . . .
what am I to say? "In love"? The word implies a totality
which was missing in my mistress, who resembled one of
those ancient Goddesses in that her attributes proliferated
through her life and were not condensed about a single
quality of heart which one could love or unlove. "Possession" is on the other hand too strong: we were human
beings not Brontë cartoons. But English lacks the distinctions which might give us (as Modern Greek does) a
word for passion-love.

Apart from all this, not knowing the content and direction of Nessim's thoughts I could in no way set his inmost
fears at rest: by telling him that Justine was merely working out with me the same obsessive pattern she had
followed out in the pages of Arnauti. She was creating a
desire of the will which, since it fed secretly on itself, must
be exhausted like a lamp—or blown out. I knew this with
only a part of my mind: but there I detected the true lack
in this union. It was not based on any repose of the will.
And yet how magically she seemed to live—a mistress so
full of wit and incantation that one wondered how one
had ever managed to love before and be content in the
quality of the loving.

At the same time I was astonished to realize that the
side of me which clave to Melissa was living its own
autonomous existence, quietly and surely belonging to her
yet not wishing her back. The letters she wrote me were
gay and full and unmarred by any shadow of reproof or
self-pity; I found in all she wrote an enlargement of her
self-confidence. She described the little sanatorium where
she was lodged with humour and a nimble eye, describing
the doctors and the other patients as a holidaymaker
might. On paper she seemed to have grown, to have
become another woman. I answered her as well as I was
able but it was hard to disguise the shiftless confusion

which reigned in my life; it was equally impossible to allude to my obsession with Justine—we were moving through a different world of flowers and books and ideas, a world quite foreign to Melissa. Environment had closed the gates to her, not lack of sensibility. "Poverty is a great cutter-off," said Justine once, "and riches a great shutter-off." But she had gained admittance to both worlds, the world of want and the world of plenty, and was consequently free to live naturally.

But here at least in the oasis one had the illusion of a beatitude which eluded one in town life. We rose early and worked on the chapel until the heat of the day began, when Nessim retired to his business papers in the little observatory and Justine and I rode down the feathery dunes to the sea to spend our time in swimming and talking. About a mile from the oasis the sea had pushed up a great coarse roundel of sand which formed a shallow-water lagoon beside which, tucked into the pectoral curve of a dune, stood a reed hut roofed with leaves, which offered the bather shade and a changing-place. Here we spent most of the day together. The news of Pursewarden's death was still fresh, I remember, and we discussed him with a warmth and awe, as if for the first time we were seriously trying to evaluate a character whose qualities had masked its real nature. It was as if in dying he had cast off from his earthly character, and taken on some of the grandiose proportions of his own writings, which swam more and more into view as the memory of the man itself faded. Death provided a new critical referent, and a new mental stature to the tiresome, brilliant, ineffectual and often tedious man with whom we had had to cope. He was only to be seen now through the distorting mirror of anecdote or the dusty spectrum of memory. Later I was to hear people ask whether Pursewarden had been tall or short, whether he had worn a moustache or not: and these simple memories were the hardest to recover and to be sure of. Some who had known him well said his eyes had been green, others that they had been brown. . . . It was amazing how quickly the human image was dissolving into the mythical image he had created of himself in his trilogy GOD IS A HUMORIST.

Here, in these days of blinding sun-light, we talked of him like people anxious to capture and fix the human memory before it quite shaded into the growing myth; we talked of him, confirming and denying and comparing, like secret agents rehearsing a cover story, for after all the fallible human being had belonged to *us*, the myth belonged to the world. It was now too that I learned of him saying, one night to Justine, as they watched Melissa dance: "If I thought there were any hope of success I would propose marriage to her tomorrow. But she is so ignorant and her mind is so deformed by poverty and bad luck that she would refuse out of incredulity."

But step by step behind us Nessim followed with his fears. One day I found the word "Beware" (Προσοχή) written in the sand with a stick at the bathing-place. The Greek word suggested the hand of Panayotis but Selim also knew Greek well.

This further warning was given point for me by an incident which occurred very shortly afterwards when, in search of a sheet of notepaper on which to write to Melissa, I strayed into Nessim's little observatory and rummaged about on his desk for what I needed. I happened to notice that the telescope barrel had been canted downwards so that it no longer pointed at the sky but across the dunes towards where the city slumbered in its misty reaches of pearl cloud. This was not unusual, for trying to catch glimpses of the highest minarets as the airs condensed and shifted was a favourite pastime. I sat on the three-legged stool and placed my eye to the eye-piece, to allow the faintly trembling and vibrating image of the landscape to assemble for me. Despite the firm stone base on which the tripod stood the high magnification of the lens and the heat haze between them contributed a feathery vibration to the image which gave the landscape the appearance of breathing softly and irregularly. I was astonished to see—quivering and jumping, yet pin-point clear—the little reed hut where not an hour since Justine and I had been lying in each other's arms, talking of Purse-

warden. A brilliant yellow patch on the dune showed up
the cover of a pocket *King Lear* which I had taken out
with me and forgotten to bring back; had the image not
trembled so I do not doubt but that I should have been
able to read the title on the cover. I stared at this image
breathlessly for a long moment and became afraid. It was
as if, all of a sudden, in a dark but familiar room one
believed was empty a hand had suddenly reached out and
placed itself on one's shoulder. I tip-toed from the observatory with the writing pad and pencil and sat in the
arm-chair looking out at the sea, wondering what I could
say to Melissa.

* * * * *

That autumn, when we struck camp and returned to the
city for its winter season, nothing had been decided; the
feeling of crisis had even diminished. We were all held
there, so to speak, in the misty solution of everyday life
out of which futurity was to crystallize whatever drama
lay ahead. I was called upon to begin my new job for Scobie and addressed myself helplessly to the wretched
boustrophedon upon which Balthazar continued to in-
struct me, in between bouts of chess. I admit that I tried
to allay my pangs of conscience in the matter by trying at
first to tell Scobie's office the truth—namely that the
Cabal was a harmless sect devoted to Hermetic philosophy and that its activities bore no reference to espionage.
In answer to this I was curtly told that I must not believe
their obvious cover-story but must try to break the code.
Detailed reports of the meetings were called for and these
I duly supplied, typing out Balthazar's discourses on Ammon and Hermes Trismegistus with a certain peevish
pleasure, imagining as I did so the jaded government servants who would have to wade through the stuff in damp
basements a thousand miles away. But I was paid and
paid well; for the first time I was able to send Melissa a
little money and to make some attempt to pay Justine
what I owed her.

It was interesting, too, to discover which of my acquaintances were really part of the espionage grape-

vine. Mnemjian, for example, was one; his shop was a clearing-post for general intelligence concerning the city, and was admirably chosen. He performed his duties with tremendous care and discretion, and insisted on shaving me free of charge; it was disheartening to learn much later on that he patiently copied out his intelligence summaries in triplicate and sold copies to various other intelligence services.

Another interesting aspect of the work was that one had the power to order raids to be made on the house of one's friends. I enjoyed very much having Pombal's apartment raided. The poor fellow had a calamitous habit of bringing official files home to work on in the evening. We captured a whole set of papers which delighted Scobie for they contained detailed memoranda upon French influence in Syria, and a list of French agents in the city. I noticed on one of these lists the name of the old furrier, Cohen.

Pombal was badly shaken by this raid and went about looking over his shoulder for nearly a month afterwards, convinced that he was being shadowed. He also developed the delusion that one-eyed Hamid had been paid to poison him and would only eat food cooked at home after I had first tasted it. He was still waiting for his cross and his transfer and was very much afraid that the loss of the files would prejudice both, but as we had thoughtfully left him the classification-covers he was able to return them to their series with a minute to say that they had been burnt "according to instructions."

He had been having no small success lately with his carefully graduated cocktail-parties—into which he occasionally introduced guests from the humbler spheres of life like prostitution or the arts. But the expense and boredom were excruciating and I remember him explaining to me once, in tones of misery, the origin of these functions. "The cocktail-party—as the name itself indicates—was originally invented by dogs. They are simply bottom-sniffings raised to the rank of formal ceremonies." Nevertheless he persevered in them and was rewarded by the favours of his Consul-General whom, despite his contempt, he still regarded with a certain childish awe. He even persuaded Justine, after much humourous pleading, to put in an appearance at one of these functions in order to further his plans for crucifixion. This gave us a chance to study Pordre and the small diplomatic circle of Alexandria—for the most part people who gave the impression of being painted with an air-brush, so etiolated and diffused did their official personalities seem to me.

Pordre himself was a whim rather than a man. He was born to be a cartoonist's butt. He had a long pale spoiled face, set off by a splendid head of silver hair which he used to affect. But it was a lackey's countenance. The falseness of his gestures (his exaggerated solicitude and friendship for the merest acquaintances) grated disagreeably and enabled me to understand both the motto my friend had composed for the French Foreign Office and also the epitaph which he once told me should be placed on the tomb of his Chief. ("His mediocrity was his salvation.") All this, of course, was some years before Pordre became famous through his negotiations over the French Fleet. I cannot believe however that the person, such as it was, suffered any change: his character was as thin as a single skin of goldleaf—the veneer of culture which diplomats are in a better position to acquire than most men.

The party went off to perfection, and a dinner invitation from Nessim threw the old diplomat into a transport of pleasure which was not feigned. It was well known that the King was a frequent guest at Nessim's table and the old man was already writing a despatch in his mind which began with the words: "Dining with the King last week I brought the conversation round to the question of. . . . . He said. . . . I replied. . . ." His lips began to move, his eyes to unfocus themselves, as he retired into one of those public trances for which he was famous, and from which he would awake with a start to astonish his interlocutors with a silly cod's smile of apology.

For my part I found it strange to revisit the little tank-like flat where I had passed nearly two years of my life; to recall that it was here, in this very room, that I had first encountered Melissa. It had undergone a great transformation at the hands of Pombal's latest mistress. She had insisted upon its being panelled and painted off-white with a maroon skirting-board. The old armchairs whose stuffing used to leak slowly out of the rents in their sides had been re-upholstered in some heavy damask material with a pattern of *fleur-de-lis* while the three ancient sofas had been banished completely to make floor-space. No doubt they had been sold or broken up. "Somewhere," I thought in quotation from a poem by the old poet, "somewhere those wretched old things must still be knocking about." How grudging memory is, and how bitterly she clutches the raw material of her daily work.

Pombal's gaunt bedroom had become vaguely *fin de siècle* and was as clean as a new pin. Oscar Wilde might have admitted it as a set for the first act of a play. My own room had reverted once more to a box-room, but the bed was still there standing against the wall by the iron sink. The yellow curtain had of course disappeared and had been replaced by a drab piece of white cloth. I put my hand to the rusted iron frame of the old bed and was stabbed to the heart by the memory of Melissa turning her candid eyes upon me in the dusky half-light of the little room. I was ashamed and surprised by my grief. And when Justine came into the room behind me I kicked the door shut and immediately began to kiss her lips and hair and forehead, squeezing her almost breathless in my arms lest she should surprise the tears in my eyes. But she knew at once, and returning my kisses with that wonderful ardour that only friendship can give to our actions, she murmured: "I know. I know."

Then softly disengaging herself she led me out of the room and closed the door behind us. "I must tell you about Nessim," she said in a low voice. "Listen to me. On Wednesday, the day before we left the Summer Palace, I went for a ride alone by the sea. There was a big flight of herring-gulls over the shoreline and all of a sudden I saw the car in the distance rolling and scrambling down the dunes towards the sea with Selim at the wheel. I couldn't

make out what they were doing. Nessim was in the back.
I thought she would surely get stuck, but no: they raced
down to the water's edge where the sand was firm and
began to speed along the shore towards me. I was not on
the beach but in a hollow about fifty yards from the sea.
As they came racing level with me and the gulls rose I
saw that Nessim had the old repeating-gun in his hands.
He raised it and fired again and again into the cloud of
gulls, until the magazine was exhausted. Three or four
fell fluttering into the sea, but the car did not stop. They
were past me in a flash. There must have been a way back
from the long beach to the sandstone and so back on to
the main road because when I rode in half an hour later
the car was back. Nessim was in his observatory. The
door was locked and he said he was busy. I asked Selim
the meaning of this scene and he simply shrugged his
shoulders and pointed at Nessim's door. 'He gave me the
orders,' was all he said. But, my dear, if you had seen
Nessim's face as he raised the gun. . . ." And thinking of
it she involuntarily raised her long fingers to her own
cheeks as if to adjust the expression on her own face. "He
looked mad."

In the other room they were talking politely of world
politics and the situation in Germany. Nessim had perched
himself gracefully on Pordre's chair. Pombal was swallowing yawns which kept returning distressingly enough
in the form of belches. My mind was still full of Melissa. I had sent her some money that afternoon and
the thought of her buying herself some fine clothes—or
even spending it in some foolish way—warmed me.
"Money," Pombal was saying playfully to an elderly
woman who had the appearance of a contrite camel.
"One should always make sure of a supply. For only with
money can one make more money. Madame certainly
knows the Arabic proverb which says: 'Riches can buy
riches, but poverty will scarcely buy one a leper's kiss.' "

"We must go," said Justine, and staring into her warm
dark eyes as I said good-bye I knew that she divined
how full of Melissa my mind was at the moment; it gave
her handshake an added warmth and sympathy.

I suppose it was that night, while she was dressing for dinner that Nessim came into her room and addressed her reflection in the spade-shaped mirror. "Justine," he said firmly, "I must ask you not to think that I am going mad or anything like that but—has Balthazar ever been more than a friend to you?" Justine was placing a cigale made of gold on the lobe of her left ear; she looked up at him for a long second before answering in the same level, equable tone: "No, my dear."

"Thank you."

Nessim stared at his own reflection for a long time, boldly, comprehensively. Then he sighed once and took from the waistcoat-pocket of his dress-clothes a little gold key, in the form of an ankh. "I simply cannot think how this came into my possession," he said, blushing deeply and holding it up for her to see. It was the little watch-key whose loss had caused Balthazar so much concern. Justine stared at it and then at her husband with a somewhat startled air. "Where was it?" she said.

"In my stud-box."

Justine went on with her toilette at a slower pace, looking curiously at her husband who for his part went on studying his own features with the same deliberate rational scrutiny. "I must find a way of returning it to him. Perhaps he dropped it at a meeting. But the strange thing is. . . ." He sighed again. "I don't remember." It was clear to them both that he had stolen it. Nessim turned on his heel and said: "I shall wait for you downstairs." As the door closed softly behind him Justine examined the little key with curiosity.

* * * * *

At this time he had already begun to experience that great cycle of historical dreams which now replaced the dreams of his childhood in his mind, and into which the City now threw itself—as if at last it had found a responsive subject through which to express the collective desires, the collective wishes, which informed its culture. He would wake to see the towers and minarets printed on the exhausted, dust-powdered sky, and see as if *en montage* on them the giant footprints of the historical memory which lies behind the recollections of individual personality, its mentor and guide: indeed its inventor, since man is only an extension of the spirit of place.

These disturbed him for they were not at all the dreams of the night-hours. They overlapped reality and interrupted his waking mind as if the membrane of his consciousness had been suddenly torn in places to admit them.

Side by side with these constructions—Palladian galleries of images drawn from his reading and meditation on his own past and the city's—there came sharper and sharper attacks of unreasoning hatred against the very Justine he had so seldom known, the comforting friend and devoted lover. They were of brief duration but of such fierceness that, rightly regarding them as the obverse of the love he felt for her, he began to fear not for her safety but for his own. He became afraid of shaving, in the sterile white bathroom every morning. Often the little barber noticed tears in the eyes of his subject as he noiselessly spread the white apron over him.

But while the gallery of historical dreams held the foreground of his mind the figures of his friends and acquaintances, palpable and real, walked backwards and forwards among them, among the ruins of classical Alexandria, inhabiting an amazing historical space-time as living personages. Laboriously, like an actuary's clerk he recorded all he saw and felt in his diaries, ordering the impassive Selim to type them out.

He saw the Mouseion, for example, with its sulky, heavily-subsidized artists working to a mental fashion-plate of its founders: and later among the solitaries and wise men the philosopher, patiently wishing the world into a special private state useless to anyone but himself— for at each stage of development each man resumes the whole universe and makes it suitable to his own inner nature: while each thinker, each thought fecundates the whole universe anew.

The inscriptions on the marbles of the Museum murmured to him as he passed like moving lips. Balthazar and Justine were there waiting for him. He had come to meet them, dazzled by the moonlight and drenching shadow of the colonnades. He could hear their voices in the darkness and he thought, as he gave the low whistle which Justine would always recognize as his: "It is mentally vulgar to spend one's time being so certain of first principles as Balthazar is." He heard the elder man saying: "And morality is nothing if it is merely a form of good behaviour."

He walked slowly down through the arches towards them. The marble stones were barred with moonlight and shadow like a zebra. They were sitting on a marble sarcophagus-lid while somewhere in the remorseless darkness of the outer court someone was walking up and down on the springy turf lazily whistling a phrase from an aria of Donizetti. The gold cigales at Justine's ears transformed her at once into a projection from one of his dreams and indeed he saw them both dressed vaguely in robes carved heavily of moonlight. Balthazar in a voice tortured by the paradox which lies at the heart of all religion was saying: "Of course in one sense even to preach the gospel is evil. This is one of the absurdities of human logic. At least it is not the gospel but the preaching which involves us with the powers of darkness. That is why the Cabal is so good for us; it posits nothing beyond a science of Right Attention."

They had made room for him on their marble perch but here again, before he could reach them the fulcrum of his vision was disturbed and other scenes gravely intervened, disregarding congruence and period, disregarding historic time and common probability.

He saw so clearly the shrine the infantry built to Aphrodite of the Pigeons on that desolate alluvial coast. They were hungry. The march had driven them all to extremities, sharpening the vision of death which inhabits the soldier's soul until it shone before them with an unbearable exactness and magnificence. Baggage-animals dying for lack of fodder and men for lack of water. They dared not pause at the poisoned springs and wells. The wild asses, loitering so exasperatingly just out

of bowshot, maddened them with the promise of meat
they would never secure as the column evolved across the
sparse vegetation of that thorny coast. They were supposed to be marching upon the city despite the omens.
The infantry marched in undress though they knew it to
be madness. Their weapons followed them in carts which
were always lagging. The column left behind it the sour
smell of unwashed bodies—sweat and the stale of oxen:
Macedonian slingers-of-the-line farting like goats.

Their enemies were of a breath-taking elegance—
cavalry in white armour which formed and dissolved
across the route of their march like clouds. At close range
one saw they were men in purple cloaks, embroidered
tunics and narrow silk trousers. They wore gold chains
round their intricate dark necks and bracelets on their
javelin-arms. They were as desirable as a flock of women.
Their voices were high and fresh. What a contrast they
offered to the slingers, case-hardened veterans of the
line, conscious only of winters which froze their sandals
to their feet or summers whose sweat dried the leather
underfoot until it became as hard as dry marble. A gold
bounty and not passion had entrained them in this ad-
venture which they bore with the stoicism of all wage-
earners. Life had become a sexless strap sinking deeper
and ever deeper into the flesh. The sun had parched and
cured them and the dust had rendered them voiceless.
The brave plumed helmets which they had been issued
were too hot to wear at midday. Africa, which they had
somehow visualized as an extension of Europe—an extension of terms, of references to a definitive past—had already asserted itself as something different: a forbidding
darkness where the croaking of ravens matched the dry
exclamations of spiritless men, and rationed laughter
fashioned from breath simply the chittering of baboons.

Sometimes they captured someone—a solitary frightened man out hunting hares—and were amazed to see
that he was human like themselves. They stripped his rags
and stared at human genitals with an elaborate uncompre-
hending interest. Sometimes they despoiled a township or
a rich man's estate in the foothills, to dine on pickled

dolphin in jars (drunken soldiers feasting in a barn
among the oxen, unsteadily wearing garlands of wild
nettles and drinking from captured cups of gold or horn).
All this was before they even reached the desert. . . .

Where the paths had crossed they had sacrificed to
Heracles (and in the same breath murdered the two
guides, just to be on the safe side); but from that
moment everything had begun to go wrong. Secretly
they knew they would never reach the city and invest it.
And God! Never let that winter bivouac in the hills be
repeated. The fingers and noses lost by frostbite! The
raids! In his memory's memory he could still hear the
squeaking munching noise of the sentry's footsteps all
winter in the snow. In this territory the enemy wore
fox-skins on their heads in a ravenous peak and long hide
tunics which covered their legs. They were silent, belonging uniquely as the vegetation did to these sharp
ravines and breath-stopping paths of the great watershed.

With a column on the march memory becomes an
industry, manufacturing dreams which common ills unite
in a community of ideas based on privation. He knew
that the quiet man there was thinking of the rose found
in her bed on the day of the Games. Another could not
forget the man with the torn ear. The wry scholar pressed
into service felt as dulled by battle as a chamberpot at a
symposium. And the very fat man who retained the curious personal odour of a baby; the joker whose sallies kept
the vanguard in a roar? He was thinking of a new depila-
tory from Egypt, of a bed trade-marked Heracles for softness, of white doves with clipped wings fluttering round a
banqueting-table. All his life he had been greeted at the
brothel door by shouts of laughter and a hail of slippers.
There were others who dreamed of less common pleasures—hair dusty with white lead, or else schoolboys in
naked ranks marching two abreast at dawn to the school
of the Harpmaster, through falling snow as thick as meal.
At vulgar country Dionysia they carried amid roars the
giant leather phallus, but once initiated took the
proffered salt and the phallus in trembling silence. Their
dreams proliferated in him, and hearing them he opened

memory to his consciousness royally, prodigally, as one might open a major artery.

It was strange to move to Justine's side in that brindled autumn moonlight across such an unwholesome tide of memories: he felt his physical body displacing them by its sheer weight and density. Balthazar had moved to give him room and he was continuing to talk to his wife in low tones. (They drank the wine solemnly and sprinkled the lees on their garments. The generals had just told them they would never get through, never find the city.) And he remembered so vividly how Justine, after making love, would sit cross-legged on the bed and begin to lay out the little pack of Tarot cards which were always kept on the shelf among the books—as if to compute the degree of good fortune left them after this latest plunge into the icy underground river of passion which she could neither subdue nor slake. ("Minds dismembered by their sexual part," Balthazar had said once, "never find peace until old age and failing powers persuade them that silence and quietness are not hostile.")

Was all the discordance of their lives a measure of the anxiety which they had inherited from the city or the age? "O my God," he almost said, "why don't we leave this city, Justine, and seek an atmosphere less impregnated with the sense of deracination and failure?" The words of the old poet came into his mind, pressed down like the pedal of a piano, to boil and reverberate around the frail hope which the thought had raised from its dark sleep.*

"My problem," he said to himself quietly, feeling his forehead to see if he had a fever, "is that the woman I loved brought me a faultless satisfaction which never touched her own happiness;" and he thought over all the delusions which were now confirming themselves in physical signs. I mean: he had beaten Justine, beaten her until his arm ached and the stick broke in his hands. All this was a dream of course. Nevertheless on waking he had found his whole arm aching and swollen. What

could one believe when reality mocked the imagination
by its performance?

At the same time, of course, he fully recognized that
suffering, indeed all illness, was itself an acute form of
self-importance, and all the teachings of the Cabal came
like a following wind to swell his self-contempt. He could
hear, like the distant reverberations of the city's memory,
the voice of Plotinus speaking, not of flight away from intolerable temporal conditions but towards a new light, a
new city of Light. "This is no journey for the feet, however. Look into yourself, withdraw into yourself and look."
But this was the one act of which he now knew himself
forever incapable.

It is astonishing for me, in recording these passages to
recall how little of all this interior change was visible on
the surface of his life—even to those who knew him
intimately. There was little to put one's finger on—only a
sense of hollowness in the familiar—as of a well-known
air played slightly out of key. It is true that at this period
he had already begun to entertain with a prodigality
hitherto unknown to the city, even among the richest
families. The great house was never empty now. The great
kitchen-quarters where we so often boiled ourselves an
egg or a glass of milk after a concert or a play—dusty and
deserted then—were now held by a permanent garrison of
cooks, surgical and histrionic, capped in floury steeples.
The upper rooms, tall staircase, galleries and salons echoing to the mournful twining of clocks were patrolled now
by black slaves who moved as regally as swans about important tasks. Their white linen, smelling of the goose-
iron, was spotless—robes divided by scarlet sashes punctuated at the waist by clasps of gold fashioned into turtles'
heads: the rebus Nessim had chosen for himself. Their
soft porpoise eyes were topped by the conventional scarlet
flower-pots, their gorilla hands were cased in white gloves.
They were as soundless as death itself.

If he had not so far outdone the great figures of
Egyptian society in lavishness he might have been
thought to be competing with them for advancement.
The house was perpetually alive to the cool fern-like

patterns of a quartet, or to the foundering plunge of saxophones crying to the night like cuckolds.

The long beautiful reception-rooms had been pierced with alcoves and unexpected corners to increase their already great seating-capacity and sometimes as many as two or three hundred guests sat down to elaborate and meaningless dinners—observing their host lost in the contemplation of a rose lying upon an empty plate before him. Yet his was not a remarkable distraction for he could offer to the nonentities of common conversation a smile—surprising as one who removes an upturned glass to show, hidden by it, some rare entomological creature whose scientific name he had not learned.

What else is there to add? The small extravagances of his dress were hardly noticeable in one whose fortune had always seemed oddly matched against a taste for old flannel trousers and tweed coats. Now in his ice-smooth sharkskin with the scarlet cummerbund he seemed only what he should always have been—the richest and most handsome of the city's bankers: those true foundlings of the gut. People felt that at last he had come into his own. This was how someone of his place and fortune should live. Only the diplomatic corps smelt in this new prodigality a run of hidden motives, a plot perhaps to capture the King, and began to haunt his drawing-room with their studied politenesses. Under the slothful or foppish faces one was conscious of curiosity stirring, a desire to study Nessim's motives and designs, for nowadays the King was a frequent visitor to the great house.

Meanwhile all this advanced the central situation not at all. It was as if the action which Nessim had been contemplating grew with such infinite slowness, like a stalactite, that there was time for all this to fill the interval—the rockets ploughing their furrows of sparks across the velvet sky, piercing deeper and ever deeper into the night where Justine and I lay, locked in each other's arms and minds. In the still water of the fountains one saw the splash of human faces, ignited by these gold and scarlet stars as they rose hissing into heaven like thirsty swans. In the darkness, her warm hand on my arm, I could watch the autumn sky thrown into convulsions of coloured light with the calm of someone for whom the whole unmerited pain of the human world had receded and diffused itself—as pain does when it goes on too long, spreading from a specific member to flood a whole area of the body or the mind. The lovely grooves of the rockets upon the dark sky filled us only with the sense of a breath-taking congruence to the whole nature of the world of love which was soon to relinquish us.

This particular night was full of a rare summer lightning; and hardly had the display ended when from the desert to the east a thin crust of thunder formed like a scab upon the melodious silence. A light rain fell, youthful and refreshing, and all at once the darkness was full of figures hurrying back into the shelter of the lamplit houses, dresses held ankle-high and voices raised in shrill pleasure. The lamps printed for a second their bare bodies against the transparent materials which sheathed them. For our part we turned wordlessly into the alcove behind the sweet-smelling box-hedges and lay down upon the stone bench carved in the shape of a swan. The laughing chattering crowd poured across the entrance of the alcove towards the light; we lay in the cradle of darkness feeling the gentle prickle of the rain upon our faces. The last fuses were being defiantly lit by men in dinner-jackets and through her hair I saw the last pale comets gliding up into the darkness. I tasted, with the glowing pleasure of the colour in my brain, the warm guiltless pressure of her tongue upon mine, her arms upon mine. The magnitude of this happiness—we could not speak but gazed abundantly at each other with eyes full of unshed tears.

From the house came the dry snap of champagne-corks and the laughter of human beings. "Never an evening alone now."

"What is happening to Nessim?"

"I no longer know. When there is something to hide one becomes an actor. It forces all the people round one to act as well."

The same man, it was true, walked about on the surface of their common life—the same considerate, gentle, punctual man: but in a horrifying sense every-thing had changed, he was no longer there. "We've abandoned each other," she said in a small expiring whisper and drawing herself closer pressed to the very hilt of sense and sound the kisses which were like summaries of all we had shared, held precariously for a moment in our hands, before they should overflow into the sur-rounding darkness and forsake us. And yet it was as if in every embrace she were saying to herself: "Perhaps through this very thing, which hurts so much and which I do not want ever to end—maybe through this I shall find my way back to Nessim." I was filled suddenly by an intolerable depression.

Later, walking about in the strident native quarter with its jabbing lights and flesh-wearing smells, I won-dered as I had always wondered, where time was lead-ing us. And as if to test the validity of the very emotions upon which so much love and anxiety could base them-selves I turned into a lighted booth decorated by a strip of cinema poster—the huge half-face of a screen-lover, meaningless as the belly of a whale turned upwards in death—and sat down upon the customer's stool, as one might in a barber's shop, to wait my turn. A dirty curtain was drawn across the inner door and from behind it came faint sounds, as of the congress of creatures unknown to science, not specially revolting—indeed interesting as the natural sciences are for those who have abandoned any claims of cultivating a sensibility. I was of course drunk by this time and exhausted—drunk as much on Justine as upon the thin-paper-bodied *Pol Roget*.

There was a tarbush lying upon the chair beside me and absently I put it on my head. It was faintly warm and sticky inside and the thick leather lining clung to my forehead. "I want to know what it really means," I told myself in a mirror whose cracks had been pasted over with the trimmings of postage stamps. I meant of course the whole portentous scrimmage of sex itself, the act of penetration which could lead a man to despair for the sake of a creature with two breasts and *le croissant* as the picturesque Levant slang has it. The sound within had increased to a sly groaning and squeaking—a combustible human voice adding itself to the jostling of an ancient wooden-slatted bed. This was presumably the identical undifferentiated act which Justine and I shared with the common world to which we belonged. How did it differ? How far had our feelings carried us from the truth of the simple, devoid beast-like act itself? To what extent was the treacherous mind—with its interminable *catalogue raisonné* of the heart—responsible? I wished to answer an unanswerable question; but I was so desperate for certainty that it seemed to me that if I surprised the act in its natural state, motivated by scientific money and not love, as yet undamaged by the idea, I might surprise the truth of my own feelings and desires. Impatient to deliver myself from the question I lifted the curtain and stepped softly into the cubicle which was fitfully lighted by a buzzing staggering paraffin lamp turned down low.

The bed was inhabited by an indistinct mass of flesh moving in many places at once, vaguely stirring like an ant-heap. It took me some moments to define the pale and hairy limbs of an elderly man from those of his partner—the greenish-hued whiteness of convex woman with a boa-constrictor's head—a head crowned with spokes of toiling black hair which trailed over the edges of the filthy mattress. My sudden appearance must have suggested a police raid for it was followed by a gasp and complete silence. It was as if the ant-hill had suddenly become deserted. The man gave a groan and a startled half-glance in my direction and then as if to escape detection buried his head between the immense breasts of the woman. It was impossible to explain to them that I was investigating nothing more particular than the act upon which they were engaged. I advanced to the bed firmly, apologetically, and with what must have seemed a vaguely scientific air of detachment I took the rusty bed-rail in my hands and stared down, not upon them for I was hardly conscious of their existence, but upon myself and Melissa, myself and Justine. The woman turned a pair of large gauche charcoal eyes upon me and said something in Arabic.

They lay there like the victims of some terrible accident, clumsily engaged, as if in some incoherent experimental fashion they were the first partners in the history of the human race to think out this peculiar means of communication. Their posture, so ludicrous and ill-planned, seemed the result of some early trial which might, after centuries of experiment, evolve into a disposition of bodies as breathlessly congruent as a ballet-position. But nevertheless I recognized that this had been fixed immutably, for all time—this eternally tragic and ludicrous position of engagement. From this sprang all those aspects of love which the wit of poets and madmen had used to elaborate their philosophy of polite distinctions. From this point the sick, the insane started growing; and from here too the disgusted and dispirited faces of the long-married, tied to each other back to back, so to speak, like dogs unable to disengage after coupling.

The peal of soft cracked laughter I uttered surprised me, but it reassured my specimens. The man raised his face a few inches and listened attentively as if to assure himself that no policeman could have uttered such a laugh. The woman re-explained me to herself and smiled "Wait one moment," she cried, waving a white blotched hand in the direction of the curtain. "I will not be long." And the man, as if reprimanded by her tone, made a few convulsive movements, like a paralytic attempting to walk—impelled not by the demands of pleasure but by the purest courtesy. His expression betrayed an access of politeness—as of someone rising in a crowded tram to surrender his place to a *multilé de la guerre*. The woman grunted and her fingers curled up at the edges.

Leaving them there, fitted so clumsily together, I stepped laughing out into the street once more to make a circuit of the quarter which still hummed with the derisive, concrete life of men and women. The rain had stopped and the damp ground exhaled the tormentingly lovely scent of clay, bodies and stale jasmine. I began to

walk slowly, deeply bemused, and to describe to myself
in words this whole quarter of Alexandria for I knew that
soon it would be forgotten and revisited only by those
whose memories had been appropriated by the fevered
city, clinging to the minds of old men like traces of
perfume upon a sleeve: Alexandria, the capital of
Memory.

The narrow street was of baked and scented terra
cotta, soft now from rain but not wet. Its whole length
was lined with the coloured booths of prostitutes whose
thrilling marble bodies were posed modestly each before
her doll's house, as before a shrine. They sat on three-
legged stools like oracles wearing coloured slippers, out
in the open street. The originality of the lighting gave
the whole scene the colours of deathless romance, for
instead of being lit from above by electric light the whole
street was lit by a series of stabbing carbide-lamps standing upon the ground: throwing thirsty, ravishing violet
shadows upwards into the nooks and gables of the dolls'
houses, into the nostrils and eyes of its inhabitants, into
the unresisting softness of that furry darkness. I walked
slowly among these extraordinary human blooms, reflecting that a city like a human being collects its predispositions, appetites and fears. It grows to maturity, utters its prophets, and declines into hebetude, old age or
the loneliness which is worse than either. Unaware that
their mother city was dying, the living still sat there in
the open street like caryatids supporting the darkness, the
pains of futurity upon their very eyelids; sleeplessly
watching, the immortality-hunters, throughout the whole
fatidic length of time.

Here was a painted booth entirely decorated by *fleur-
de-lis* carefully and correctly drawn upon a peach-
coloured ground in royal blue. At its door sat a giant
bluish child of a Negress, perhaps eighteen years of age,
clad in a red flannel nightgown of a vaguely mission-
house *allure*. She wore a crown of dazzling narcissus on
her black woolen head. Her hands were gathered hum-
bly in her lap—an apron full of chopped fingers. She
resembled a heavenly black bunny sitting at the entrance

of a burrow. Next door a woman fragile as a leaf, and
next her one like a chemical formula rinsed out by
anaemia and cigarette smoke. Everywhere on these
brown flapping walls I saw the basic talisman of the
country—imprint of a palm with outspread fingers,
seeking to ward off the terrors which thronged the
darkness outside the lighted town. As I walked past them
now they uttered, not human monetary cries, but the soft
cooing propositions of doves, their quiet voices filling the
street with a cloistral calm. It was not sex they offered in
their monotonous seclusion among the yellow flares, but
like the true inhabitants of Alexandria, the deep forgetfulness of parturition, compounded of physical pleasures
taken without aversion.

The dolls' houses shivered and reeled for a second as
the wind of the sea intruded, pressing upon loose fragments of cloth, unfastened partitions. One house lacked
any backcloth whatever and staring through the door one
caught a glimpse of a courtyard with a stunted palm-
tree. By the light thrown out from a bucket of burning
shavings three girls sat on stools, dressed in torn kimonos,
talking in low tones and extending the tips of their
fingers to the elf-light. They seemed as rapt, as remote as
if they had been sitting around a camp fire on the
steppes.

(In the back of my mind I could see the great banks of
ice—snowdrifts in which Nessim's champagne-bottles lay,
gleaming bluish-green like aged carp in a familiar pond.
And as if to restore my memory I smelt my sleeves for
traces of Justine's perfume.)

I turned at last into an empty cafe where I drank
coffee served by a Saidi whose grotesque squint seemed
to double every object he gazed upon. In the far corner,
curled up on a trunk and so still that she was invisible at
first sat a very old lady smoking a *narguileh* which from
time to time uttered a soft air-bubble of sound like the
voice of a dove. Here I thought the whole story through
from beginning to end, starting in the days before I ever
knew Melissa and ending somewhere soon in an idle
pragmatic death in a city to which I did not belong; I say

that I thought it through, but strangely enough I thought
of it not as a personal history with an individual accent so
much as part of the historical fabric of the place. I
described it to myself as part and parcel of the city's
behavior, completely in keeping with everything that
had gone before, and everything that would follow it. It
was as if my imagination had become subtly drugged by
the ambience of the place and could not respond to
personal, individual assessments. I had lost the capacity
to feel even the thrill of danger. My sharpest regret,
characteristically enough, was for the jumble of
manuscript notes which might be left behind. I had
always hated the incomplete, the fragmentary. I decided
that they at least must be destroyed before I went a step
further. I rose to my feet—only to be struck by a sudden
realization that the man I had seen in the little booth had
been Mnemjian. How was it possible to mistake that
misformed back? This thought occupied me as I re-
crossed the quarter, moving towards the larger thorough-
fares in the direction of the sea. I walked across this
mirage of narrow intersecting alleys as one might walk
across a battlefield which had swallowed up all the
friends of one's youth; yet I could not help in delighting
at every scent and sound—a survivor's delight. Here at one
corner stood a flame-swallower with his face turned up to
the sky, spouting a column of flames from his mouth
which turned black with flapping fumes at the edges and
bit a hole in the sky. From time to time he took a swig
at a bottle of petrol before throwing back his head once
more and gushing flames six feet high. At every corner
the violet shadows fell and foundered, striped with human experience—at once savage and tenderly lyrical. I
took it as a measure of my maturity that I was filled no
longer with despairing self-pity but with a desire to be
claimed by the city, enrolled among its trivial or tragic
memories—if it so wished.

It was equally characteristic that by the time I reached
the little flat and disinterred the grey exercise books in
which my notes had been scribbled I thought no longer of
destroying them. Indeed I sat there in the lamp-light and

added to them while Pombal discoursed on life from the other easy chair.

"Returning to my room I sit silent, listening to the heavy tone of her scent: a smell perhaps composed of flesh, faeces and herbs, all worked into the dense brocade of her being. This is a peculiar type of love for I do not feel that I possess her—nor indeed would wish to do so. It is as if we joined each other only in self-possession, became partners in a common stage of growth. In fact we outrage love, for we have proved the bonds of friendship stronger. These notes, however they may be read, are intended only as a painstaking affectionate commentary on a world into which I have been born to share my most solitary moments—those of coitus—with Justine. I can get no nearer to the truth.

"Recently, when it had been difficult to see her for one reason or another, I found myself longing so much for her that I went all the way down to Pietrantoni to try and buy a bottle of her perfume. In vain. The good-tempered girl-assistant dabbed my hands with every make she had in stock and once or twice I thought that I had discovered it. But no. Something was always missing— I suppose the flesh which the perfume merely costumed. The undertow of the body itself was the missing factor. It was only when in desperation I mentioned Justine's name that the girl turned immediately to the first perfume we had tried. 'Why did you not say so at first?' she asked with an air of professional hurt; everyone, her tone implied, knew the perfume Justine used except myself. It was unrecognizable. Nevertheless I was surprised to discover that *Jamais de la vie* was not among the most expensive or exotic of perfumes.

"(When I took home the little bottle they found in Cohen's waistcoat-pocket the wraith of Melissa was still there, imprisoned. She could still be detected.)"

Pombal was reading aloud the long terrible passage from *Moeurs* which is called "The Dummy Speaks." In all these fortuitous collisions with the male animal I had never known release, no matter what experiences I had submitted my body to. I always see in the mirror the image of an ageing fury crying: *"J'ai raté mon propre amour—mon amour à moi. Mon amour-propre, mon propre amour. Je l'ai raté. Je n'ai jamais souffert, jamais eu de joie simple et candid."*

He paused only to say: "If this is true you are only taking advantage of an illness in loving her," and the remark struck me like the edge of an axe wielded by someone of enormous and unconscious strength.

* * * * *

When the time for the great yearly shoot on Lake Mareotis came round Nessim began to experience a magical sense of relief. He recognized at last that what had to be decided would be decided at this time and at no other. He had the air of a man who has fought a long illness successfully. Had his judgment indeed been so faulty even though it had not been conscious? During the years of his marriage he had repeated on every day the words, "I am so happy"—fatal as the striking of a grandfather-clock upon which silence is forever encroaching. Now he could say so no longer. Their common life was like some cable buried in the sand which, in some inexplicable way, at a point impossible to discover, had snapped, plunging them both into an unaccustomed and impenetrable darkness.

The madness itself, of course, took no account of circumstances. It appeared to superimpose itself not upon personalities tortured beyond the bounds of endurance but purely upon a given situation. In a real sense we all shared it, though only Nessim acted it out, exemplified it in the flesh, as a person. The short period which preceded the great shoot on Mareotis lasted for perhaps a month—certainly for very little more. Here again to those who did not know him nothing was obvious. Yet the delusions multiplied themselves at such a rate that in his own records they give one the illusion of watching bacteria under a microscope—the pullulation of healthy cells, as in cancer, which have gone off their heads, renounced their power to repress themselves.

The mysterious series of code messages transmitted by

the street names he encountered showed definite irrefutable signs of a supernatural agency at work full of the threat of unseen punishment—though whether for himself or for others he could not tell. Bathazar's treatise lying withering in the window of a bookshop and the *same day* coming upon his father's grave in the Jewish cemetery—with those distinguishing names engraved upon the stone which echoed all the melancholy of European Jewry in exile.

Then the question of noises in the room next door: a sort of heavy breathing and the sudden simultaneous playing of three pianos. These, he knew, were not delusions but links in an occult chain, logical and persuasive only to the mind which had passed beyond the frame of causality. It was becoming harder and harder to pretend to be sane by the standards of ordinary behavior. He was going through the *Devastatio* described by Swedenborg.

The coal fires had taken to burning into extraordinary shapes. This could be proved by relighting them over again to verify his findings—terrifying landscapes and faces. The mole on Justine's wrist was also troubling. At meal times he fought against his desire to touch it so feverishly that he turned pale and almost fainted.

One afternoon a crumpled sheet began breathing and continued for a space of about half an hour, assuming the shape of the body it covered. One night he woke to the soughing of great wings and saw a bat-like creature with the head of a violin resting upon the bed-rail.

Then the counter-agency of the powers of good—a message brought by a ladybird which settled on the notebook in which he was writing; the music of Weber's *Pan* played *every day* between three and four on a piano in an adjoining house. He felt that his mind had become a battle-ground for the forces of good and evil and that his task was to strain every nerve to recognize them, but it was not easy. The phenomenal world had begun to play tricks on him so that his senses were beginning to accuse reality itself of inconsistency. He was in peril of a mental overthrow.

Once his waistcoat started ticking as it hung on the

back of a chair, as if inhabited by a colony of foreign heartbeats. But when investigated it stopped and refused to continue for the benefit of Selim whom he had called into the room. The same day he saw his initials in gold upon a cloud reflected in a shop-window in the Rue St. Saba. *Everything seemed proved by this.*

That same week a stranger was seated in the corner always reserved by Balthazar in the Café Al Aktar sipping an *arak*—the *arak* he had intended to order. The figure bore a strong yet distorted resemblance to himself as he turned in the mirror, unfolding his lips from white teeth in a smile. He did not wait but hurried to the door.

As he walked the length of Rue Fuad he felt the entire pavement turn to sponge beneath his feet; he was foundering waist-deep in it before the illusion vanished. At two-thirty that afternoon he rose from a feverish sleep, dressed and set off to confirm an overpowering intuition that both Pastroudi and the Café Dordali were empty. They were, and the fact filled him with triumphant relief; but it was short-lived, for on returning to his room he felt all of a sudden as if his heart were being expelled from his body by the short mechanical movements of an air-pump. He had come to hate and fear this room of his. He would stand for a long time listening until the noise came again—the slither of wires being uncoiled upon the floor and the noise of some small animal, its shrieks being stifled, as it was bundled into a bag. Then distinctly the noise of suitcase-hasps being fastened with a snap and the breathing of someone who stood against the wall next door listening for the least sound. Nessim removed his shoes and tip-toed to the bay-window in an attempt to see into the room next door. His assailant, it seemed to him, was an elderly man, gaunt and sharp-featured, with the sunk reddish eyes of a bear. He was unable to confirm this. Then, waking early on the very morning upon which the invitations for the great shoot must be issued he saw with horror from the bedroom window two suspicious-looking men in Arab dress tying a rope to a sort of windlass on the roof. They pointed to him and spoke together in low tones. Then they began to lower

something heavy, wrapped in a fur coat, into the open
street below. His hands trembled as he filled in the large
white squares of pasteboard with that flowing script, se-
lecting his names from the huge type-written list which
Selim had left on his desk. Nevertheless he smiled as
well when he recalled how large a space was devoted in
the local press each year to this memorable event—the
great shoot on Mareotis. With so much to occupy him he
felt that nothing should be left to chance and though
the solicitous Selim hovered near, he pursued his lips and
insisted on attending to all the invitations himself. My
own, charged with every presage of disaster, stared at me
now from the mantelpiece. I gazed at it, my attention
scattered by nicotine and wine, recognizing that here, in
some indefinable way, was the solution towards which we
all had moved. ("Where science leaves off nerves begin."
Moeurs.)

"Of course you will refuse. You will not go?" Justine
spoke so sharply that I understood that her gaze had
followed mine. She stood over me in the misty early
morning light, and between sentences cocked an ear
towards the heavily-breathing wraith of Hamid behind
the door. "You are not to tempt providence. Will you?
Answer me." And as if to make persuasion certain she
slipped off her skirt and shoes and fell softly into bed
beside me—warm hair and mouth, and the treacherous
nervous movements of a body which folded against one
as if hurt, as if tender from unhealed wounds. It seemed
to me then—and the compulsion had nothing of bravado
in it—it seemed to me then that I could no longer deprive
Nessim of the satisfaction he sought of me, or indeed the
situation of its issue. There was, too, underneath it all a
vein of relief which made me feel almost gay until I saw
the grave sad expression of my companion-in-arms. She
lay, staring out of those wonderfully expressive dark
eyes, as if from a high window in her own memory. She
was looking, I knew, into the eyes of Melissa—into the
troubled candid eyes of one who, with every day of
increasing danger, moved nearer and nearer to us. After
all, the one most to be wounded by the issue Nessim

might be contemplating was Melissa—who else? I
thought back along the iron chain of kisses which Justine
had forged, steadily back into memory, hand over fist,
like a mariner going down an anchor-chain into the
darkest depths of some great stagnant harbour, memory.

From among many sorts of failure each selects the one
which least compromises his self-respect: which lets him
down the lightest. Mine had been in art, in religion, and
in people. In art I had failed (it suddenly occurred to me
at this moment) because I did not believe in the discrete
human personality. ("Are people," writes Pursewarden,
"continuously themselves, or simply over and over again
so fast that they give the illusion of continuous features—
the temporal flicker of old silent film?") I lacked a belief
in the true authenticity of people in order to successfully
portray them. In religion? Well, I found no religion worth
while which contained the faintest grain of propitiation—
and which can escape the charge? *Pace* Balthazar it
seemed to me that all churches, all sects, were at the best
mere academies of self-instruction against fear. But the
last, the worst failure (I buried my lips in the dark living
hair of Justine), the failure with people: it had been
brought about by a gradually increasing detachment of
spirit which, while it freed me to sympathize, forbade me
possession. I was gradually, inexplicably, becoming more
and more deficient in love, yet better and better at
self-giving—the best part of loving. This, I realized
with horror, was the hold I now had over Justine. As a
woman, a natural possessive, she was doomed to try and
capture the part of myself which was forever beyond
reach, the last painful place of refuge which was for me
laughter, and friendship. This sort of loving had made
her, in a way, desperate for I did not depend on her; and
the desire to possess can, if starved, render one absolutely possessed in the spirit oneself. How difficult it is to
analyse these relationships which lie under the mere skin
of our actions; for loving is only a sort of skin-language,
sex a terminology merely.

And further to render down this sad relationship
which had caused me so much pain—I saw that pain

itself was the only food of memory: for pleasure ends in
itself—all they had bequeathed me was a fund of permanent health—life-giving detachment. I was like a dry-cell
battery. Uncommitted, I was free to circulate in the
world of men and women like a guardian of the true
rights of love—which is not passion, nor habit (they only
qualify it) but which is the divine trespass of an immor-
tal among mortals—Aphrodite-in-arms. Beleaguered thus,
I was nevertheless defined and realized in myself by the
very quality which (of course) hurt me most: selfless-
ness. *This* is what Justine loved in me—not my personality. Women are sexual robbers, and it was this treasure of
detachment she hoped to steal from me—the jewel
growing in the toad's head. It was the signature of this
detachment she saw written across my life with all its
haphazardness, discordance, disorderliness. My value
was not in anything I achieved or anything I owned.
Justine loved me because I presented to her something
which was indestructible—a person already formed who
could not be broken. She was haunted by the feeling that
even while I was loving her I was wishing at the same
time only to die! This she found unendurable.

And Melissa? She lacked of course the insight of Justine into my case. She only knew that my strength
supported her where she was at her weakest—in her
dealings with the world. She treasured every sign of my
human weakness—disorderly habits, incapacity over
money affairs, and so on. She loved my weaknesses
because there she felt of use to me; Justine brushed all
this aside as unworthy of her interest. She had detected
another kind of strength. I interested her only in this one
particular which I could not offer her as a gift nor she
steal from me. This is what is meant by possession—to be
passionately at war for the qualities in one another: to
contend for the treasures of each other's personalities.
But how can such a war be anything but destructive and
hopeless?

And yet, so entangled are human motives: it would be
Melissa herself who had driven Nessim from his refuge
in the world of fantasy towards an action which he knew

we would all bitterly regret—our death. For it was she
who, overmastered by the impulse of her unhappiness
one night, approached the table at which he sat, before
an empty champagne-glass, watching the cabaret with a
pensive air: and blushing and trembling in her false
eyelashes, blurted out eight words, *"Your wife is no
longer faithful to you"*—a phrase which stood quivering in
his mind from then on, like a thrown knife. It is true that
for a long time now his dossiers had been swollen with
reports of this dreaded fact but these reports were like
newspaper-accounts of a catastrophe which had occurred
a long way off, in a country which one had not visited.
Now he was suddenly face to face with an eye-witness,
a victim, a survivor. . . . The resonance of this one phrase
refecundated his powers of feeling. The whole dead tract
of paper suddenly rose up and screeched at him.

Melissa's dressing-room was an evil-smelling cubicle
full of the coiled pipes which emptied the lavatories. She
had a single poignant strip of cracked mirror and a little
shelf dressed with the kind of white paper upon which
wedding-cakes are built. Here she always set out the
jumble of powders and crayons which she misused so
fearfully.

In this mirror the image of Selim blistered and flick-
ered in the dancing gas-jets like a spectre from the underworld. He spoke with an incisive finish which was a
copy of his master's; in this copied voice she could feel
some of the anxiety the secretary felt for the only human
being he truly worshipped, and to whose anxieties he
reacted like a planchette.

Melissa was afraid now, for she knew that offence
given to the great could, by the terms of the city, be
punished swiftly and dreadfully. She was aghast at what
she had done and fought back a desire to cry as she
picked off her eyelashes with trembling hands. There
was no way of refusing the invitation. She dressed in her
shabby best and carrying her fatigue like a heavy pack
followed Selim to the great car which stood in deep
shadow. She was helped in beside Nessim. They moved

off slowly into the dense crepuscular evening of an
Alexandria which, in her panic, she no longer recognized. They scouted a sea turned to sapphire and turned
inland, folding up the slums, towards Mareotis and the
bituminous slag-heaps of Mex where the pressure of the
headlights now peeled off layer after layer of the
darkness, bringing up small intimate scenes of Egyptian
life—a drunkard singing, a biblical figure on a mule with
two children escaping from Herod, a porter sorting sacks—
swiftly, like someone dealing cards. She followed these
familiar sights with emotion, for behind lay the desert, its
emptiness echoing like a seashell. All this time her companion had not spoken, and she had not dared to risk so
much as a glance in his direction.

Now when the pure steely lines of the dunes came up
under the late moon Nessim drew the car to a standstill.
Groping in his pocket for his cheque-book he said in a
trembling voice, his eyes full of tears: "What is the price
of your silence?" She turned to him and, seeing for the
first time the gentleness and sorrow of that dark face,
found her fear replaced by an overwhelming shame.
She recognized in his expression the weakness for the good
which could never render him an enemy of her kind.
She put a timid hand on his arm and said: "I am so
ashamed. Please forgive me. I did not know what I was
saying." And her fatigue overcame her so that her emotion which threatened her with tears turned to a yawn.
Now they stared at one another with a new understanding, recognizing each other as innocents. For a minute it
was almost as if they had fallen in love with each other
from sheer relief.

The car gathered momentum again like their silence—
and soon they were racing across the desert towards the
steely glitter of stars, and a horizon stained black with
the thunder of surf. Nessim, with this strange sleepy
creature at his side, found himself thinking over and over
again: "Thank God I am not a genius—for a genius has
nobody in whom he can confide."

The glances he snatched at her enabled him to study
her, and to study me in her. Her loveliness must have

disarmed and disturbed him as it had me. It was a
beauty which filled one with the terrible premonition
that it had been born to be a target for the forces of
destruction. Perhaps he remembered an anecdote of Pursewarden's in which she figured, for the latter had found
her as Nessim himself had done, in the same stale cabaret; only on this particular evening she had been
sitting in a row of dance-hostesses selling dance-tickets.
Pursewarden, who was gravely drunk, took her to the
floor and, after a moment's silence, addressed her in his
sad yet masterful way: *"Comment vous défendez-vous
contre la solitude?"* he asked her. Melissa turned upon him
an eye replete with all the candour of experience and
replied softly: *"Monsieur, je suis devenue la solitude
même."* Pursewarden was sufficiently struck to remember and repeat this passage later to his friends, adding:
"I suddenly thought to myself that here was a woman
one might very well love." Yet he did not, as far as I
know, take the risk of revisiting her, for the book was
going well, and he recognized in the kindling of this
sympathy a trick being played on him by the least intent
part of his nature. He was writing about love at the time
and did not wish to disturb the ideas he had formed on
the subject. ("I cannot fall in love," he made a character
exclaim, "for I belong to that ancient secret society—the
Jokers!"; and elsewhere speaking about his marriage he
wrote: "I found that as well as displeasing another I also
displeased myself; now, alone, I have only myself to
displease. Joy!")

Justine was still standing over me, watching my face as
I composed these scorching scenes in my mind. "You will
make some excuse," she repeated hoarsely. "You will not
go." It seemed to me impossible to find a way out of this
predicament. "How *can* I refuse?" I said. "How can
you?"

They had driven across that warm, tideless desert
night, Nessim and Melissa, consumed by a sudden sympathy for each other, yet speechless. On the last scrap
before Bourg El Arab he switched off the engine and let

the car roll off the road. "Come," he said, "I want to show you Justine's Summer Palace."

Hand in hand they took the road to the little house. The caretaker was asleep but he had the key. The rooms smelt damp and uninhabited, but were full of light reflected from the white dunes. It was not long before he had kindled a fire of thorns in the great fireplace, and taking his old *abba* from the cupboard he clothed himself in it and sat down before it saying: "Tell me now, Melisssa, who sent you to persecute me?" He meant it as a joke but forgot to smile, and Melissa turned crimson with shame and bit her lip. They sat there for a long time enjoying the firelight and the sensation of sharing something—their common hopelessness.

(Justine stubbed out her cigarette and got slowly out of bed. She began to walk slowly up and down the carpet. Fear had overcome her and I could see that it was only with an effort that she overcame the need for a characteristic outburst. "I have done so many things in my life," she said to the mirror. "Evil things, perhaps. But never inattentively, never wastefully. I've always thought of acts as messages, wishes from the past to the future, which invited self-discovery. Was I wrong? Was I wrong?" It was not to me she addressed the question now but to Nessim. It is so much easier to address questions intended for one's husband to one's lover. "As for the dead," she went on after a moment, "I have always thought that the dead think of us as dead. They have rejoined the living after this trifling excursion into quasi-life." Hamid was stirring now and she turned to her clothes in a panic. "So you must go," she said sadly, "and so must I. You are right. We must go." And then turning to the mirror to complete her toilet she added: "Another grey hair," studying that wicked fashionable face.

Watching her thus, trapped for a moment by a rare sunbeam on the dirty window-pane, I could not help reflecting once more that in her there was nothing to control or modify the intuition which she had developed out of a nature gorged upon introspection: no education, no resources of intellection to battle against the imperatives of a violent heart. Her gift was the gift one finds occasionally in ignorant fortune-tellers. Whatever passed for thought in her was borrowed—even the remark about the dead which occurs in *Moeurs;* she had picked out what was significant in books not by reading them but by listening to the matchless discourses of Balthazar, Arnauti, Pursewarden, upon them. She was a walking abstract of the writers and thinkers whom she had loved or admired—but what clever woman is more?)

Nessim now took Melissa's hands between his own (they lay there effortless, cool, like wafers) and began to question her about me with an avidity which might have easily suggested that his passion was not Justine, but myself. One always falls in love with the love-choice of the person one loves. What would I not give to learn all that she told him, striking ever more deeply into his sympathies with her candours, her unexpected reserves? All I know is that she concluded stupidly, "Even now they are not happy: they quarrel dreadfully: Hamid told me so when last I met him." Surely she was experienced enough to recognize in these reported quarrels the very subject-matter of our love? I think she saw only the selfishness of Justine—that almost deafening lack of interest in other people which characterized my tyrant. She utterly lacked the charity of mind upon which Melissa's good opinion alone could be grounded. She was not really human—nobody wholly dedicated to the ego is. What on earth could I see in her?—I asked this question of myself for the thousandth time. Yet Nessim, in beginning to explore and love Melissa as an extension of Justine, delineated perfectly the human situation. Melissa would hunt in him for the qualities which she imagined I must have found in his wife. The four of us were unrecognized complementaries of one another, inextricably bound together. ("We who have travelled much and loved much: we who have—I will not say suffered for we have always recognized through suffering our own self-sufficiency—only we appreciate the complexities of tenderness, and understand how narrowly love and friendship are related." *Moeurs.*)

They talked now as a doomed brother and sister might, renewing in each other the sense of relief which comes to those who find someone to share the burden of unconfessed preoccupations. In all this sympathy an unexpected shadow of desire stirred within them, a wraith merely, the stepchild of confession and release. It foreshadowed, in a way, their own love-making, which was to come, and which was so much less ugly than ours—mine and Justine's. Loving is so much truer when sympathy and not desire makes the match; for it leaves no wounds. It was already dawn when they rose from their conversation, stiff and cramped, the fire long since out, and marched across the damp sand to the car, scouting the pale lavender light of dawn. Melissa had found a friend and patron; as for Nessim, he was transfigured. The sensation of a new sympathy had enabled him, magically, to become his own man again—that is to say, a man who could act (could murder his wife's lover if he so wished)!

Driving along that pure and natal coastline they watched the first tendrils of sunlight uncoil from horizon to horizon across the dark self-sufficient Mediterranean sea whose edges were at one and the same moment touching lost hallowed Carthage and Salamis in Cyprus.

Presently, where the road dips down among the dunes to the sea-shore Nessim once more slowed down and involuntarily suggested a swim. Changed as he was he felt a sudden desire that Melissa should see him naked, should approve the beauty which for so long had lain, like a suit of well-cut clothes in an attic cupboard, forgotten.

Naked and laughing, they waded out hand in hand, into the icy water feeling the tame sunlight glowing on their backs as they did so. It was like the first morning since the creation of the world. Melissa, too, had shed with her clothes the last residual encumbrance of the flesh, and had become the dancer she truly was; for nakedness always gave her fulness and balance: the craft she lacked in the cabaret.

They lay together for a long time in perfect silence, seeking through the darkness of their feelings for the way forward. He realized that he had won an instant compliance from her—that she was now his mistress in everything.

They set off together for the city, feeling at the same time happy and ill-at-ease—for both felt a kind of hollowness at the heart of their happiness. Yet since they were reluctant to surrender each other to the life which awaited them they lagged, the car lagged, their silence lagged between endearments.

At last Nessim remembered a tumbledown café in Mex where one could find a boiled egg and coffee. Early though it was the sleepy Greek proprietor was awake and set chairs for them under a barren fig-tree in a backyard full of hens and their meagre droppings. All around them towered corrugated iron wharves and factories. The sea was present only as a dank and resonant smell of hot iron and tar.

He set her down at last on the street-corner she named and said good-bye in a "wooden perfunctory" sort of way—afraid perhaps that some of his own office employees might oversee him. (This last is my own conjecture as the words "wooden" and "perfunctory," which occur in his diaries, seem somehow out of place.) The inhuman bustle of the city intervened once more, committing them to past feelings and preoccupations. For her part, yawning, sleepy and utterly natural as she was, she left him only to turn into the little Greek church and set a candle to the saint. She crossed herself from left to right as the orthodox custom is and brushed back a lock of hair with one hand as she stooped to the ikon, tasting in its brassy kiss all the consolation of a forgotten childhood habit. Then wearily she turned to find Nessim standing before her. He was deathly white and staring at her with a sweet burning curiosity. She at once understood everything. They embraced with a sort of anguish, not kissing, but simply pressing their bodies together, and he all at once began to tremble with fatigue. His teeth began to chatter. She drew him to a choir stall where he sat for some abstracted moments, struggling to speak, and drawing his hand across his forehead like someone who is re-

covering from drowning. It was not that he had anything
to say to her, but this speechlessness made him fear that
he was experiencing a stroke. He croaked: "It is terribly
late, nearly half past six." Pressing her hand to his stubbled cheek he rose and like a very old man groped his
way back through the great doors into the sunlight,
leaving her sitting there gazing after him.

Never had the early dawn-light seemed so good to
Nessim. The city looked to him as brilliant as a precious
stone. The shrill telephones whose voices filled the great
stone buildings in which the financiers really lived,
sounded to him like the voices of great fruitful mechanical birds. They glittered with a pharaonic youthfulness.
The trees in the park had been rinsed down by an
unaccustomed dawn rain. They were covered in bril-
liants and looked like great contented cats at their toilet.

Sailing upwards to the fifth floor in the lift, making
awkward attempts to appear presentable (feeling the
dark stubble on his chin, retying his tie) Nessim ques-
tioned his reflection in the cheap mirror, puzzled by the
whole new range of feelings and beliefs these brief scenes
had given him. Under everything, however, aching like a
poisoned tooth or finger, lay the quivering meaning of
those eight words which Melissa had lodged in him. In a
dazed sort of way he recognized that Justine was dead to
him—from a mental picture she had become an engraving, a locket which one might wear over one's heart
forever. It is always bitter to leave the old life for the
new—and every woman is a new life, compact and self-
contained and *sui generis*. As a person she had suddenly
faded. He did not wish to possess her any longer but to
free himself from her. From a woman she had become a
situation.

He rang for Selim and when the secretary appeared he
dictated to him a few of the duller business letters with a
calm so surprising that the boy's hand trembled as he
took them down in his meticulous crowsfoot shorthand.
Perhaps Nessim had never been more terrifying to Selim
than he appeared at this moment, sitting at his great

polished desk with the gleaming battery of telephones ranged before him.

Nessim did not meet Melissa for some time after this episode but he wrote her long letters, all of which he destroyed in the lavatory. It seemed necessary to him, for some fantastic reason, to explain and justify Justine to her and each of these letters began with a long painful exegesis of Justine's past and his own. Without this preamble, he felt, it would be impossible ever to speak of the way in which Melissa had moved and captivated him. He was defending his wife, of course, not against Melissa who had uttered no criticism of her (apart from the one phrase) but against all the new doubts about her which emerged precisely from his experience with Melissa. Just as my own experience of Justine had illuminated and re-evaluated Melissa for me so he looking into Melissa's grey eyes saw a new and unsuspected Justine born therein. You see, he was now alarmed at the extent to which it might become possible to hate her. He recognized now that hate is only unachieved love. He felt envious when he remembered the single-mindedness of Pursewarden who on the flyleaf of the last book he gave Balthazar had scribbled the mocking words:

Pursewarden on Life
N.B. Food is for eating
Art is for arting
Women for ——
Finish
RIP

And when next they met, under very different circumstances. . . . But I have not the courage to continue. I have explored Melissa deeply enough through my own mind and heart and cannot bear to recall what Nessim found in her—pages covered with erasures and emendations. Pages which I have torn from his diaries and destroyed. Sexual jealousy is the most curious of animals and can take up a lodgement anywhere, even in memory. I avert my face from the thought of Nessim's shy

kisses, of Melissa's kisses which selected in Nessim only
the nearest mouth to mine. . . .

From a crisp packet I selected a strip of pasteboard on
which, after so many shame-faced importunities, I had
persuaded a local jobbing printer to place my name and
address, and taking up my pen wrote:

> mr ———— accepts with pleasure the
> kind invitation of mr ———— to a duck
> shoot on Lake Mareotis.

It seemed to me that now one might learn some
important truths about human behaviour.

* * * * *

Autumn has settled at last into the clear winterset.
High seas flogging the blank panels of stone along the
Corniche. The migrants multiplying on the shallow
reaches of Mareotis. Waters moving from gold to grey,
the pigmentation of winter.

The parties assemble at Nessim's house towards twilight—a prodigious collection of cars and shooting-brakes.
Here begins the long packing and unpacking of wicker
baskets and gun-bags, conducted to the accompaniment
of cocktails and sandwiches. Costumes burgeon. Compari-
son of guns ad cartridges, conversation inseparable from
a shooter's life, begin now, rambling, inconsequent, wise.
The yellowish moonless dusk settles; the angle of the
sunlight turns slowly upwards into the vitreous lilac of
the evening sky. It is brisk weather, clear as waterglass.

Justine and I are moving through the spiderweb of our
preoccupations like people already parted. She wears the
familiar velveteen costume—the coat with its deeply cut
and slanted pockets: and the soft *velours* hat pulled down
over her brows—a schoolgirl's hat: leather jack-boots. We
do not look directly at each other any more, but talk with
a hollow impersonality. I have a splitting headache. She
has urged upon me her own spare gun—a beautiful light

twelve by Purdey, ideal for such an impractised hand and
eye as mine.

There is laughter and clapping as lots are drawn for
the make-up of the various parties. We will have to take
up widely dispersed positions around the lake, and those
who draw the western butts will have to make a long
detour by road through Mex and the desert fringes. The
leaders of each party draw paper strips in turn from a
hat, each with a guest's name written upon it. Nessim
has already drawn Capodistria who is clad in a natty
leather jerkin with velvet cuffs, khaki gaberdine plus-fours
and check socks. He wears an old tweed hat with a cock-
pheasant's feather in it, and is festooned with bandoliers
full of cartridges. Next comes Ralli the old Greek general,
with ash-coloured bags under his eyes and darned riding-
breeches; Pallis the French chargé d'affaires in a sheepskin coat; lastly myself.

Justine and Pombal are joining Lord Errol's party. It
is clear now that we are to be separated. All of a sudden,
for the first time, I feel real fear as I watch the expressionless glitter of Nessim's eyes. We take our various
places in the shooting-brakes. Selim is doing up the
straps of a heavy pigskin gun-case. His hands tremble.
With all the dispositions made the cars start up with
a roar of engines, and at this signal a flock of servants
scamper out of the great house with glasses of cham-
pagne to offer us as a stirrup-cup. This diversion enables
Justine to come across to our car and under the
pretext of handing me a packet of smokeless cartridges to
press my arm once, warmly, and to fix me for a half-
second with those expressive black eyes shining now
with an expression I might almost mistake for relief. I try
to form a smile with my lips.

We move off steadily with Nessim at the wheel and
catch the last rays of the sunset as we clear the town to
run along the shallow dunelands towards Aboukir. Everyone is in excellent spirits, Ralli talking nineteen to the
dozen and Capodistria keeping us entertained with anecdotes of his fabulous mad father. ("His first act on going
mad was to file a suit against his two sons accusing them

of wilful and persistent illegitimacy.") From time to time
he raises a finger to touch the cotton compress which is
held in position over his left eye by the black patch.
Pallis has produced an old deer-stalker with large ear-
flaps which make him look like a speculative Gallic
rabbit. From time to time in the driving mirror I catch
Nessim's eye and he smiles.

The dusk has settled as we come to the shores of the
lake. The old hydroplane whimpers and roars as it waits
for us. It is piled high with decoys. Nessim assembles a
couple of tall duck-guns and tripods before joining us in
the shallow punt to set off across the reed-fringed wilderness of the lake to the desolate lodge where we are to
spend the night. All horizons have been abruptly cut off
now as we skirt the darkening channels in our noisy
craft, disturbing the visitants of the lake with the roar of
our engines; the reeds tower over us, and everywhere the
sedge hassocks of islands rise out of the water with their
promise of cover. Once or twice a long vista of water
opens before us and we catch sight of the flurry of birds
rising—mallard trailing their webs across the still surface.
Nearer at hand the hither-and-thithering cormorants
keep a curiosity-shop with their long slave-to-appetite
beaks choked with sedge. All round us now, out of sight
the teeming colonies of the lake are settling down for the
night. When the engines of the hydroplane are turned off
the silence is suddenly filled with groaning and gnatting
of duck.

A faint green wind springs up and ruffles the water
round the little wooden hut on the balcony of which sit
the loaders waiting for us. Darkness has suddenly fallen,
and the voices of the boatmen sound hard, sparkling,
gay. The loaders are a wild crew; they scamper from
island to island with shrill cries, their *galabeahs* tucked
up round their waists, impervious to the cold. They seem
black and huge, as if carved from the darkness. They
pull us up to the balcony one by one and then set off in
shallow punts to lay their armfuls of decoys while we
turn to the inner room where paraffin lamps have already been lit. From the little kitchen comes the encour-

aging smell of food which we sniff appreciatively as we divest ourselves of our guns and bandoliers, and kick off our boots. Now the sportsmen fall to backgammon or tric-trac and bag-and-shot talk, the most delightful and absorbing masculine conversation in the world. Ralli is rubbing pigsfat into his old much-darned boots. The stew is excellent and the red wine has put everyone in a good humour.

By nine however most of us are ready to turn in; Nessim is busy in the darkness outside giving his last instructions to the loaders and setting the rusty old alarm clock for three. Capodistria alone shows no disposition to sleep. He sits, as if plunged in reflection, sipping his wine and smoking a cheroot. We speak for a while about trivialities; and then all of a sudden he launches into a critique of Pursewarden's third volume which has just appeared in the bookshops. "What is astonishing," he says, "is that he presents a series of spiritual problems as if they were commonplaces and illustrates them with his characters. I have been thinking over the character of Parr the sensualist. He resembles me so closely. His apology for a voluptuary's life is fantastically good—as in the passage where he says that people only see in us the contemptible skirt-fever which rules our actions but completely miss the beauty-hunger underlying it. To be so struck by a face sometimes that one wants to devour it feature by feature. Even making love to the body beneath it gives no surcease, no rest. What is to be done with people like us?" He sighs and abruptly begins to talk about Alexandria in the old days. He speaks with a new resignation and gentleness about those far-off days across which he sees himself moving serenely, so effortlessly as a youth and a young man. "I have never got to the bottom of my father. His view of things was mordant, and yet it is possible that his ironies concealed a wounded spirit. One is not an ordinary man if one can say things so pointed that they engage the attention and memory of others. As once in speaking of marriage he said: 'In marriage they legitimized despair,' and, 'Every kiss is the conquest of a repulsion.' He struck me as having a co-

herent view of life but madness intervened and all I have
to go on is the memory of a few incidents and sayings.
I wish I could leave behind as much."

I lie awake in the narrow wooden bunk for a while
thinking over what he has been saying: all is darkness
now and silence save for the low rapid voice of Nessim
on the balcony outside talking to the loaders. I cannot
catch the words. Capodistria sits for a while in the
darkness to finish his cheroot before climbing heavily into
the bunk under the window. The others are already
asleep to judge by the heavy snoring of Ralli. My fear has
given place to resignation once more; now at the borders
of sleep I think of Justine again for a moment before
letting the memory of her slide into the limbo which is
peopled now only with far-away sleepy voices and the
rushing sighing waters of the great lake.

It is pitch-dark when I awake at the touch of Nessim's
gentle hand shaking my shoulder. The alarm clock has
failed us. But the room is full of stretching yawning
figures climbing from their bunks. The loaders have been
curled up asleep like sheep-dogs on the balcony outside.
They busy themselves in lighting the paraffin lamps
whose unearthly glare is to light our desultory breakfast
of coffee and sandwiches. I go down the landing
stage and wash my face in the icy lake-water. Utter
blackness all around. Everyone speaks in low voices, as if
weighed down by the weight of the darkness. Snatches
of wind make the little lodge tremble, built as it is on
frail wooden stilts over the water.

We are each allotted a punt and a gun-bearer. "You'll
take Faraj," says Nessim. "He's the most experienced and
reliable of them." I thank him. A black barbaric face
under a soiled white turban, unsmiling, spiritless. He
takes my equipment and turns silently to the dark punt.
With a whispered farewell I climb in and seat myself.
With a little swing of the pole Faraj drives us out into the
channel and suddenly we are scoring across the heart of
a black diamond. The water is full of stars, Orion down,
Capella tossing out its brilliant sparks. For a long while
now we crawl upon this diamond-pointed star-floor in

silence save for the suck and lisp of the pole in the mud.
Then we turn abruptly into a wider channel to hear a
string of wavelets pattering against our prow while
draughts of wind fetch up from the invisible sea-line
tasting of salt.

Premonitions of the dawn are already in the air as we
cross the darkness of this lost world. Now the approaches
to the empty water ahead are shivered by the faintest
etching of islands, sprouts of beard, reeds and sedge.
And on all sides now comes the rich plural chuckle of
duck and the shrill pinched note of the gulls to the sea-
board. Faraj grunts and turns the punt towards a nearby
island. Reaching out upon the darkness my hands grasp
the icy rim of the nearest barrel into which I laboriously
climb. The butts consist merely of a couple of dry wood-
slatted barrels tied together and festooned with tall reeds
to make them invisible. The loader holds the punt steady
while I disembarrass him of my gear. There is nothing to
do now but to sit and wait for the dawn which is rising
slowly somewhere, to be born from this black expressionless darkness.

It is bitterly cold now and even my heavy greatcoat
seems to offer inadequate protection. I have told Faraj
that I will do my own loading as I do not want him
handling my spare gun and cartridges in the next barrel. I
must confess to a feeling of shame as I do so, but it sets
my nerves at rest. He nods with an expressionless face
and stands off with the punt in the next cluster of reeds,
camouflaged like a scarecrow. We wait now with our faces
turned towards the distant reaches of the lake—it seems
for centuries.

Suddenly at the end of the great couloir my vision is
sharpened by a pale disjunctive shudder as a bar of
buttercup-yellow thickening gradually to a ray falls slowly through the dark masses of cloud to the east. The
ripple and flurry of the invisible colonies of birds around
us increases. Slowly, painfully, like a half-open door the
dawn is upon us, forcing back the darkness. A minute
more and a stairway of soft kingcups slides smoothly
down out of heaven to touch in our horizons, to give

eye and mind an orientation in space which it has been
lacking. Faraj yawns heavily and scratches himself. Now
rose-madder and warm burnt gold. Clouds move to green
and yellow. The lake has begun to shake off its sleep. I see
the black silhouette of teal cross my vision eastward. "It
is time," murmurs Faraj; but the minute hand of my wrist
watch shows that we still have five minutes to go. My
bones feel as if they have been soaked in the darkness. I
feel suspense and inertia struggling for possession of my
sleepy mind. By agreement there is to be no shooting before four-thirty. I load slowly and dispose my bandolier
across the butt next me within easy reach. "It is time,"
says Faraj more urgently. Nearby there is a plop and a
scamper of some hidden birds. Out of sight a couple of
coot squat in the middle of the lake pondering. I am about
to say something when the first chapter of guns opens
from the south—like the distant click of cricket-balls.

Now solitaries begin to pass, one, two, three. The light
grows and waxes, turning now from red to green. The
clouds themselves are moving to reveal enormous cavities
of sky. They peel the morning like a fruit. Four separate
arrowheads of duck rise and form two hundred yards
away. They cross me trimly at an angle and I open up
with a tentative right barrel for distance. As usual they
are faster and higher than they seem. The minutes are
ticking away in the heart. Guns open up nearer to hand,
and by now the lake is in a general state of alert. The
ducks are coming fairly frequently now in groups, three,
five, nine: very low and fast. Their wings purr, as they
feather the sky, their necks reach. Higher again in
mid-heaven there travel the clear formations of mallard,
grouped like aircraft against the light, ploughing a soft
slow flight. The guns squash the air and harry them as
they pass, moving with a slow curling bias towards the
open sea. Even higher and quite out of reach come
chains of wild geese, their plaintive honking sounding
clearly across the now sunny waters of Mareotis.

There is hardly time to think now: for teal and wid-
geon like flung darts whistle over me and I begin to shoot
slowly and methodically. Targets are so plentiful that it

is often difficult to choose one in the split second during
which it presents itself to the gun. Once or twice I catch
myself taking a snap shot into a formation. If hit squarely
a bird staggers and spins, pauses for a moment, and then
sinks gracefully like a handkerchief from a lady's hand.
Reeds close over the brown bodies, but now the tireless
Faraj is out poling about like mad to retrieve the birds.
At times he leaps into the water with his *galabeah* tucked
up to his midriff. His features blaze with excitement.
From time to time he gives a shrill whoop.

They are coming in from everywhere now, at every
conceivable angle and every speed. The guns bark and
jumble in one's ears as they drive the birds backwards
and forwards across the lake. Some of the flights though
nimble are obviously war-weary after heavy losses; other
solitaries seem quite out of their minds with panic. One
young and silly duck settles for a moment by the punt,
almost within reach of Faraj's hands, before it suddenly
sees danger and spurts off in a slither of foam. In a modest
way I am not doing too badly though in all the excitement
it is hard to control oneself and to shoot deliberately. The
sun is fairly up now and the damps of the night have been
dispersed. In an hour I shall be sweating again in these
heavy clothes. The sun shines on the ruffled waters of
Mareotis where the birds still fly. The punts by now will
be full of the sodden bodies of the victims, red blood
running from the shattered beaks on to the floor-boards,
marvellous feathers dulled by death.

I eke out my remaining ammunition as best I can
but already by quarter past eight I have fired the last
cartridge; Faraj is still at work painstakingly tracking
down stragglers among the reeds with the single-mindedness of a retriever. I light a cigarette, and for the first time
feel free from the shadow of omens and premonitions—free
to breathe, to compose my mind once more. It is extraordinary how the prospect of death closes down upon the
free play of the mind, like a steel shutter, cutting off the
future which alone is nourished by hopes and wishes. I
feel the stubble on my unshaven chin and think longingly
of a hot bath and a warm breakfast. Faraj is still tireless-

ly scouting the islands of sedge. The guns have slackened,
and in some quarters of the lake are already silent. I think
with a dull ache of Justine, somewhere out there across the
sunny water. I have no great fear for her safety for she has
taken as her own gun-bearer my faithful servant Hamid.

I feel all at once gay and light-hearted as I shout to
Faraj to cease his explorations and bring back the punt.
He does so reluctantly and at last we set off across the
lake, back through the channels and corridors of reed
towards the lodge.

"Eight brace no good," says Faraj, thinking of the large
professional bags we will have to face when Ralli and
Capodistria return. "For me it is very good," I say. "I am
a rotten shot. Never done as well." We enter the thickly
sown channels of water which border the lake like miniature canals.

At the end, against the light, I catch sight of another
punt moving towards us which gradually defines itself
into the familiar figure of Nessim. He is wearing his old
moleskin cap with the ear-flaps up and tied over the top.
I wave but he does not respond. He sits abstractedly in
the prow of the punt with his hands clasped about his
knees. "Nessim," I shout. "How did you do? I got eight
brace and one lost." The boats are nearly abreast now, for
we are heading towards the mouth of the last canal
which leads to the lodge. Nessim waits until we are
within a few yards of each other before he says with a
curious serenity, "Did you hear? There's been an accident. Capodistria . . ." and all of a sudden my heart
contracts in my body. "Capodistria?" I stammer. Nessim
still has the curious impish serenity of someone resting
after a great expenditure of energy. "He's dead," he says,
and I hear the sudden roar of the hydroplane engines
starting up behind the wall of reeds. He nods towards the
sound and adds in the same still voice: "They are taking
him back to Alexandria."

A thousand conventional commonplaces, a thousand
conventional questions spring to my mind, but for a long
time I can say nothing.

On the balcony the others have assembled uneasily,

almost shamefacedly; they are like a group of thoughtless schoolboys for whom some silly prank has ended in the death of one of their fellows. The furry cone of noise from the hydroplane still coats the air. In the middle distance one can hear shouts and the noise of car-engines starting up. The piled bodies of the duck, which would normally be subject matter for gloating commentaries, lie about the lodge with anachronistic absurdity. It appears that death is a relative question. We had only been prepared to accept a certain share of it when we entered the dark lake with our weapons. The death of Capodistria hangs in the still air like a bad smell, like a bad joke.

Ralli had been sent to get him and had found the body lying face down in the shallow waters of the lake with the black eye-patch floating near him. It was clearly an accident. Capodistria's loader was an elderly man, thin as a cormorant, who sits now hunched over a mess of beans on the balcony. He cannot give a coherent account of the business. He is from Upper Egypt and has the weary half-crazed expression of a desert father.

Ralli is extremely nervous and is drinking copious draughts of brandy. He retells his story for the seventh time, simply because he must talk in order to quieten his nerves. The body could not have been long in the water, yet the skin was like the skin of a washerwoman's hands. When they lifted it to get it into the hydroplane the false teeth slipped out of the mouth and crashed on to the floor-boards frightening them all. This incident seems to have made a great impression on him. I suddenly feel overcome with fatigue and my knees start to tremble. I take a mug of hot coffee and, kicking off my boots, crawl into the nearest bunk with it. Ralli is still talking with deafening persistence, his free hand coaxing the air into expressive shapes. The others watch him with a vague and dispirited curiosity, each plunged in his own reflections. Capodistria's loader is still eating noisily like a famished animal, blinking in the sunlight. Presently a punt comes into view with three policemen perched precariously in it. Nessim watches their antics with an imperturbability flavoured ever so slightly with satisfac-

tion; it is as if he were smiling to himself. The clatter of
boots and musket-butts on the wooden steps, and up they
come to take down our depositions in their notebooks.
They bring with them a grave air of suspicion which hovers over us all. One of them carefully manacles Capodistria's loader before helping him into the punt. The servant
puts out his wrists for the iron cuffs with a bland uncom-
prehending air such as one sees on the faces of old apes
when called upon to perform a human action which they
have learned but not understood.

It is nearly one o'clock before the police have finished
their business. The parties will all have ebbed back from
the lake by now to the city where the news of Capodistria's death will be waiting for them. But this is not to be
all.

One by one we struggle ashore with our gear. The
cars are waiting for us, and now begins a long chaffering
session with the loaders and boatmen who must be paid
off; guns are broken up and the bag distributed; in all
this incoherence I see my servant Hamid advancing tim-
idly through the crowd with his good eye screwed up
against the sunlight. I think he must be looking for me but
no: he goes up to Nessim and hands him a small blue envelope. I want to describe this exactly. Nessim takes it
absently with his left hand while his right is reaching into
the car to place a box of cartridges in the glove-box. He
examines the superscription once thoughtlessly and then
once more with marked attention. Then keeping his eyes
on Hamid's face he takes a deep breath and opens the
envelope to read whatever is written on the half sheet of
notepaper. For a minute he studies it and then replaces
the letter in the envelope. He looks about him with a
sudden change of expression, as if he suddenly felt sick
and was looking about for a place where he might be so.
He makes his way through the crowd and putting his
head against a corner of mud wall utters a short panting
sob, as a runner out of breath. Then he turns back to
the car, completely controlled and dry-eyed, to complete
his packing. This brief incident goes completely unre-
marked by the rest of his guests.

Clouds of dust rise now as the cars begin to draw away towards the city; the wild gang of boatmen shout and wave and treat us to carved watermelon smiles studded with gold and ivory. Hamid opens the car door and climbs in like a monkey. "What is it?" I say, and folding his small hands apologetically towards me in an attitude of supplication which means "Blame not the bearer of ill tidings," he says in a small conciliatory voice: "Master, the lady has gone. There is a letter for you in the house."

It is as if the whole city had crashed about my ears: I walk slowly to the flat, aimlessly as survivors must walk about the streets of their native city after an earthquake, surprised to find how much that had been familiar has changed. Rue Piroua, Rue de France, the Terbana Mosque (cupboard smelling of apples), Rue Sidi Abou El Abbas (water-ices and coffee), Anfouchi, Ras El Tin (Cape of Figs), Ikingi Mariut (gathering wild flowers together, convinced she cannot love me), equestrian statue of Mohammed Ali in the square. . . . General Earle's comical little bust, killed Sudan 1885. . . . An evening multitudinous with swallows . . . the tombs at Kom El Shugafa, darkness and damp soil, both terrified by the darkness. . . . Rue Fuad as the old Canopic Way, once Rue Rosette. . . . Hutchinson disturbed the whole water-disposition of the city by cutting the dykes. . . . The scene in *Moeurs* where he tries to read her the book he is writing about her. "She sits in the wicker chair with her hands in her lap, as if posing for a portrait, but with a look of ever-growing horror on her face. As last I can stand it no longer, and I throw down the manuscript in the fireplace, crying out: 'What are they worth, since you understand nothing, these pages written from a heart pierced to the quick?' " In my mind's eye I can see Nessim racing up the great staircase to her room to find a distraught Selim contemplating the empty cupboards and a dressing table swept clean as if by a blow from a leopard's paw.

In the harbour of Alexandria the sirens whoop and wail. The screws of ships crush and crunch the green oil-coated waters of the inner bar. Idly bending and inclining, effortlessly breathing as if in the rhythm of the earth's own systole and diastole, the yachts turn their spars against the sky. Somewhere in the heart of experience there is an order and a coherence which we might purprise if we were attentive enough, loving enough, or patient enough. Will there be time?

THE DISAPPEARANCE of Justine was something new to be borne. It changed the whole pattern of our relationship. It was as if she had removed the keystone to an arch: Nessim and I, left among the ruins, so to speak were faced with the task of repairing a relationship which she herself had invented and which her absence now rendered hollow, echoing with a guilt which would, I thought, henceforward always overshadow affection.

His suffering was apparent to everyone. That expressive face took on a flayed unhealthy look—the pallor of a church martyr. In seeing him thus I was vividly reminded of my own feelings during the last meeting with Melissa before she left for the clinic in Jerusalem. The candour and gentleness with which she said: "The whole thing is gone. . . . It may never come back. . . . At least this separation." Her voice grew furry and moist, blurring the edges of the words. At this time she was quite ill. The lesions had opened again. "Time to reconsider ourselves. . . . If only I were Justine. . . . I know you thought of her when you made love to me. . . . Don't deny it. . . . I know my darling. . . . I'm even jealous of your imagination. . . . Horrible to have self-reproach heaped on top of other miseries. . . . Never mind." She blew her nose shakily and managed a smile. "I need rest so badly . . . . And now Nessim has fallen in love with me" I put my hand over her sad mouth. The taxi throbbed on remorselessly, like someone living on his nerves. All round us walked the wives of the Alexandrians, smartly turned out, with the air of well-lubricated phantoms. The driver watched us in the mirror like a spy. The emotions of white people, he perhaps was thinking, are odd and excite prurience. He watched as one might watch cats making love.

"I shall never forget you."

"Nor I. Write to me."

"I shall always come back if you want."

"Never doubt it. Get well, Melissa, you must get well. I'll wait for you. A new cycle will begin. It is all there inside me, intact. I feel it."

The words that lovers use at such times are charged with distorting emotions. Only their silences have the cruel precision which aligns them to truth. We were silent, holding hands. She embraced me and signalled to the driver to set off.

"With her going the city took on an unnerving strangeness for him," writes Arnauti. "Wherever his memory of her turned a familiar corner she re-created herself swiftly, vividly, and superimposed those haunted eyes and hands on the streets and squares. Old conversations leaped up and hit him among the polished tabletops of cafés where once they had sat, gazing like drunkards into each other's eyes. Sometimes she appeared walking a few paces ahead of him in the dark street. She would stop to adjust the strap of a sandal and he would overtake her with beating heart—only to find it was someone else. Particular doors seemed just about to admit her. He would sit and watch them doggedly. At other times he was suddenly seized by the irresistible conviction that she was about to arrive on a particular train, and he hurried to the station and breasted the crowd of passengers like a man fording a river. Or he might sit in the stuffy waiting-room of the airport after midnight watching the departures and arrivals, in case she were coming back to surprise him. In this way she controlled his imagination and taught him how feeble reason was; and he carried the consciousness of her going heavily about with him—like a dead baby from which one could not bring oneself to part."

The night after Justine went away there was a freak thunder-storm of tremendous intensity. I had been wan-

dering about in the rain for hours, a prey not only to
feelings which I could not control but also to remorse for
what I imagined Nessim must be feeling. Frankly, I
hardly dared to go back to the empty flat, lest I should
be tempted along the path Pursewarden had already
taken so easily, with so little premeditation. Passing Rue
Fuad for the seventh time, coatless and hatless in that
blinding downpour, I happened to catch sight of the
light in Clea's high window and on an impulse rang the
bell. The front door opened with a whine and I stepped
into the silence of the building from the dark street with
its booming of rain gutters and the splash of overflowing
manholes.

She opened the door to me and at a glance took in my
condition. I was made to enter, peel off my sodden
clothes and put on the blue dressing-gown. The little
electric fire was a blessing, and Clea set about making
me hot coffee.

She was already in pyjamas, her gold hair combed out
for the night. A copy of *A Rebours* lay face down on
the floor beside the ash-tray with the smouldering cigarette in it. Lighting kept flashing fitfully at the window,
lighting up her grave face with its magnesium flashes.
Thunder rolled and writhed in the dark heavens outside
the window. In this calm it was possible partly to exor-
cise my terrors by speaking of Justine. It appeared she
knew all—nothing can be hidden from the curiosity of the
Alexandrians. She knew all about Justine, that is to say.

"You will have guessed," said Clea in the middle of all
this, "that Justine was the woman I told you once I loved
so much."

This cost her a good deal to say. She was standing with
a coffee cup in one hand, clad in her blue-striped
pyjamas by the door. She closed her eyes as she spoke, as
if she were expecting a blow to fall upon the crown of
her head. Out of the closed eyes came two tears which
ran slowly down on each side of her nose. She looked like
a young stag with a broken ankle. "Ah! let us not speak
of her any more," she said at last in a whisper. "She will
never come back."

Later I made some attempt to leave but the storm was
still at its height and my clothes still impossibly sodden.
"You can stay here," said Clea, "with me;" and she added
with a gentleness which brought a lump into my throat
"But please—I don't know how to say this—please don't
make love to me."

We lay together in that narrow bed talking of Justine
while the storm blew itself out, scourging the window-
panes of the flat with driven rain from the seafront. She
was calm now with a sort of resignation which had a
moving eloquence about it. She told me many things
about Justine's past which only she knew: and she spoke
of her with a wonder and tenderness such as people
might use in talking of a beloved yet infuriating queen.
Speaking of Arnauti's ventures into psycho-analysis she
said with amusement: "She was not really clever, you
know, but she had the cunning of a wild animal at bay.
I'm not sure she really understood the object of these
investigations. Yet though she was evasive with the doctors she was perfectly frank with her friends. All that
correspondence about the words 'Washington D.C.,' for
example, which they worked so hard on—remember?
One night while we were lying here together I asked her
to give me her free associations from the phrase. Of
course she trusted my discretion absolutely. She replied
unerringly (it was clear she had already worked it out
though she would not tell Arnauti): 'There is a town
near Washington called Alexandria. My father always
talked of going to visit some distant relations there. They
had a daughter called Justine who was exactly my age.
She went mad and was put away. She had been raped
by a man.' I then asked her about D.C. and she said, 'Da
Capo. Capodistria.' "

I do not know how long this conversation lasted or how
soon it melted into sleep, but we awoke next morning in
each other's arms to find that the storm had ceased. The
city had been sponged clean. We took a hasty breakfast
and I made my way towards Mnemjian's shop for a
shave through streets whose native colours had been
washed clean by the rain so that they glowed with

warmth and beauty in that soft air. I still had Justine's letter in my pocket but I did not dare to read it again lest I destroy the peace of mind which Clea had given me. Only the opening phrase continued to echo in my mind with an obstinate throbbing persistence: "If you should come back alive from the lake you will find this letter waiting for you."

On the mantelpiece in the drawing-room of the flat there is another letter offering me a two-year contract as a teacher in a Catholic school in Upper Egypt. I sit down at once without thinking and draft my acceptance. This will change everything once more and free me from the streets of the city which have begun to haunt me of late so that I dream that I am walking endlessly up and down, hunting for Melissa among the dying flares of the Arab quarter.

With the posting of this letter of acceptance a new period will be initiated, for it marks my separation from the city in which so much has happened to me, so much of momentous importance: so much that has aged me. For a little while, however, life will carry its momentum forwards by hours and days. The same streets and squares will burn in my imagination as the Pharos burns in history. Particular rooms in which I have made love, particular café tables where the pressure of fingers upon a wrist held me spellbound, feeling through the hot pavements the rhythms of Alexandria transmitted upwards into bodies which could only interpret them as famished kisses, or endearments uttered in voices hoarse with wonder. To the student of love these separations are a school, bitter yet necessary to one's growth. They help one to strip oneself mentally of everything save the hunger for more life.

Now, too, the actual framework of things is undergoing a subtle transformation, for other partings are also beginning. Nessim is going to Kenya for a holiday. Pombal has achieved crucifixion and a posting to the Chancery in Rome where I have no doubt he will be happier. A series of leisurely farewell parties have begun to serve the purposes of all of us; but they are heavy with the absence of the one person whom nobody ever mentions any more—Justine. It is clear too that a world war is slowly creeping upon us across the couloirs of history—doubling our claims upon each other and upon life. The sweet sickly smell of blood hangs in the darkening air and contributes a sense of excitement, of fondness and frivolity. This note has been absent until now.

The chandeliers in the great house whose ugliness I have come to hate, blaze over the gatherings which have been convened to say farewell to my friend. They are all there, the faces and histories I have come to know so well, Sveva in black, Clea in gold, Gaston, Claire, Gaby. Nessim's hair I notice has during the last few weeks begun to be faintly touched with grey. Ptolemeo and Fuad are quarrelling with all the animation of old lovers. All around me the typical Alexandrian animation swells and subsides in conversations as brittle and frivolous as spun glass. The women of Alexandria in all their stylish wickedness are here to say good-bye to someone who has captivated them by allowing them to befriend him. As for Pombal himself, he has grown fatter, more assured since his elevation in rank. His profile now has a certain Neronian cast. He is professing himself worried about me in *sotto voce;* for some weeks we have not met properly, and he has only heard about my schoolmastering project tonight. "You should get out," he repeats, "back to Europe. This city will undermine your will. And what has Upper Egypt to offer? Blazing heat, dust, flies, a menial occupation. . . . After all you are not Rimbaud."

The faces surging round us sipping toasts prevent my answering him, and I am glad of it for I have nothing to say. I gaze at him with a portentous numbness, nodding my head. Clea catches my wrist and draws me aside to whisper: "A card from Justine. She is working in a Jewish *kibbutz* in Palestine. Shall I tell Nessim?"

"Yes. No. I don't know."

"She asks me not to."

"Then don't."

I am too proud to ask if there is any message for me. The company has started to sing the old song "For He's a

Jolly Good Fellow" in a variety of times and accents.
Pombal has turned pink with pleasure. I gently shake off
Clea's hand in order to join in the singing. The little
Consul-General is fawning and gesticulating over Pombal; his relief at my friend's departure is so great that he
has worked himself up into a paroxysm of friendship and
regret. The English consular group has the disconsolate
air of a family of moulting turkeys. Madame de Venuta is
beating time with an elegant gloved hand. The black
servants in their long white gloves move swiftly from
group to group of the guests like eclipses of the moon. If
one were to go away, I catch myself thinking, to Italy
perhaps or to France: to start a new sort of life: not a
city life this time, perhaps an island in the Bay of
Naples. . . . But I realize that what remains unresolved in
my life is not the problem of Justine but the problem of
Melissa. In some curious way the future, if there is one,
has always been vested in her. Yet I felt powerless to influence it by decisions or even hopes. I feel that I must
wait patiently until the shallow sequences of our history
match again, until we can fall into step once more. This
may take years—perhaps we will both be grey when the
tide sudenly turns. Or perhaps the hope will die stillborn,
broken up like wreckage by the tides of events. I have so
little faith in myself. The money Pursewarden left is still
in the bank—I have not touched a penny of it. For such
a sum we might live for two years in some cheap spot in
the sun.

Melissa still writes the spirited nonchalant letters
which I have such difficulty in answering save by whining retorts about my circumstances or my improvidence.
Once I leave the city it will be easier. A new road will
open. I will write to her with absolute frankness, telling
her all I feel—even those things which I believe her
forever incapable of understanding properly. "I shall
return in the spring." Nessim is saying to the Baron
Thibault, "and take up my summer quarters at Abu Sir. I
am determined to slack off for about two years. I've been
working too hard at business and it isn't worth it."
Despite the haunted pallor of his face one cannot help

seeing in him a new repose, a relaxation of the will; the
heart may be distracted, but the nerves are at last at rest.
He is weak, as a convalescent is weak; but he is no longer
ill. We talk and joke quietly for while; it is clear that our
friendship will repair itself sooner or later—for we now
have a common fund of unhappiness upon which to
draw. "Justine," I say, and he draws in his breath slightly,
as if one had run a small thorn under his fingernail,
"writes from Palestine." He nods quickly and motions
me with a small gesture. "I know. We have traced her.
There is no need to . . . I'm writing to her. She can stay
away as long as she wishes. Come back in her own good
time." It would be foolish to deprive him of the hope
and the consolation it must give him, but I know now
that she will never return on the old terms. Every phrase
of her letter to me made this clear. It is not us she had
abandoned so much but a way of life which threatened
her reason—the city, love, the sum of all that we had
shared. What had she written to him, I wondered, as I
recalled the short sobbing breath he had drawn as he
leaned against the whitewashed wall?

*   *   *   *   *

On these spring mornings while the island slowly
uncurls from the sea in the light of an early sun I walk
about on the deserted beaches, trying to recover my
memories of the two years spent in Upper Egypt. It is
strange when everything about Alexandria is so vivid
that I can recover so little of that lost period. Or perhaps
it is not so strange—for compared to the city life I had
lived my new life was dull and uneventful. I remember
the back-breaking sweat of school work: walks in the flat
rich fields with their bumper crops feeding upon dead
men's bones: the black silt-fed Nile moving corpulently
through the Delta to the sea: the bilharzia-ridden peas-
antry whose patience and nobility shown through their
rags like patents of dispossessed royalty: village patriachs
intoning: the blind cattle turning the slow globe of their
waterwheels, blindfolded against monotony—how small
can a world become? Throughout this period I read

nothing, thought nothing, was nothing. The fathers of the
school were kindly and left me alone in my spare time,
sensing perhaps my distaste for the cloth, for the appara-
tus of the Holy Office. The children of course were a
torment—but then what teacher of sensibility does not
echo in his heart the terrible words of Tolstoy: "Whenever I enter a school and see a multitude of children,
ragged thin and dirty but with their clear eyes and
sometimes angelic expressions, I am seized with restless-
ness and terror, as though I saw people drowning?"

Unreal as all correspondence seemed, I kept up a
desultory contact with Melissa whose letters arrived
punctually. Clea wrote once or twice, and surprisingly
enough old Scobie who appeared to be rather annoyed
that he should miss me as much as he obviously did. His
letters were full of fantastic animadversion against Jews
(who were always referred to jeeringly as "snipcocks")
and, surprisingly enough, to passive pederasts (whom he
labelled "Herms," i.e. Hermaphrodites). I was not surprised to learn that the Secret Service had gravelled him,
and he was now able to spend most of the day in bed
with what he called a "bottle of wallop" at his elbow. But
he was lonely, hence his correspondence.

These letters were useful to me. My feeling of unreality had grown to such a pitch that at times I distrusted
my own memory, finding it hard to believe that there had
ever been such a town as Alexandria. Letters were a
lifeline attaching me to an existence in which the greater
part of myself was no longer engaged.

As soon as my work was finished I locked myself in my
room and crawled into bed; beside it lay the green jade
box full of hashish-loaded cigarettes. If my way of life
was noticed or commented upon at least I left no
loophole for criticism in my work. It could be hard to
grudge me simply an inordinate taste for solitude. Father
Racine, it is true, made one or two attempts to rouse me.
He was the most sensitive and intelligent of them all and
perhaps felt that my friendship might temper his own
intellectual loneliness. I was sorry for him and regretted
in a way not being able to respond to these overtures.

But I was afflicted by a gradually increasing numbness, a mental apathy which made me shrink from contact. Once or twice I accompanied him for a walk along the river (he was a botanist) and heard him talk lightly and brilliantly on his own subject. But my taste for the landscape, its flatness, its unresponsiveness to the seasons had gone stale. The sun seemed to have scorched up my appetite for everything—food, company and even speech. I preferred to lie in bed staring at the ceiling and listening to the noises around me in the teachers' block: Father Gaudier sneezing, opening and shutting drawers; Father Racine playing a few phrases over and over again on his flute; the ruminations of the organ mouldering away among its harmonies in the dark chapel. The heavy cigarettes soothed the mind, emptying it of every preoccupation.

One day Gaudier called to me as I was crossing the close and said that someone wished to speak to me on the telephone. I could hardly comprehend, hardly believe my ears. After so long a silence who would telephone? Nessim perhaps?

The telephone was in the Head's study, a forbidding room full of elephantine furniture and fine bindings. The receiver, crepitating slightly, lay on the blotter before him. He squinted slightly and said with distaste: "It is a woman from Alexandria." I thought it must be Melissa but to my surprise Clea's voice suddenly swam up out of the incoherence of memory: "I am speaking from the Greek Hospital. Melissa is here, very ill indeed. Perhaps even dying."

Undeniably my surprise and confusion emerged as anger. "But she would not let me tell you before. She didn't want you to see her ill—so thin. But I simply must now. Can you come quickly? She will see you now."

In my mind's eye I could see the jogging night train with its interminable stoppings and startings in dust-blown towns and villages—the dirt and the heat. It would take all night. I turned to Gaudier and asked his permission to absent myself for the whole week-end. "In exceptional cases we do grant permission," he said thoughtful-

ly. "If you were going to be married, for example, or if
someone was seriously ill." I swear that the idea of
marrying Melissa had not entered my head until he
spoke the words.

There was another memory, too, which visited me now
as I packed my cheap suitcase. The rings, Cohen's rings,
were still in my stud-box wrapped in brown paper. I
stood for a while looking at them and wondering if inanimate objects also had a destiny as human beings have.
These wretched rings, I thought—why, it was as if they
had been anxiously waiting here all the time like human
beings; waiting for some shabby fulfilment on the finger
of someone trapped into a *marriage de convenance*. I put
the poor things in my pocket.

Far off events, transformed by memory, acquire a
burnished brilliance because they are seen in isolation,
divorced from the details of before and after, the fibres
and wrappings of time. The actors, too, suffer a transformation; they sink slowly deeper and deeper into the
ocean of memory like weighted bodies, finding at every
level a new assessment, a new evaluation in the human
heart.

It was not anquish I felt so much at Melissa's defec-
tion, it was rage, a purposeless fury based, I imagine, in
contrition. The enormous vistas of the future which in all
my vagueness I had nevertheless peopled with images of
her had gone by default now; and it was only now that I
realized to what an extent I had been nourishing myself
on them. It had all been there like a huge trust fund, an
account upon which I would one day draw. Now I was
suddenly bankrupt.

Balthazar was waiting for me at the station in his little
car. He pressed my hand with rough and ready sympathy as he said, in a matter of fact voice: "She died last
night poor girl. I gave her morphia to help her away.
Well." He sighed and glanced sideways at me. "A pity
you are not in the habit of shedding tears. *Ça aurait été
un soulagement.*"

"*Soulagement grotesque.*"

"*Approfondir les émotions . . . les purger.*"

"*Tais-toi,* Balthazar, shut up."

"She loved you I suppose."

"*Je le sais.*"

"*Elle parlait de vous sans cesse. Cléa a été avec elle toute la semaine.*"

"*Assez.*"

Never had the city looked so entrancing in that soft morning air. I took the light wind from the harbour on my stubbled cheek like the kiss of an old friend. Mareotis glinted here and there between the palm-tops, between the mud huts and the factories. The shops along Rue Fuad seemed to have all the glitter and novelty of Paris. I had, I realized, become a complete provincial in Upper Egypt. Alexandria seemed a capital city. In the trim garden nurses were rolling their prams and children their hoops. The trams squashed and clicked and rattled. "There is something else," Balthazar was saying as we raced along. "Melissa's child, Nessim's child. But I suppose you know all about it. It is out at the summer villa. A little girl."

I could not take all this in, so drunk was I on the beauty of the city which I had almost forgotten. Outside the Municipality and professional scribes sat at their stools, inkhorns, pens and stamped paper beside them. They scratched themselves, chattering amiably. We climbed the low bluff on which the hospital stood after threading the long bony spine of the Canopic Way. Balthazar was still talking as we left the lift and started to negotiate the long white corridors of the second floor.

"A coolness has sprung up between Nessim and myself. When Melissa came back he refused to see her out of a sort of disgust which I found inhuman, hard to comprehend. I don't know. . . . As for the child he is trying to get it adopted. He has come almost to hate it, I suppose. He thinks Justine will never come back to him so long as he has Melissa's child. For my part," he added more slowly, "I look at it this way: by one of those fearful displacements of which only love seems capable the

child Justine lost was given back by Nessim not to her
but to Melissa. Do you see?"

The sense of ghostly familiarity which was growing
upon me now was due to the fact that we were approaching the little room in which I had visited Cohen
when he was dying. Of course Melissa must be lying in
the same narrow iron bed in the corner by the wall. It
would be just like real life to imitate art at this point.

There were some nurses in the room busy whispering
round the bed, arranging screens; but at a word from
Balthazar they scattered and disappeared. We stood arm
in arm in the doorway for a moment looking in. Melissa
looked pale and somehow wizened. They had bound up
her jaw with tape and closed the eyes so that she looked
as if she had fallen asleep during a beauty treatment. I
was glad her eyes were closed; I had been dreading their
glance.

I was left alone with her for a while in the huge silence
of that whitewashed ward and all of a sudden I found
myself suffering from acute embarrassment. It is hard to
know how to behave with the dead; their enormous
deafness and rigidity is so studied. One becomes awkward as if in the presence of royalty. I coughed behind
my hand and walked up and down the ward stealing
little glances at her out of the corner of my eye, remembering the confusion which had once beset me when she
called upon me with a gift of flowers. I would have liked
to slip Cohen's rings on her fingers but they had already
swathed her body in bandages and her arms were bound
stiffly to her sides. In this climate bodies decompose so
quickly that they have to be almost unceremoniously
rushed to the grave. I said "Melissa" twice in an uncertain
whisper bending my lips to her ear. Then I lit a cigarette
and sat down beside her on a chair to make a long study
of her face, comparing it to all the other faces of Melissa
which thronged my memory and had established their
identity there. She bore no resemblance to any of them—
and yet she set them off, concluded them. This white
little face was the last term of a series. Beyond this point
there was a locked door.

At such times one gropes about for a gesture which will match the terrible marble repose of the will which one reads on the faces of the dead. There is nothing in the whole ragbag of human emotions. "Terrible are the four faces of love," wrote Arnauti in another context. I mentally told the figure on the bed that I would take the child if Nessim would part with her, and this silent agreement made I kissed the high pale forehead once and left her to the ministrations of those who would parcel her up for the grave. I was glad to leave the room, to leave a silence so elaborate and forbidding. I suppose we writers are cruel people. The dead do not care. It is the living who might be spared if we could quarry the message which lies buried in the heart of all human experience.

("In the old days the sailing ships in need of ballast would collect tortoises from the mainland and fill great barrels with them, alive. Those that survived the terrible journey might be sold as pets for children. The putrefying bodies of the rest were emptied into the East India Docks. There were plenty more where they came from.")

I walked lightly effortlessly about the town like an escaped prisoner. Mnemjian had violet tears in his violet eyes as he embraced me warmly. He settled down to shave me himself, his every gesture expressing an emollient sympathy and tenderness. Outside on the pavements drenched with sunlight walked the citizens of Alexandria each locked into a world of personal relationships and fears, yet each seeming to my eyes infinitely remote from those upon which my own thoughts and feelings were busy. The city was smiling with a heart-breaking indifference, a *cocotte* refreshed by the darkness.

There remained only one thing to do now, to see Nessim. I was relieved to learn that he was due to come into town that evening. Here again time had another surprise in store for me for the Nessim who lived in my memories of two years before had changed.

He had aged like a woman—his hips and face had both broadened. He walked now with his weight distributed comfortably on the flats of his feet as if his body had already submitted to a dozen pregnancies. The queer litheness of his step had gone. Moreover he radiated now a flabby charm mixed with concern which made him at first all but unrecognizable. A foolish authoritativeness had replaced the delightful old diffidence.

I had hardly time to capture and examine these new impressions when he suggested that we should visit the Etoile together—the night-club where Melissa used to dance. It had changed hands, he added, as if this somehow excused our visiting it on the very day of her funeral. Shocked and surprised as I was I agreed without hesitation, prompted both by curiosity as to his own feelings and a desire to discuss the transaction which concerned this mythical child.

When we walked down the narrow airless stairway into the white light of the place a cry went up and the girls came running to him from every corner like cockroaches. It appeared that he was well known now as an habitué. He opened his arms to them with a shout of laughter, turning to me for approval as he did so. Then taking their hands one after another he pressed them voluptuously to the breast pocket of his coat so that they might feel the outlines of the thick wallet he now carried, stuffed with banknotes. This gesture at once reminded me of how, when I was accosted one night in the dark streets of the city by a pregnant woman and trying to make my escape, she took my hand, as if to give me an idea of the pleasure she was offering (or perhaps to emphasize her need) and pressed it upon her swollen abdomen. Now, watching Nessim, I suddenly recalled the tremulous beat of the foetal heart in the eighth month.

It is difficult to describe how unspeakably strange I found it to sit beside this vulgar double of the Nessim I had once known. I studied him keenly but he avoided my eye and confined his conversation to laboured commonplaces which he punctuated by yawns that were one by one tapped away behind ringed fingers. Here and there, however, behind this new façade stirred a hint of

the old diffidence but buried—as a fine physique may get
buried in the mountain of fat. In the washroom Zoltan
the waiter confided in me: "He has become truly himself
since his wife went away. All Alexandria says so." The
truth was that he had become like all Alexandria.

Late that night the whim seized him to drive me to
Montaza in the late moonlight; we sat in the car for a
long time in silence, smoking, gazing out at the moonlit
waves hobbling across the sand bar. It was during this
silence that I apprehended the truth about him. He had
not really changed inside. He had merely adopted a new
mask.

       ❖   ❖   ❖   ❖   ❖

In the early summer I received a long letter from Clea
with which this brief introductory memorial to Alexandria may well be brought to a close.

"You may perhaps be interested in my account of a
brief meeting with Justine a few weeks ago. We had, as
you know, been exchanging occasional cards from our
respective countries for some time past, and hearing that
I was due to pass through Palestine into Syria she herself
suggested a brief meeting. She would come, she said, to
the border station where the Haifa train waits for half an
hour. The settlement in which she works is somewhere
near at hand, she could get a lift. We might talk for a
while on the platform. To this I agreed.

"At first I had some difficulty in recognizing her. She
has gone a good deal fatter in the face and has chopped
off her hair carelessly at the back so that it sticks out in
rats' tails. I gather that for the most part she wears it
done up in a cloth. No trace remains of the old elegance
or *chic*. Her features seem to have broadened, become
more classically Jewish, lip and nose inclining more towards each other. I was shocked at first by the glittering
eyes and the quick incisive way of breathing and talking
—as if she were feverish. As you can imagine we were
both mortally shy of each other.

"We walked out of the station along the road and sat
down on the edge of a dry ravine, a wadi, with a few
terrified-looking spring flowers about our feet. She gave

the impression of already having chosen this place for
our interview: perhaps as suitably austere. I don't know.
She did not mention Nessim or you at first but spoke only
about her new life. She had achieved, she claimed, a new
and perfect happiness through 'community-service': the
air with which she said this suggested some sort of religious conversation. Do not smile. It is hard, I know, to
be patient with the weak. In all the back-breaking sweat
of the Communist settlement she claimed to have achieved
a 'new humility.' (Humility! The *last trap* that awaits the
ego in search of absolute truth. I felt disgusted but said
nothing.) She described the work of the settlement coarse-
ly, unimaginatively, as a peasant might. I noticed that
those once finely-tended hands were callused and rough.
I suppose people have a right to dispose of their bodies as
they think fit, I said to myself, feeling ashamed because I
must be radiating cleanliness and leisure, good food and
baths. By the way, she is not a Marxist as yet—simply a
work-mystic after the manner of Panayotis at Abu Sir.
Watching her now and remembering the touching and
tormenting person she had once been for us all I found it
hard to comprehend the change into this tubby little
peasant with the hard paws.

"I suppose events are simply a sort of annotation of our
feelings—the one might be deduced from the other. Time
carries us (boldly imagining that we are discrete egos
modelling our own personal futures)—time carries us
forward by the momentum of those feelings inside us of
which we ourselves are least conscious. Too abstract for
you? Then I have expressed the idea badly. I mean, in
Justine's case, having become cured of the mental aberrations brought about by her dreams, her fears, she has
been deflated like a bag. For so long the fantasy occupied the foreground of her life that now she is dispossessed of her entire stock-in-trade. It is not only that the
death of Capodistria has removed the chief actor in this
shadow-play, her chief gaoler. The illness itself had kept
her on the move, and when it died it left in its place total
exhaustion. She has, so to speak, extinguished with her
sexuality her very claims on life, almost her reason.

People driven like this to the very boundaries of freewill
are forced to turn somewhere for help, to make absolute
decisions. If she had not been an Alexandrian (i.e. scep-
tic) this would have taken the form of religious conver-
sion. How is one to say these things? It is not a question
of growing to be happy or unhappy. A whole block of
one's life suddenly falls into the sea, as perhaps yours did
with Melissa. But (this is how it works in life, the
retributive law which brings good for evil and evil for
good) her own release also released Nessim from the
inhibitions governing his passional life. I think he always
felt that so long as Justine lived he would never be able
to endure the slightest human relationship with anyone
else. Melissa proved him wrong, or at least so he thought;
but with Justine's departure the old heartsickness
cropped up and he was filled with overwhelming disgust
for what he had done to her—to Melissa.

"Lovers are never equally matched—do you think?
One always overshadows the other and stunts his or her
growth so that the overshadowed one must always be
tormented by a desire to escape, to be free to grow.
Surely this is the only tragic thing about love?

"So that if from another point of view Nessim did plan
Capodistria's death (as has been widely rumoured and
believed) he could not have chosen a more calamitous
path. It would indeed have been wiser to kill you.
Perhaps he hoped in releasing Justine from the succubus
(as Arnauti before him) he would free her for himself.
(He said so once—you told me.) But quite the opposite
has happened. He has granted her a sort of absolution, or
poor Capodistria unwittingly did—with the result that
she thinks of him now not as a lover but as a sort of
arch-priest. She speaks of him with a *reverence* which
would horrify him to hear. She will never go back, how
could she? And if she did he would know at once that he
had lost her forever—for those who stand in a confession-
al relationship to ourselves can never love us, never truly
love us.

"(Of you Justine said simply, with a slight shrug: 'I
had to put him out of my mind.')

"Well, these are some of the thoughts that passed through my mind as the train carried me down through the orange groves to the coast; they were thrown into sharp relief by the book I had chosen to read on the journey, the last volume of *God Is a Humorist*. How greatly Pursewarden has gained in stature since his death! It was before as if he stood between his own books and our understanding of them. I see now that what we found enigmatic about the man was due to a fault in ourselves. An artist does not live a personal life as we do, he hides it, forcing us to go to his books if we wish to touch the true source of his feelings. Underneath all his preoccupations with sex, society, religion, etc. (all the staple abstractions which allow the forebrain to chatter) there is, quite simply, a man *tortured beyond endurance by the lack of tenderness in the world*.

"And all this brings me back to myself, for I too have been changing in some curious way. The old self-sufficient life has transformed itself into something a little hollow, a little empty. It no longer answers my deepest needs. Somewhere deep inside a tide seems to have turned in my nature. I do not know why but it is towards you, my dear friend, that my thoughts have turned more and more of late. Can one be frank? Is there a friendship possible this side of love which could be sought and found? I speak no more of love—the word and its conventions have become odious to me. But is there a friendship possible to attain which is deeper even, limitlessly deep, and yet wordless, idealess? It seems somehow necessary to find a human being to whom one can be faithful, not in the body (I leave that to the priests) but in the culprit mind? But perhaps this is not the sort of problem which will interest you much these days. Once or twice I have felt the absurd desire to come to you and offer my services in looking after the child perhaps. But it seems clear now that you do not really need anybody any more, and that you value your solitude above all things. . . ."

There are a few more lines and then the affectionate superscription.

*   *   *   *   *   *

The cicadas are throbbing in the great plains, and the summer Mediterranean lies before me in all its magnetic blueness. Somewhere out there, beyond the mauve throbbing line of the horizon lies Africa, lies Alexandria, maintaining its tenuous grasp on one's affections through memories which are already refunding themselves slowly into forgetfulness; memory of friends, of incidents long past. The slow unreality of time begins to grip them, blurring the outlines—so that sometimes I wonder whether these pages record the actions of real human beings; or whether this is not simply the story of a few inanimate objects which precipitated drama around them—I mean a black patch, a green fingerstall, a watch-key and a couple of dispossessed wedding-rings....

Soon it will be evening and the clear night sky will be dusted thickly with summer stars. I shall be here, as always, smoking by the water. I have decided to leave Clea's last letter unanswered. I no longer wish to coerce anyone, to make promises, to think of life in terms of compacts, resolutions, convenants. It will be up to Clea to interpret my silence according to her own needs and desires, to come to me if she has need or not, as the case may be. Does not everything depend on our interpretation of the silence around us? So that....

CONSEQUENTIAL DATA

* * *

Land-scape tones: steep skylines, low cloud, pearl ground with shadows in oyster and violet. Accidie. On the lake gun-metal and lemon. Summer: sand lilac sky. Autumn: swollen bruise greys. Winter: freezing white sand, clear skies, magnificent starscapes.

* * *

CHARACTER-SQUEEZES

Sveva Magnani: pertness, malcontent.
Georges Pombal: honey-bear, fleshy opiates.
Teresa di Petromonti: farded Berenice.
Pfolomeo Dandolo: astronomer, astrologer, Zen.
Fuad El Said: black moon-pearl.
Josh Scobie: piracy.
Justine Hosnani: arrow in darkness.
Clea Montis: still waters of pain.
Gaston Phipps: nose like a sock, black hat.
Ahmed Zananiri: pole-star criminal.
Nessim Hosnani: smooth gloves, face frosted glass.
Melissa Artemis: patron of sorrow.
S. Balthazar: fables, work, unknowing.

* * *

Pombal asleep in full evening dress. Beside him on the bed a chamber-pot full of banknotes he had won at the Casino.

* * *

Da Capo: "To bake in sensuality like an apple in its jacket."

* * *

Spoken impromptu by Gaston Phipps:
*   "The lover like a cat with fish*
*   Longs to be off and will not share his dish."*

223

*Accident or attempted murder? Justine racing along the desert
road to Cairo in the Rolls when suddenly the lights give out.
Sightless, the great car swarms off the road and whistling like
an arrow buries inself in a sand-dune. It looked as if the wires
had been filed down to a thread. Nessim reached her within
half an hour. They embrace in tears. (From her diary.)*

* * *

*Balthazar on Justine: "You will find that her formidable man-
ner is constructed on a shaky edifice of childish timidities."*

* * *

Clea always has a horoscope cast before any decision reached.

* * *

*Clea's account of the horrible party; driving with Justine they
had seen a brown cardboard box by the road. They were late
so they put it in the back and did not open it until they reached
the garage. Inside was dead baby wrapped in newspaper. What
to do with this wizened homunculus? Perfectly formed organs.
Guests were due to arrive, they had to rush. Justine slipped it
into drawer of the hall desk. Party a great success.*

* * *

*Pursewarden on the "n-dimensional novel" trilogy: "The nar-
rative momentum forward is counter-sprung by references
backwards in time, giving the impression of a book which is
not travelling from a to b but standing above time and turning
slowly on its own axis to comprehend the whole pattern.
Things do not all lead forward to other things: some lead backwards to things which have passed. A marriage of past and
present with the flying multiplicity of the future racing towards one. Anyway, that was my idea. . . ."*

* * *

*"Then how long will it last, this love?" (in jest).
"I don't know."
"Three weeks, three years, three decades . . . ?"*

* * *

*"You are like all the others . . . trying to shorten eternity with
numbers," spoken quietly, but with intense feeling.*

Conundrum: a peacock's eye. Kisses, so amateurish they resembled an early form of printing.

* * *

Of poems: "I like the soft thudding of Alexandrines" (Nessim).

* * *

Clea and her old father whom she worships. White haired, erect, with a sort of haunted pity in his eyes for the young unmarried goddess he has fathered. Once a year on New Year's Eve they dance at the Cecil, stately, urbanely. He waltzes like a clockwork man.

* * *

Pombal's love for Sveva: based on one gay message which took his fancy. When he awoke she'd gone, but she had neatly tied his dress tie to his John Thomas, a perfect bow. This message so captivated him that he at once dressed and went round to propose marriage to her because of her sense of humour.

* * *

Pombal was at his most touching with his little car which he loved devotedly. I remember him washing it by moonlight very patiently.

* * *

Justine: "Always astonished by the force of my own emotions—tearing the heart out of a book with my fingers like a fresh loaf."

* * *

Places: street with arcade: awnings: silverware and doves for sale. Pursewarden fell over a basket and filled the street with apples.

* * *

Message on the corner of a newspaper. Afterwards the closed cab, warm bodies, night volume of jasmine.

* * *

A basket of quail burst open in the bazaar. They did not try to escape but spread out slowly like spilt honey. Easily recaptured.

Postcard from Balthazar: "*Scobie's death was the greatest fun. How he must have enjoyed it. His pockets were full of love-letters to his aide Hassan, and the whole vice squad turned out to sob at his grave. All these black gorillas crying like babies. A very Alexandrian demonstration of affection. Of course the grave was too small for the coffin. The grave-diggers had knocked off for lunch, so a scratch team of policemen was brought into action. Usual muddle. The coffin fell over on its side and the old man nearly rolled out. Shrieks. The padre was furious. The British Consul nearly died of shame. But all Alexandria was there and a good time was had by all.*"

* * *

Pombal walking in stately fashion down Rue Fuad, dead drunk at ten in the morning, clad in full evening dress, cloak and opera hat—but bearing on his shirt-front, written in lipstick, the words: "Torche-cul des républicains."

* * *

(Museum)
Alexander wearing the horns of Ammon (Nessim's madness). He identified himself with A. because of the horns?

* * *

Justine reflecting sadly on the statue of Berenice mourning her little daughter whom the Priests deified: "Did that assuage her grief I wonder? Or did it make it more permanent?"

* * *

Tombstone of Apollodorus giving his child a toy. "Could bring tears to one's eyes." (Pursewarden) "They are all dead. Nothing to show for it."

* * *

Aurelia beseeching Petesouchos the crocodile god. . . .

* * *

Lioness Holding a Golden flower. . . .

* * *

Ushabti . . . little serving figures which are supposed to work for the mummy in the underworld.

Somehow even Scobie's death did not disturb our picture of him. I had already seen him long before in Paradise—the soft conklin-coloured yams like the haunches of newly cooked babies: the night falling with its deep-breathing blue slur over Tobago, softer than parrot-plumage. Paper flamingoes touched with gold-leaf, rising and falling on the sky, touched by the kneening of the bruise-dark water-bamboos. His little hut of reeds with the cane bed, beside which still stands the honoured cake-stand of his earthly life. Clea once asked him: "Do you not miss the sea, Scobie?" and the old man replied simply, without hesitation, "Every night I put to sea in my dreams."

* * *

I copied out and gave her the two translations from Cavafy which had pleased her though they were by no means literal. By now the Cavafy canon has been established by the fine thoughtful translations of Mavrogordato and in a sense the poet has been freed for other poets to experiment with; I have tried to transplant rather than translate—with what success I cannot say.

THE CITY

*You tell yourself I'll be gone
To some other land, some other sea,
To a city lovelier far than this
Could ever have been or hoped to be—
Where every step now tightens the noose:
A heart in a body buried and out of use:
How long, how long must I be here
Confined among these dreary purlieus
Of the common mind? Wherever now I look
Black ruins of my life rise into view.
So many years have I been here
Spending and squandering and nothing gained.
There's no new land, my friend, no
New sea; for the city will follow you,
In the same streets you'll wander endlessly,
The same mental suburbs slip from youth to age,
In the same house go white at last—
The city is a cage.
No other places, always this
Your earthly landfall, and no ship exists*

To take you from yourself. Ah! don't you see
Just as you've ruined your life in this
One plot of ground you've ruined its worth
Everywhere now—over the whole earth?

THE GOD ABANDONS ANTONY

When suddenly at darkest midnight heard,
The invisible company passing, the clear voices,
Ravishing music of invisible choirs—
Your fortunes having failed you now,
Hopes gone aground, a lifetime of desires
Turned into smoke. Ah! do not agonize
At what is past deceiving
But like a man long since prepared
With courage say your last good-byes
To Alexandria as she is leaving.
Do not be tricked and never say
It was a dream or that your ears misled,
Leave cowards their entreaties and complaints,
Let all such useless hopes as these be shed,
And like a man long since prepared,
Deliberately, with pride, with resignation
Befitting you and worthy of such a city
Turn to the open window and look down
To drink past all deceiving
Your last black rapture from the mystical throng,
And say farewell, farewell to Alexandria leaving.

NOTES IN THE TEXT

Page 4. "The Poet of the city." C. P. Cavafy.

Page 5. "The old man." C. P. Cavafy

Page 28. Caballi. The astral bodies of men who died a premature death. "They imagine to perform bodily actions while in fact they have no physical bodies but act in their thoughts." *Paracelsus.*

Page 29. "Held the Gnostic doctrine that creation is a mistake. . . . He imagines a primal God, the centre of a divine harmony, who sent out manifestations of him in pairs of male and female. Each pair was inferior to its predecessor and Sophia ('wisdom') the female of the thirtieth pair, least perfect of all. She showed her imperfection not, like Lucifer, by rebelling from God, but by desiring too ardently to be united to him. She fell through love."

E. M. Forster, *Alexandria.*

Page 30. Quotation from Paracelsus.

Page 43. Taphia, Egyptian "Red Biddy."

Page 45. Greek text Όταν θά βγῶ, ἄν δέν ἔχης φιλενάδα, φώναξέ με.

Page 73. Amr, Conqueror of Alexandria, was a poet and soldier. Of the Arab invasion E. M. Forster writes: "Though they had no intention of destroying her, they destroyed her, as a child might watch. She never functioned again properly for over 1,000 years."

Page 162. A translation of 'The City' is among the 'Workpoints.'